BELOW
THE FOLD

Also By R. G. Belsky

The Clare Carlson Mysteries
Yesterday's News

The Gil Malloy Series
Blonde Ice
Shooting for the Stars
The Midnight Hour
The Kennedy Connection

Other Novels
Loverboy
Playing Dead

BELOW THE FOLD

A Clare Carlson Mystery

R. G. BELSKY

OCEANVIEW PUBLISHING
SARASOTA, FLORIDA

ISBN 978-1-60809-324-3

Cover Design by Christian Fuenfhausen

Published in the United States of America by Oceanview Publishing

Sarasota, Florida

www.oceanviewpub.com

10 9 8 7 6 5 4 3 2 1

PRINTED IN THE UNITED STATES OF AMERICA

For Laura Morgan

"All things truly wicked start from an innocence."
—ERNEST HEMINGWAY

PROLOGUE

She was thinking about money when the killer came knocking on her door.

How much money she was going to have. And where she was going to spend it. South America. Mexico. The Caribbean. Maybe even some really faraway paradise like Tahiti, where she could lie on the beach and laugh about everything that had happened to her in New York City.

New York was all right, but she'd kind of worn out her welcome. It was time to move on to bigger and better conquests, no question about that.

The thing was, she'd beaten New York. They all thought she was finished here, but she'd used the adversity to beat them at their own game and come out triumphant again.

She was always smarter than anyone else.

She believed that right up until the very end.

That's why the last emotion she would ever feel wasn't fear or panic or confusion. It was astonishment.

"My God, I'm going to die," she thought as the blows rained down upon her.

Then there was just darkness . . .

OPENING CREDITS

THE RULES ACCORDING TO CLARE

EVERY HUMAN LIFE is supposed to be important, everyone should matter. That's what we all tell ourselves, and it's a helluva noble concept. But it's not true. Not in the real world. And certainly not in the world of TV news where I work.

Especially when it comes to murder.

Murder is a numbers game for me. It operates on what is sometimes cynically known in the media as the Blonde White Female Syndrome. My goal is to find a murder with a sexy young woman victim to put on the air. Sex sells. Sex, money, and power. That translates into big ratings numbers, which translates into more advertising dollars. These are the only murder stories really worth doing.

The amazing thing to me is not that there is so much news coverage of these types of stories. It's that there are people who actually question whether they should be big news stories. These critics dredge up the age-old argument about why some murders get so much more play in the media than all the other murders that happen every day.

I don't understand these people.

Because the cold, hard truth—and everyone knows this, whether they want to admit it or not—is that not everybody is equal when it comes to murder.

Not in life.

And certainly not in death.

It reminds me of the ongoing debate that happens every time Sirhan Sirhan—the man who killed Robert F. Kennedy—comes up for a parole hearing. There are those who point out that he's already served fifty years in jail. They argue that many other killers have served far less time before being paroled. Sirhan Sirhan should be treated equally, they say, because the life of Robert F. Kennedy is no more or less important than the life of any other crime victim. Me, I think Sirhan Sirhan should be kept caged up in a four-foot by six-foot cell as long as he lives—which hopefully will be to a hundred so he can suffer every minute of it. For God's sakes, people, he killed Robert—freakin'—Kennedy!

And so, to those who think that we in the media make too big a deal out of some of these high-profile murder stories, I say that's completely and utterly ridiculous. I reject that argument completely. I won't even discuss it.

* * *

Now let me tell you something else.

Everything I just said there is a lie.

The truth is there really is no magic formula for murder in the TV news business. No simple way to know from the beginning if a murder story is worth covering or not. No easy answer to the question of how much a human life is worth—or what the impact will be of that person's death by a violent murder.

When I started out working at a newspaper years ago, I sat next to a veteran police reporter on the overnight shift. There was an old-fashioned wire machine that would print out police slips of murders that happened during the night. Most of them involved down-market victims in bad neighborhoods whose deaths clearly would never make the paper.

But he would dutifully call the police on each one and ask questions like: "Tell me about the body of that kid you found in the Harlem pool room—was he a MENSA candidate or what?" Or, "The woman you found dead in the alley behind the housing project—any chance she might be Julia Roberts or a member of the British Royal Family?"

I asked him once why he even bothered to make the calls since none of these murders seemed ever worth writing about in the paper.

"Hey, you never know," he said.

It was good advice back then, and it still is today. I try to teach it to all my reporters in the TV newsroom that I run now. Check every murder out. Never assume anything about a murder story. Follow the facts and the evidence on every murder—on every crime story—because you can never be certain where that trail might take you.

Okay, I don't always follow my own advice in the fast-paced, ratings-obsessed world of TV news where I make my living.

And usually it does turn out to be just a waste of time.

But every once in a while, well . . .

Hey, you never know.

PART I

DORA & GRACE

CHAPTER 1

THE NEWS MEETING at Channel 10 was my favorite part of the day. That's when we talked about the stories to decide which ones to put on the air.

"Here's your talker of the day, Clare," said Maggie Lang, my assignment editor. "A guy goes into the hospital for hemorrhoid surgery. He's real nervous and has a lot of gas buildup. While he's on the operating table, he involuntarily lets go of a big fart. An oxygen unit catches fire, there's an explosion, and the entire operating team gets blown backward by the force of the blast."

"Boom!" I said.

"The poor schmuck's lying there with half his rear end gone. The hospital's looking at a big malpractice suit."

"I guess the operation backfired, huh?" one of the editors said.

"Maybe we should start calling New York the windy city now instead of Chicago," another one quipped.

Everyone at the meeting laughed.

"All right, we'll use it," I said. "But do it short and play it straight. No giggling on air, no bad puns. We'll play it at the very end of the newscast."

My name is Clare Carlson, and I'm the news director at Channel 10 now. But I used to be a reporter. Not an on-air TV reporter, but a real reporter at a newspaper that sadly doesn't exist anymore. I was a pretty damn good reporter too. Even won a Pulitzer Prize a long time ago. Yep, Clare Carlson, Pulitzer Prize winner. That's got a nice sound to it, huh? And I still think of myself at heart as a reporter, not a news executive. I guess that's why I liked this meeting so much. It gave me a chance to get away from budget planning, ad sales, rating demographics, and—at least for a little while—just be a journalist again and worry about the stories.

"What's our lead story going to be?" I asked everyone.

"Probably the chaos at Penn Station," Maggie said. "There was another derailment there this morning. No one really got hurt, but they had to cancel most of the trains. The delays getting in and out of the city are supposed to extend into the evening rush hour too. There's great video of angry commuters packed in there waiting for the trains—yelling at conductors, demanding answers, chanting for someone to be fired over this latest commuter mess there. One of the angry passengers even assaulted an information clerk who couldn't give him an answer as to when his train might be running again. That video's already gone viral on social media. We could start off with it and then go with all the other commuter chaos footage."

I looked around the room.

"Does everyone agree that's a good story for us to lead the broadcast with tonight?" I asked.

"Yes," said Dani Blaine, one of the Channel 10 co-anchors.

"No," said Brett Wolff, the other co-anchor.

"Well, that about covers all the possibilities," I said.

Brett and Dani didn't like each other. Well, that's not totally true. Actually, they did like each other . . . a bit too much. A few months earlier, they'd engaged in a torrid off-camera love affair.

But then Brett broke it off, and so there was a lot of anger and bitterness and sexual tension between them now. They were still professional on the air but feuded constantly behind the scenes. The bottom line here though was they were one of the most popular anchor teams in town, so I had to make it work. Just another fun part of my job.

"We led with trains delays all last week," Brett said. "Do we really want to do that again?"

"We had our highest ratings in months too," Dani pointed out. "More viewers, more website hits, more social media response, and an overall bigger market share than anyone else in town."

"Uh, I think she just answered your question, Brett," I said.

Score one for Dani.

I turned to Steve Stratton, our Channel 10 sports guy.

"What's going on in sports?" I asked him now,

"The Jets have offered their first draft choice $50 million."

"Fifty—friggin'—million?"

"Yeah, but that's not really the story. The story is the guy turned it down."

I told Stratton to come up with some kind of visual graphic to put on air that broke down $50 million into numbers that people would understand. How many houses could you buy with it? How many cars? How many boats? How many college educations? How many doctor visits and trips to the dentist? I wanted our viewers to understand the enormity of the sum.

"What else is there?" I said.

"The mayor's office says they have a new plan to balance the budget by the end of the year," an editor suggested.

There were groans around the room. Budget stories didn't translate well into TV news. They didn't translate well into any kind of news.

"Didn't they say that last year?" someone asked.

"They said it during the Giuliani administration," I said.

"Well, the mayor also has an appearance scheduled this afternoon at the groundbreaking ceremony for a pool in the Bronx. With the new *Sports Illustrated* swimsuit model. In a swimsuit."

"The mayor or the model?" an editor said, laughing.

"Now we're talking real journalism," another one said.

"Can he bring the swimsuit chick to the next budget meeting?" someone suggested.

The news meeting usually went on for nearly an hour. I always tried to keep it like this—freewheeling, funny, encouraging people to speak up and throw out their ideas. We went through a lot of other possible stories—police stuff, weather, some features and everything else needed to put out a TV newscast.

I was just about to wrap up the meeting when Maggie Lang said she had another story she wanted to discuss.

"It's a crime story," she said.

"Crime is good," I told her.

"A woman was murdered."

"What's her name?"

"I don't know."

"So what's the angle?"

"She was a homeless woman."

There were groans around the room. Even louder than for the budget story. I wanted to groan too, but I didn't. Maggie was young—still in her twenties—but I probably trusted her more than anyone else at the station.

"Look, we're always doing stories about the homeless issue in the city," Maggie said. "But always just people talking numbers and political positions about the issue. This is the real thing. A woman who was murdered on the streets of New York City. Sure, no one cares about her, right? But someone must have cared about her once. What if we do a profile on this woman—find out how she wound up dying alone the way she did?

"I knew her. Well, that is I used to see her on the street. You probably did too. She would stand in front of the coffee shop down the street from our building and hold the door open for people in hopes of getting a handout. I went inside the coffee shop and asked the people there about her. They didn't know her name either. But they said she used to call herself Cinderella. No one knew exactly why.

"She was found stabbed to death in the vestibule of a bank a few blocks away. They have no idea who killed her or why, and they probably never will. She's just another forgotten homeless person dead on the streets. But what if we make her more than that? What if we turn her into a symbol of everything that's wrong and tragic and needs to be fixed about the homeless people we see all around us?

"Maybe there's even an interesting story to her too. Clare, you always preach to us about how there's a story to every murder. All we have to do is find it, you tell us. Let's find out the story behind this woman. Who was she? Why did she call herself Cinderella? Where was she and what was she doing before she started living on the street?"

Maybe it was the fact that Maggie threw my own words back at me, which made it tough for me to argue about what she was saying.

Maybe it was the name "Cinderella" that intrigued me too.

Maybe it was my reporter's curiosity and desire to do some real journalism again, to escape however briefly from the confines of TV news.

Or maybe it was a combination of all these things—plus a bit of luck—that convinced me to do what I did next.

"Okay," I said finally. "Let's find out the story of Cinderella."

CHAPTER 2

HER NAME WAS Dora Gayle. She was fifty-four years old and had lived in New York City for her entire life. Grew up in the West Village, attended college at NYU, then had a variety of jobs and lived in different locations around town until she finally wound up on the street at some point.

Those were the basic facts about her.

But they didn't really tell the story behind the sad and tragic life of the woman who called herself Cinderella.

"She told me once that she used to live in a big white house at the end of a street, with a fence around the yard and a garden in the back," one person we interviewed told us. "There was a porch too, she said. She remembered sitting on the porch with her husband and reading poetry and writing love sonnets to him. She said she was very happy. But then she would begin to cry."

We found out that Dora Gayle had grown up on Bank Street in the Village. Her mother and father, by all accounts from people still in the neighborhood who remembered them, were serious alcoholics who drank themselves to sleep every night. Dora frequently had to put them to bed and make sure they were all right, an awesome responsibility for a young girl growing up.

Maybe that's why Dora never drank herself back then. She'd seen enough of that as a child. She hated the sight of liquor. She hated the smell of it. And, most of all, she hated what it did to people like her parents.

Which made it even seem more tragic when Dora developed her own drinking problem—but that would all come later.

By the time she went to college, Dora had left the depressing surroundings of her parents' home and moved to a place on East 3rd Street. She walked each day to her classes at NYU, where she majored in English literature and became a very serious, introspective student. She read dark poetry by Sylvia Plath; listened to sad songs about death and despair; and worried about the poor and the desperate and the lonely—believing that their suffering was her own too.

Not exactly a fun date for the guys in college. Except for one thing. We found an old picture of her at NYU, and the young Dora Gayle was gorgeous. Drop dead gorgeous. She had long straight black hair that hung down to her waist. Big brown eyes. A beautiful face. Even though she hardly ever wore makeup, men were said to be captivated by her unadulterated beauty.

She told people her goal was to write serious poetry and teach literature herself one day.

No one knew much about exactly what happened to her after she left college.

But she popped up in a city Social Services report years later when she'd apparently tried to apply for government assistance. By that point, according to the report, she seemed like a totally different person from the pretty, poetry-loving student at NYU.

She'd worked in a variety of jobs—waitress, cleaning lady, department store clerk. None of them lasted very long. She'd started drinking somewhere along the line, and alcohol had completely taken over her life. She couldn't hold a job anymore.

After that, she just disappeared from the system again.

Until she turned up on the street as a homeless person.

Everyone who encountered Dora on the streets seemed to like her—and many tried their best to help her. A woman behind the counter at the coffee shop where she could often be seen holding the door for customers gave her free sandwiches and coffee from time to time. So did the owner of a nearby deli. A bartender named Jimmy Landon at a place called the Landmark Tavern said he sometimes slipped her a bottle or two.

"She was going to drink anyway," Landon explained, "and this way at least maybe she'll have a little more left over for something else. She was a very polite lady. She always said thank you to me. I wish all my customers were as pleasant as she was. There's a lot of people who wander in here looking for free drinks. But she was different. There was almost an aura of . . . well, class or dignity about her. She was smart too. She'd quote from Thoreau or Shakespeare or some other guys I never heard. I always figured she was somebody once, but then things went bad for her."

The woman from the coffee shop, Janice Aiello, was the one who first said Dora Gayle always told people her name was Cinderella.

"I never knew her real name," the woman said. "Just Cinderella. I asked her once why she called herself Cinderella. I was curious. She told me that one day a handsome prince would come and rescue her and they would live happily ever after. Just like the fairy tale."

She talked about how Dora had been a regular sight at the coffee shop each day panhandling at the front door. Holding it open and hoping for a handout from the busy people who pushed past her to get their coffee and pastry before rushing to their offices. People like me. Like Maggie had said at the news meeting that first day, the coffee shop was close to our office and I had stopped in there many mornings.

I tried to remember if I had ever seen Dora Gayle there myself and, if I had, whether I'd given her any money. I sometimes did give money to homeless panhandlers, but not a lot. There was just too many of them to worry about. It was easier for all of us to look away, pretend they didn't exist, and go on with our own lives. I understood that. But I still wished I'd given Dora Gayle some money one of those days that might have made her own sad life a little better, even if only for a brief few minutes.

Janice Aiello explained how she frequently gave Dora Gayle coffee to drink, especially when it was cold outside. Sometime she gave the homeless woman sandwiches and pastries too. The owner of the store wouldn't let her give away free coffee and food, she said. So she paid for it herself.

Janice Aiello seemed like a nice person.

Nicer than me.

"Did she talk about anything else besides her name being Cinderella when she was there?" the reporter asked.

"A bit. A lot of the time she didn't make much sense. She drank a lot. And, even when she didn't ... well, I'm not sure she was right in the head."

"Any idea what she was doing before she started living on the street?"

"Not really."

"Did she ever talk about having any family?"

"She did tell me once she had a daughter."

"Was there a name or any information about the daughter?"

Aiello shook her head no.

"I think it was a long time ago."

* * *

We got a big break when Maggie found a documentary online from a student filmmaker that included Dora Gayle. It was called

"Forgotten and Alone", and the person who did it had interviewed various homeless people on the streets of New York City. One of them was Dora Gayle.

"I like living here in the park," she said in the film, sitting on a park bench with a liquor bottle in her hand. "I don't have to deal with anyone here. I can just be left alone. Oh, sure, sometimes people look at me funny, sitting here with all these shopping bags filled with my possessions. But I don't care. People have been doing that for my entire life—or at least as long as I can remember. Mostly though, people are nice to me. I try to be nice to them too. I don't want to cause any trouble."

She took a long drink from the bottle she was holding in the video.

She said she didn't remember a lot about her life but did recall being happy once a long time ago—particularly when she was in college. It was almost like she was talking about another person and another life.

"That was such a beautiful time," she recalled to the filmmaker. "I wrote poetry back in those days, you know. It was beautiful poetry. I was in love then too. Him and me, we were so happy together."

But she didn't know what she'd done yesterday, or for much of her life since then.

"I forget things. I used to remember more, but the memories were always bad. So now I don't mind forgetting. I live here and down by the coffee shop and in the park and a few other places. I just try to get through each day with something to eat and something to drink. It seems simpler that way."

Watching the picture of the haggard-looking, disoriented woman in the documentary, it was hard to imagine this was the same person who had been such a beautiful girl in that long-ago NYU picture.

But that was the downward spiral Dora Gayle's life had taken before her death.

* * *

The details of her murder itself were sketchy. A customer had discovered her body that morning when he let himself in the bank area to use one of the ATM machines. She had been stabbed numerous times, according to the Medical Examiner's report. The time of death was estimated to be several hours earlier, sometime during the middle of the night. The assumption was she'd gone into the bank vestibule to sleep. Someone had accosted her inside for whatever reason—and then killed her. The police said it appeared to be just a random case of street violence. Which meant it was not very likely her murder would ever be solved or the killer caught.

The story was delivered on the air by Cassie O'Neal, one of Channel 10's top rated personalities. Cassie was blond and beautiful, like so many other people on TV these days. Her strength was her looks, not her reporting skills. And she'd stumbled a bit in the past when doing live breaking news. But a story like this was one she couldn't mess up too badly. I had other staffers do the reporting, and then Maggie and I wrote the whole script for the report on Dora Gayle.

Cassie ended it by saying:

"Her name was Dora Gayle. But she called herself Cinderella. She believed that one day there would be a happy ending to her story. And, in a city where people are supposed to be hard-hearted and unfeeling, Dora Gayle—aka Cinderella—touched a lot of us. She was a New York City fixture in that park and the neighborhood around it. A true New York character. Someone who got many to open up their hearts and emotions to another human being. Sadly though, there would be no happy ending for her. Instead, she died alone and violently while seeking a brief respite from her hard life on the street. Goodbye, Cinderella . . . we will miss you."

The segment ended with a picture of Dora Gayle on the screen—not the one from the documentary, but the picture of the beautiful young woman at NYU who loved poetry and still had all her dreams in front of her.

That's the way I wanted our viewers to remember Dora Gayle.

Me, too.

CHAPTER 3

I WAS HAVING dinner with my best friend, Janet Wood. We were eating at a place that was supposed to have the best stuffed lamb chops in town. The chef there had recently boasted about how proud he was of them during an interview with *New York* magazine. Janet just ordered some kind of a big salad dish though. Me, I went for the lamb chops. I didn't want to offend the chef.

I told her about the Dora Gayle story and the latest on Brett and Dani's abortive affair and a lot of other things going on at Channel 10. Janet was a lawyer and talked about a messy divorce case she was working on at the moment.

"Don't you get tired of eating that green stuff?" I asked her at one point between bites of my lamp chops.

"It's called salad."

"Whatever."

"I want to look good. Eating healthy helps me to look good and feel better too. Don't you ever think about that, Clare?"

"Nah, I just want to keep eating so I'll pack on thirty pounds and no man will ever be interested in me again. That way I can just entirely eliminate men from my life. It sure would make things a lot simpler that way."

Janet cut off a small slice of tomato, picked it up with her fork along with some lettuce and put it in her mouth. She ate like she did everything else. Precise. Impeccably neat. Always in control. She always seemed so perfect in everything she did. She had a great husband, great kids, a great career. Oh, I knew she had to have troubles somewhere in her life. But, if she did, she sure put on a great act.

"Problem?" she asked me now.

"No problem."

"What's his name?"

"Whose name?"

"The guy you just broke up with."

"C'mon, Janet, why do you always assume that I'm upset because of something that's gone wrong in my love life? That my personal life is always somehow a mess or in crisis? I have a lot of things going on in my life besides worrying about whether or not I'm having a healthy relationship with a man at the moment."

"What's his name?" Janet repeated.

* * *

His name was Alan Paulus. And it hadn't exactly been a relationship. It was really just a date. Well, actually not even a full date. We'd met at a party, then gone back to his place.

"What happened then?" Janet asked me when I told her the story.

"I asked him what he thought about our Channel 10 news show. He said he never watched any TV news. In fact, he didn't even own a TV. Didn't go on the Internet for it either. He said he got all his news from listening to public radio. I hate pretentious people like that. I decided there was no way this was going any-where long term between us."

She took another bite of her salad. I finished off my first lamb chop, then began to devour the second one. They were good. Very good. Maybe not the best lamb chops I'd ever eaten, but damn close.

"Well, at least you found out how you felt before you had sex or anything with this guy," Janet said.

"Oh, we had sex."

"You had sex."

"Of course."

"I don't understand . . . why did you have sex with him after what you just told me?"

"You kinda had to be there," I said.

"So how was it?"

"The sex?"

"Yes, the sex."

"Very good."

"So the sex was good, but you still don't want to see him again because he gets all his news from public radio—not from TV?"

"I can't be with someone who doesn't watch TV," I said. "That's one of the hard and fast Clare Carlson rules for any kind of a re-lationship. It's a real priority for me."

"You have a strange set of priorities."

"Well, they work for me."

"How do they work? You're a forty-something-year-old woman who's been divorced three times and has no man in her life right now."

"Okay, I didn't say they worked well."

The truth was, though, that Alan Paulus wasn't even the man I was really upset about. I told Janet about that now too.

"Do you remember Sam?"

"The cop who was your second ex-husband?"

"My third. But who's counting? Anyway, I was talking to someone at his precinct the other day, and he said Sam and his new wife just had a baby. I knew she was pregnant. He'd told me that the last time I talked with him. But I didn't realize she'd already had the baby. I guess the baby news kind of depressed me."

"Did you want to have a baby with Sam?"

"Not really."

"Do you want to have a baby with anyone?"

"At my age? No way."

"So why did the baby stuff impact you so much? It doesn't really make a lot of sense, Clare."

I knew the answer to that question. But it was a secret I couldn't tell to anyone. Not even Janet.

No, I didn't want to have a baby now.

You see, I already had a baby.

A long time ago.

But then I lost her.

CHAPTER 4

THERE WERE NO more answers about the Dora Gayle murder. No one was arrested for it. No potential suspects were found, questioned, or even identified. No one figured out exactly why she was in the bank vestibule in the middle of the night. Or why someone had stabbed her to death there.

Which was not really surprising.

People like Dora Gayle died in New York City all the time and then were quickly forgotten. We see them on the streets, in the subway stations, or in our parks and walk right past them as if they didn't exist. And then one day, they are gone and no one ever thinks much more about them.

But there was something about Dora Gayle—unlike other New York City crime stories—that had really gotten to me.

And I knew what it was.

The picture.

I was still haunted by that picture from NYU of the young, beautiful Dora Gayle. This wasn't actually a crime story anymore, at least not a crime story like the ones we usually covered on Channel 10. No one really cared about who killed Dora Gayle. It would wind up being a drug addict or another homeless person or someone else like that who murdered her for no real reason. That wasn't the story here. The real story I still wanted to tell was how she went from the young girl who liked to read poetry and write love sonnets to become the homeless woman who died alone in that bank vestibule.

But everywhere we went turned out to be a dead end.

Dora Gayle was just another obscure person who died an obscure death for some obscure reason.

Sure, we'd given her a few minutes of fame in death by doing her story on the air. A couple of newspapers and news websites in town picked it up—and a few of the national cable news channels did too. The Associated Press even put out a story that went out to media around the country about the sad, tragic woman who called herself Cinderella that died on the streets of New York City.

Still, most people didn't really care. We have a pretty sophisticated rating tracking system for our newscast that shows how many people are watching at any given moment. The ratings were very high for the segment before Dora Gayle, a feature about a new celebrity diet that everyone was trying. And then again for the segment afterward, an interview with a woman who'd won $20 million in the lottery by picking the numbers from her dog's birthday. But not so much for Dora Gayle.

Which meant I wasn't really doing my job. My job was to keep viewers watching the Channel 10 News every night. To get them to buy products from our advertisers. If I didn't do that . . . well, sooner or later I'd be out of a job. I understood that was the bottom line in the TV news business.

And so even I had to finally admit now that the Dora Gayle story was over. When I worked for newspapers, we called murders like this "below the fold" news. That meant they didn't get top play on the front page. It's the same with TV news. Dora Gayle just wasn't important enough for us to care about very much on the evening news.

* * *

I had plenty of other news to cover in the days and weeks after that. Something was always happening in New York City—most of it bad. There were more delays and more commuter outrage at Penn Station. A fire had wiped out a landmark building in Soho. The mayor and the governor were feuding—and both of them were mad at the City Council president.

Plenty of new murders too, and one day we got one right in the Channel 10 wheelhouse as a classic Blonde White Female Syndrome story.

"A woman stockbroker named Grace Mancuso was found beaten to death in her Upper East Side apartment," Maggie told me. "She was very pretty, very successful. The crime scene was really bad. There was blood everywhere in the apartment-bedroom, living room, and kitchen. The Medical Examiner's office says the killer kept beating her even after she must have been long dead. Nothing was taken, as far as investigators can see. It sure looks like a crime of passion."

"Any suspects?" I asked.

"Grace Mancuso had a very active love life—including a new boyfriend and an ex-lover she'd just dumped. They're all being questioned now. "

"Well, that sounds like our top story," I said.

"It gets even better, Clare. Turns out she was involved in some big financial scandal at the Wall Street firm where she worked. A whole bunch of people there are being indicted. And the Mancuso woman had recently negotiated a plea deal for her to turn state's evidence and testify against them."

Money, sex, a beautiful victim—this murder had everything we were looking for in a big story. And yes, she was even blond too.

"Let's work the hell out of it," I told Maggie. "Pictures of Grace Mancuso; video from the scene; interviews with her neighbors; co-workers at the Wall Street business that can tell us about the scandal stuff; details about her love life; and anything else you can think of. I want all hands on deck for this one."

"You got it, boss," she said.

*   *   *

I spent the next few hours doing other news director stuff.

We were starting a series of commercials for a new advertising campaign to promote the Channel 10 newscast—and we'd hired a big Madison Avenue firm to produce the promo spots for us.

The idea was to show all the members of the Channel 10 news team out there doing their jobs just like regular New Yorkers.

There were shots of our sports guy, Steve Stratton, playing stickball with a group of kids on a street in the Bronx; then interviewing players in the locker room at Yankee Stadium; and finally eating a hot dog and cheering during a game along with other die-hard baseball fans in the bleachers. For Wendy Jeffers, the woman who did the weather, we put her on the boardwalk at Coney Island talking about looking forward to the hot summer months ahead. Our traffic reporter was in a helicopter looking down from the sky at a massive traffic jam at the George Washington Bridge; the movie critic standing in the lobby of a theater munching on a tub of popcorn; and the consumer reporter waiting in line at a local store to return a broken appliance.

Those were easy, but some of the other on-air reporters were a bit more challenging. Especially Cassie O'Neal. And Janelle Wright. The two of them were our top-rated on-air reporters. Not coincidentally, both of them were very sexy and glamorous. But beauty—not brains—was their strong suit. I wanted to make sure they came across in the ad as serious journalists, not like the Barbi Twins.

The decision was to put Cassie on a crowded subway car and Janelle in a public-school cafeteria to show how dedicated they were to the important issues of transit and education. The only problem was Cassie had hardly ever been in a subway station before and couldn't figure out how to get through the turnstile, while Janelle refused to eat anything they served in the cafeteria— "I've never eaten a Sloppy Joe in my life—and I'm not about to start now," she proclaimed.

As for Brett and Dani, our two anchors, the ads showed them sitting in a comfortable living room setting—just like the viewers who would be inviting them into their living rooms for the Channel 10 News each night, Of course, I thought it might be more appropriate to shoot the spots with Brett and Dani in the bedroom, but I didn't tell that to the Madison Avenue people.

Somehow though we made it all work.

* * *

My phone rang just before the six p.m. newscast was about to start.

"Clare, I have to talk to you," a familiar voice at the other end said.

It was Sam, my ex-husband who was a cop.

"I'm a little busy right now."

"This is important."

"Okay. And listen, belated congratulations on your baby. I heard the news."

"Huh? Oh yeah, thanks. But this is concerning a story. Do you know about the Grace Mancuso murder on the East Side?"

"Sure. We're leading our newscast with it in a few minutes."

I told him all we'd found out at the scene, at the company where Mancuso worked, and from our police sources.

"There's more," he said.

"More how?"

"They found a note at the scene, Clare. They haven't gone public with it yet. But I wanted to give you a heads-up. It's about your boss."

I was confused.

"What boss?"

"Your big boss. Brendan Kaiser."

Brendan Kaiser was a media mogul who owned a lot of properties in movies, publishing, the Internet, and, of course, TV—including Channel 10, which he had bought about a year earlier.

"There was a list left behind in the Mancuso woman's apartment, apparently by the killer. We're not sure what it means. Kaiser's name is on it. And four more names. There's a politician, Bill Atwood– the guy who used to be in Congress. A well-known lawyer, Emily Lehrman. Even a police detective, a homicide lieutenant named Scott Manning. And I have no idea why the fourth name is there. You'll see what I'm talking about in a few seconds. I'm sending it to you now on email."

"Thanks, Sam. But why are you doing this for me?"

"Old times, Clare. I owe you at least that much."

"I didn't figure you thought the old times were that great."

"I gotta run. You didn't get this from me. Remember that."

He hung up. A few seconds later, I heard the ping of a new email from my computer. I opened up the message. It said:

TO THE NEW YORK CITY POLICE DEPARTMENT

Someone says there's something left to pay, for sins committed yesterday.

Grace Mancuso paid the price today for sins committed a long time ago.

I did this with a little help from my friends . . .

There was a list of names below. Like Sam had said, Brendan Kaiser, the owner of my station, Channel 10, was on that list. So were several other prominent New Yorkers I recognized. None of it made any sense. But it was the last name on the list that made the least sense of all. The list read:

Brendan Kaiser
Bill Atwood
Emily Lehrman
Scott Manning
Dora Gayle

CHAPTER 5

JACK FARON WAS the executive producer of the Channel 10 News. Faron was a pretty good guy, as far as executive producers go. Which is a bit like saying Charles Manson used to be a pretty good guy, as far as crazed, psychotic cult killers go. Still, Faron was the one who promoted me to news director from TV reporter. I was never sure if that was because he thought I'd be good as a behind-the-scenes news executive or because I was so bad on the air. But, one way or another, I owed Faron.

He walked by my office now after I finished reading the note.

"Hey, Jack, I need to show you something I just got from a source of mine," I yelled out.

He came into my office and sat down.

"You still have sources?"

"Yes, I have sources."

"Who's the source?"

"You want a name?"

"Anything."

"He's my ex-husband."

"The lawyer?"

"The cop."

"Kinda hard to keep track of your ex-husbands without a scorecard, Clare."

He smiled broadly. My turbulent marital history was a source of constant amusement for him and a lot of other people at the station. Most of the time I played along with the jokes. But I wasn't in a joking mood right now.

"This is information about Brendan Kaiser," I said.

"What does a cop know about Brendan Kaiser?"

"Kaiser's name just turned up in a murder investigation."

Faron wasn't smiling anymore.

"Turned up why?"

"I'm not sure yet."

"Are you saying he's a suspect in a murder?"

"Not at the moment."

"Well, then what . . ."

"Maybe as a potential future victim. Although I have no idea why. His name was on a note found at the crime scene of the Grace Mancuso murder that we're leading the newscast with in a few minutes. Along with several other well-known names."

I handed him a printout of the email from Sam with the note and told him about our conversation.

"None of this makes any sense," he said after he finished reading it.

"Nope."

"Why would Kaiser's name be on a list like this?"

"I have no idea."

"And what in the world could Dora Gayle—that old homeless woman murdered a few weeks ago—have to do with Kaiser or any of the other people on this list?"

I shrugged. I had no answers for him. Like he said, none of it made any sense.

"No one else knows about this?" he asked now.

"Not yet."

"But they will, right?"

"I can't imagine it won't get leaked by someone even if there's no official release of the information."

"Damn, damn, damn," Faron muttered.

Faron looked over at me then and asked the question I knew he wanted to know the answer to next.

"Are you planning on going with this on the air tonight? Telling everyone about this list with Kaiser's name on it?"

"I think you have to make that decision, Jack."

"This one's above my pay grade."

He took out his cell phone, punched in a number, and then said he urgently needed to talk to Brendan Kaiser.

Kaiser's office said he'd get back to Faron as soon as possible.

While we waited for Kaiser to call back, Faron and I watched our newscast leading off with the Grace Mancuso murder story.

Brett and Dani went through the basic details of the crime and then switched to a live feed of a press conference at police headquarters.

An NYPD spokesman said Grace Mancuso had been bludgeoned to death by as many as fifty to sixty blows. The murder instrument was a large wooden statue found at the scene—a cheap replica of the Empire State Building that looked like it was something sold at a store in Times Square or some similar place that catered to New York City tourists. A chunk of the wooden statue had broken off and couldn't be found. The larger piece, covered in blood, was lying next to Mancuso's body.

The spokesman said there was no sign of forced entry or break-in at the scene, which indicated Mancuso had let the killer in voluntarily. Her body was found when police broke into the apartment after receiving an anonymous 911 call about screams and sounds of violence coming from inside, but the time of death was actually now estimated to be twelve to eighteen hours before that call was received.

He also reported several sets of fingerprints had been found in the apartment besides Grace Mancuso's, and law enforcement authorities were running them through all possible computer data banks to see if they could be identified.

"We are operating on the premise that the motive for the murder is most likely either something in Ms. Mancuso's personal life or else related to her job on Wall Street where she had recently been involved in a financial scandal investigation. Accordingly, we are conducting interviews right now with as many of her friends and co-workers as possible."

The police spokesman did not say anything about a note with the name of Brendan Kaiser or anyone else being found at the scene.

After the live feed from the press conference was over, the Channel 10 broadcast cut back to Brett and Dani in the studio and the rest of the Channel 10 news team with our blanket coverage of the murder of Grace Mancuso.

The most interesting part came when Cassie O'Neal interviewed a neighbor at the Mancuso address who said she'd had several bizarre conversations with the dead woman in recent weeks.

"She asked me for money," the woman said. "Wanted to know if she could borrow a few thousand dollars from me. But she promised to pay it back very soon. It all seemed very strange to me. I mean, I knew she had this big job on Wall Street that paid her a lot of money. And I'd seen the inside of her apartment—it was filled with expensive furniture, closets full of designer clothes, and fancy paintings on the walls. Why did she suddenly need money in such a hurry from me?"

"Did you loan her money or find out what she needed it for?" Cassie asked.

"Of course not. I felt badly for her, but not badly enough to lend money to a neighbor I barely knew. I was a little uncomfortable about it afterward though. I kept hoping I wouldn't run into her and have to make some sort of excuse about the money all over again. But that never happened."

"You never saw her again before her death?"

"Oh, I saw her. Just a few days ago. I wasn't sure what to say, so I just apologized again for not being able to help with the loan of any money. But she didn't even want to talk about it anymore. She didn't seem to care about the loan anymore. She said she'd figured out some other way to get the money she needed."

A few minutes after the segment was over, Faron's phone rang. It was Brendan Kaiser. Faron told him about the note police had obtained and ran through whatever other facts about the murder he knew at the moment.

He tried to put the part about Kaiser's potential involvement in the case as delicately as possible.

But there was no delicate way to tell your boss—and one of the most powerful people in the country—that their name has been linked to a murder.

Me, I hated dealing with the top-level executives at the station on any story.

Even worse, I never wanted to be dealing with the top boss.

And, most of all, I didn't want to be involved in any way in giving him this kind of bad news.

The phrase "kill the messenger" kept running through my mind.

But it turned out I didn't really have much choice this time.

"He wants to see us right away," Faron said when he got off the phone.

"Us?"

"You and me both. I need you with me on this one, Clare."

CHAPTER 6

I HAD NEVER met Brendan Kaiser, even though he owned the TV station I worked for. I'd seen him once, when he bought the station eighteen months earlier and showed up briefly at Channel 10 for the official announcement to everyone here.

I thought about trying to introduce myself that day but decided not to. This was Brendan Kaiser, the legendary media giant who owned TV stations, movie studios, book and magazine publishing companies, newspapers around the world, and also a series of popular and prosperous websites. Head of the billion-dollar Kaiser Communications Corp. I wasn't intimidated very easily, but Kaiser intimidated me.

Most of his time was spent at the main Kaiser headquarters office located in a new high-rise building in Lower Manhattan.

Faron and I went through a succession of security checks there now and then rode a private elevator up to see Kaiser on the top floor of the building. During the cab ride downtown, I had decided on a plan of action for how to handle this whole thing. I would let Faron do all the talking, and I would keep my mouth shut. That way I couldn't get into any trouble.

It was an excellent plan, I decided.

And I congratulated myself for thinking of it.

What could go wrong?

*   *   *

Kaiser greeted us warmly when we were ushered into his office. He was around fifty, decent-looking with thick gray hair, but he also had a bit of a paunch I could see when he stood to greet us. There was an exercise bicycle sitting in a corner of his office, but I had the feeling Brendan Kaiser didn't spend much time on it.

"Tell me everything you know, so we can decide the best course of action here," Kaiser said as he sat down behind his desk after the introductions.

Direct. To the point. No nonsense. I liked that.

Faron ran through it all for him. The call I got from a police source about the note found with Kaiser's name on it at the crime scene; the other names on the list; and the fact that the authorities hadn't made the names—or even the existence of the list and the note—public at this time.

"Do you know any of the other people on the list, Mr. Kaiser?" Faron asked when he was done with that.

"Just one of them. Bill Atwood, the ex-congressman. He and I have met at several political functions. I can't say I know him very well. I meet a lot of politicians like Atwood in my position. There was no special relationship of any kind. I might have run into the Lehrman woman—the attorney—at some event over the years. I'm not sure. But her name seems familiar. I don't know the police officer and I certainly didn't know the homeless woman. And I never heard of Grace Mancuso until she was murdered."

"In other words, you have no idea why your name was on that list," Faron said.

"None whatsoever."

Faron nodded sympathetically.

"Who else at the station knows about this at the moment?" Kaiser asked.

"No one except the two of us, Mr. Kaiser. Clare found out from her source and came directly to me with the information. Then I notified you. I know this all must come as quite a shock to you."

"It certainly does," Kaiser said. "But the question now is what we do next. That's why I called you both here. As you said, this is all very sudden and troubling news for me to hear from you. But now I'd like to hear your ideas about what we should be doing to deal with this going forward."

My plan to remain quiet had been working perfectly so far. It sure was a good plan. A damn fine plan. But, as Mike Tyson once said, everyone has a plan until they get punched in the face.

"How long have you known?" I asked Kaiser.

"Excuse me?"

"How long have you known about your name being found at the Mancuso crime scene? I figure the police would have contacted you right away, probably at least a few hours ago. They had to find out what you might or might not know about the note. I assume you told them the same thing you told us. Then Jack here called you and told you we knew about the note at the crime scene too. You acted like this was the first you'd heard about it, because you wanted to see what our reaction would be. You wanted to know if we were planning to put it on the air. You wanted to know if you were going to have to bigfoot us as the big boss to put a lid on all this—or whether we were going to do that on our own. That's why you just played out this little 'golly, gee—this is the first I heard about this' charade here. Is that pretty much right, Mr. Kaiser?"

Faron looked like he was about to have a heart attack next to me

"Pretty much," Kaiser said softly.

"So why don't we just get to the point you really want to find out from us? About the note at the crime scene which mysteriously includes your name for some reason. How do we keep a lid on this? How do we avoid you being drawn into a messy murder case in some way? How do we contain this?"

"Okay, so how do we contain it?" Kaiser asked me.

"We don't," I responded.

"Uh, what Clare means is . . ." Faron started to say.

Kaiser interrupted him.

"Let her say what she means," he said.

"Mr. Kaiser, you must realize this is going to come out in the media," I told him. "Sooner or later, probably sooner. I know about it. Faron knows. People in the police department know. They talk to other reporters too. Reporters from other stations, newspapers, and all the TMZ-like websites that have sprouted up out there too. Bottom line here is there are three possible reasons you're on that list: 1) You're a potential victim next; 2) you're a possible murder suspect in this; or 3) it was completely random and has no direct connection with you. I'm assuming—I'm really, really hoping—that it's reason No. 3. So our plan should be this: We don't try to contain it. We break the story ourselves. Total transparency. We—or more specifically you—have nothing to hide. We're the station that tells the news as it is, even if we have some kind of personal interest. Even if the story is about our own boss."

There was a long silence after I was finished. Kaiser didn't say anything. Faron didn't say anything. I was beginning to wish I hadn't said anything. But Kaiser finally nodded and smiled at me.

"Go ahead. I'm still listening."

"We break it on the 11 o'clock news tonight. Everyone will pick it up. The other stations, the papers, all the websites—but it will be *our* story right from the beginning."

"We could have Brett and Dani make the announcement at the top of the newscast," Faron said, jumping on board with my idea now. "They're very respected and trusted in the news business."

Kaiser shook his head no.

"I want you to break the story," he told me.

"On the air?"

"Yes."

"Why me?"

"It was your idea, you should be the one to do it."

"All right, I guess I can. But I still don't understand why—"

"There's more," Kaiser said. "I have one more condition if I agree to go ahead with this. But it's a big condition."

I wasn't sure where this was going, but I was about to find out.

"I want you to be the reporter on this. I want you to go on air and talk about any stories we do on this. I want you to handle all the reporting—or at least the bulk of it. I want you to be the face of Channel 10 on the screen breaking whatever news comes out of this in the coming days."

I looked over at Faron. Now he was the quiet one in the room, and it was up to me to say something significant or meaningful or perceptive.

"Why me?" I said again.

It was the only thing I could think of.

"I read up on you. You won a Pulitzer Prize as a newspaper reporter. You did a great job reporting on a lot of other big stories. You're the best reporter we have here. And I want the best. This is about me and I want answers. I want to know why I've been dragged into all this. I want to know who's behind this. I need to use the best possible tools I have at my disposal to get those answers. That's why I want you to cover the story first hand for us."

I hesitated before answering. Normally, I would have jumped at the chance to get back out there reporting a big story myself again. Normally, reporting was the thing I loved to do best. But these weren't normal times for me. I finally told Kaiser I'd do it, but he picked up on my reluctance.

"C'mon, Carlson." He smiled. "Maybe you'll win another Pulitzer. What have you got to lose? Do you have something more important to do right now than throw yourself into this story?"

Actually, I did.

But I couldn't tell Brendan Kaiser what it was.

I couldn't tell anyone.

CHAPTER 7

A LIFETIME AGO, when I was a nineteen-year-old college freshman, I had a baby girl after a one-night stand with a guy I never saw again. I gave the baby up for adoption. I didn't think about it much for a long time after that.

Then, eleven years later, I met my daughter again. Briefly. Her name was Lucy, and she lived with a family named Devlin right here in New York City. Neither she nor the Devlins knew that I was really Lucy's biological mother. Soon after that she was kidnapped and presumed murdered in a sensational New York City crime story. It rivaled the disappearance of six-year-old Etan Patz during the seventies as the most famous missing child case in the city's history.

I covered the story as a newspaper reporter—still never telling anyone about my relationship with Lucy Devlin—and won a Pulitzer Prize and became a pretty big media star because of it. Did I feel any guilt over profiting on my dead daughter? Sure, but I sublimated that guilt to someplace deep down inside me just like I did when I gave her up for adoption.

Last year, I discovered the shocking news that my daughter might still be alive.

I then compromised my journalistic integrity to cover up a powerful politician's role in Lucy's disappearance—and other likely crimes—in order to get him to tell me how to find her.

He still has not done that.

So I had become increasingly consumed over the past few months over what to do next—and by the questions that haunted me along with this.

These questions were:

1) Was my daughter alive?

2) Where was she?

3) What would happen if I ever did meet her?

The consequences of this act of giving birth—which I'd barely thought about when I was nineteen—had become the most important thing in my life as a forty-five-year-old woman.

Even more important than a big story involving Grace Mancuso and Dora Gayle and Brendan Kaiser and all the rest.

But, like I said, I couldn't tell anyone that.

Not even my best friend, Janet.

I had brought it up in a general way with Janet recently. I'd been struggling to find an intelligent, reasonable way to track down my daughter if she was still alive. I couldn't think of any intelligent, reasonable way to do that. So I decided I'd try something stupid. I was that desperate.

"Whatever happened to that guy Todd Schacter you got acquitted?" I asked Janet.

"The computer hacker?"

"Right."

Janet shrugged.

"He's probably online right now stealing someone else's private information, just like he did last time."

Todd Schacter had been arrested after breaking into a Fortune 500 company's computer files. He published on his website all the details of the company's top officers—including salaries, expense accounts, cars and other perks, plus even their home addresses in case disgruntled stockholders wanted to show up at their door to complain.

"If you thought what he did was illegal, why did you represent him?" I asked.

"I'm a lawyer. I represent people who are guilty and innocent. That's what a lawyer does."

"How did you get him acquitted anyway?"

"Did you ever hear of the First Amendment?"

"Vaguely."

"Well, I just stretched the First Amendment a bit."

I asked her a few more questions about Schacter and then I got to the point.

"Can you tell me how to contact him?"

"Why?"

"I want to hire him."

"For what?"

"Do you remember Elliott Grayson? Our former federal prosecutor and now U.S. Senator?"

"Sure, I do. You had an affair with him last year. Then you covered him in that missing girl case. Lucy Devlin."

She knew nothing, of course, about Lucy Devlin being my biological daughter—the daughter I'd given up at birth years earlier.

Or that Elliott Grayson was the politician I'd made a secret deal with last November that helped him get elected to the Senate in return for information on my daughter.

I'd discovered that Grayson had been involved in Lucy's long-ago kidnapping off a Manhattan street—ostensibly as a kind of vigilante justice act to save her from an abusive family situation—as well as several other missing child cases. But I had never told anyone about this or aired the story. In return, Grayson promised to tell me how to find Lucy after the election was over. Except he'd never done that. I'd tried everything to force him to tell me the truth about my daughter, but none of it had worked.

"I need someone to hack into Grayson's computer files."

"Jesus!"

"Yeah, I know. I figured that would be your reaction.'

"Why?"

"I can't tell you that."

"I'm your best friend."

"That's why I can't tell you."

Janet shook her head.

"He's a U.S. Senator. You could get yourself in real legal trouble with this, Clare."

"Then I'll hire you to defend me."

"How would I do that?"

"Ever hear of a little something called the First Amendment?" I smiled.

She sighed.

"Listen, this guy Schacter is really scary. I mean he spies on anyone's records. I was concerned for a while that he was going through my files and my records and my bank accounts."

"Sounds like the person I'm looking for."

"What do you think is in Elliott Grayson's computer files that's so important? No, wait a minute . . . don't tell me. I don't want to know."

"I'm not asking you to do anything illegal, Janet. Just put me in touch with Schacter. Or you don't even have to do that. Just let me know some way to contact him. You don't have to be involved at all."

Janet took out her phone, looked up his information, and clicked on it. She held up the phone screen so I could see and copy it. I had to do it by hand. She refused to even send an email to me with it that might leave some kind of trail back to her if this all went bad.

"Be careful, Clare," she said after she put the phone away. "I know what you're doing must be important to you. But this is a slippery slope you're going down here, my friend."

She was right about that.

It sure was a slippery slope

Slipperier than she could imagine.

CHAPTER 8

THE FIRST THING I decided to do on the Grace Mancuso/Brendan Kaiser story was find out more about the people involved. All the people on the note found next to Mancuso's body, plus Mancuso herself. Accumulate as much information as I could on them. Then see if there was a connection or link I could find between these six seemingly disparate lives that might somehow explain the note.

And so, on the morning after I broke the story on air for Channel 10 about the bizarre note at the crime scene, I started digging on this. I'd worked out an agreement with Faron that I'd still function as news editor for as long as the story took, but he would take over a lot of the day-to-day duties so I could focus on reporting. I also had free rein to use any of the station's reporting staff to help me. Kaiser had balked at this initially, saying he only wanted me doing this story because of the sensitive nature of it for him. But I convinced him it was necessary that I use the station's reporting resources. He finally agreed, as long as all the information came through me.

I have to admit there was a part of me that was grateful to be able to work on a big story like this.

Working on a big story has always been an escape for me from the problems in my life—bad romances, failed marriages, and even a missing daughter. I threw myself into my reporting to avoid having to deal with whatever was bothering me. A big story made my problems fade into the background, at least for a while. A big story kept my mind focused on other things. A big story always made everything better for me.

Maggie had already started a lot of the research. By the time I got to my office a little after eight a.m., she had compiled files of information on all six of the people:

*Bill Atwood, former U.S. Congressman who was now a college president

*Emily Lehrman, high-profile defense attorney

*Scott Manning, NYPD homicide detective

*Dora Gayle, homeless woman found murdered several days earlier

*Brendan Kaiser, media mogul who owned Channel 10

*Grace Mancuso, the murder victim

I took a sip of the coffee I'd bought on my way—at the same store where Dora Gayle used to panhandle at the door, which seemed a bit sad for me—and began going through the information with Maggie.

*   *   *

We started with Bill Atwood. Much of his life was already pretty well known from his years on the public scene. For a while, he'd been the golden boy of American politics. A Rhodes scholar. A successful businessman for several years. After that, he went into public service—getting elected first to statewide office, then to Congress by an overwhelming majority of the voters.

He'd led a charmed life. His father was a wealthy real estate developer and a real mover and shaker in New York politics. Young

Atwood grew up in a Sutton Place penthouse apartment; summered on Nantucket and in Europe; and attended Princeton before going to England on the Rhodes scholarship. He then had become a successful real estate developer himself before going into politics.

On the home front, he was married with a daughter. His wife, Nancy, was a formidable presence in her own right, a major player in both the New York political and cultural scene. Their daughter, Miranda, had been on the dean's list with academic honors at Yale, where she also was a star athlete.

"Then it all began to fall apart," Maggie said. "An intern in his congressional office filed a complaint against him for sexual harassment. She claimed Atwood propositioned her numerous times, made lewd remarks to her, and tried to fondle and touch her inappropriately. When she rejected his advances, she claimed, he ended her internship and gave the job to another young girl. She also told salacious stories she'd found out about Atwood and other women in his office.

"The women began coming out of the woodwork after that. Another intern who said she'd slept with him a dozen times. A stewardess who said she'd had a two-year affair with him. A Washington lobbyist who claimed he'd come on to her after a late-night meeting, then paid her to keep quiet. The House Ethics Committee eventually announced that Atwood had 'agreed to resign' from Congress to avoid any further action."

He left Washington, but he didn't leave the public eye. Within a few months, he was back. He went on the lecture tour, commanding $100,000 per appearance. He helped raise funds for other candidates and the party too, with a seemingly endless succession of benefits and appearances around the country. Then, a year ago, he was named president of Benson College in New York City. There was some opposition from educators who felt he wasn't a proper role model for students. But the board of the school and the alumni and most of the student body embraced him wholeheartedly. He was a popular guy, a charismatic figure who could put their school on the map.

And that's just what he'd done. There were speeches, TV appearances, fund-raisers—he even wrote a best-selling book about U.S. politics. Bill Atwood was a happening guy again. People knew what he had done, but somehow it didn't seem to bother them. A recent poll had showed that a majority of people would vote for him again if he ever ran for another public office.

*   *   *

Emily Lehrman was the kind of rich, super-successful lawyer who made people mad.

There was an interview with her in a legal magazine in which she almost seemed to flaunt her role as a poster girl for everything that people hated about the profession.

"My job is to win cases and make money doing it," she told the interviewer. "It's that simple. I don't care whether my client is guilty, innocent or somewhere in between. I represent anyone that wants to pay me for the best legal representation that money can buy. What I'm doing is what everyone else does in other professions. Making money. I just make more of it than most other people do."

"Charming woman, huh?" Maggie said.

"I guess that's why people love lawyers so much."

It turned out that Lehrman wasn't always that money-hungry though. At first, after graduating from law school, she went into public defender practice in New York. Her specialty had been representing tenants—most of them poor—against unscrupulous landlords. There were several small newspaper articles from that period of her cases. One involved representing a homeless man who'd been arrested for vagrancy. She also worked extensively with tenants who'd been evicted as well as squatters—people living illegally in condemned or otherwise uninhabitable buildings because they had no place else to go.

"After that there was nothing about her for a few years until she suddenly turned up representing a mobster with a long record on a gun possession charge," Maggie said. "These days she's in the media a lot in connection with a series of high profile cases. Underworld figures, drug czars, and big-money white collar crime. Weird, isn't it? Almost as if there were two Emily Lehrmans. Except there wasn't. I checked with the American Bar Association."

So what happened? Why did it take Emily Lehrman so long to figure out where the money was?

More importantly, what did any of this have to do with the story? I sure didn't know.

* * *

Scott Manning was a decorated police officer who had been with the NYPD for more than twenty years.

He graduated from the police academy at the top of his class and started working as a uniformed patrolman. He did well on the street, moving up to detective and then sergeant and finally homicide lieutenant—with lots of commendations along the way. He lived with his wife and three children in Staten Island, where he was a volunteer fireman in the community and also helped to coach Little League on Saturdays. At first glance, Scott Manning seemed to be a good cop and a good father and an all-around good guy.

Or was he?

He'd been placed on restricted duty after a controversial death involving him and his partner. A nineteen-year-old named Manny

Nazario had been arrested as a suspect in a series of brutal attacks on women and the elderly. While he was in the holding cell on the second floor of the precinct, he somehow went out a window and was found unconscious on the street below.

At first, it seemed as if he'd simply tried to escape and been unlucky when he hit the pavement, since his injuries seemed far beyond what would be expected from a two-story fall. He was taken to the hospital, where he was not expected to survive. But Nazario regained consciousness and insisted, according to family members at his bedside, that he was not trying to escape. He claimed that a cop had pushed him out the window.

He also said the cop had beaten him up before that, which accounted for the severity of his injuries. He identified the cop as one of the detectives who'd arrested him. Sergeant Tommy Bratton—Manning's partner. Then he lapsed back into a coma and died three days later. Bratton denied all the charges and his partner, Scott Manning, backed up his story.

There was a lot of outrage by community leaders who said the department was covering up police brutality. Both Bratton and Manning were then taken off active duty until a further investigation was conducted. In the midst of all this furor, Bratton died of a heart attack. At his funeral, the eulogy was delivered by his partner, Manning, who praised him as "a good cop, my partner, my friend, my brother in blue."

* * *

There were no surprises with Dora Gayle.

We pretty much knew all the information about her from the stuff we'd already reported on the murder. I was still struck by the fact, though, that she was the only person who seemed out of place on this list—the only one who wasn't either rich or successful or prominent in their field.

We went back to the park, the coffee shop and the other places she spent her time without learning anything new. I even sent a reporter and camera crew to the bank where she had died. They took some video of customers lined up there to use the ATM machines. That's where she'd been found dead. Presumably she'd gone into the bank entrance to sleep where it was warm, and someone had followed her inside and murdered her for God knows what reason.

The Channel 10 crew interviewed the bank manager, still looking for any kind of morsel of interest. His name was Jason Wincott.

"We've always had a lot of transients who try to camp out there," Wincott said. "The outer door is locked, of course. But they wait for someone to go in or out to the ATMs using their pass card, then just follow them inside and stay. That's what must have happened the other night with this woman."

"I guess she must have wanted someplace warm to spend the night," the reporter said.

"Only thing is it wasn't that cold. It was the first really nice early spring night of the year. Temperature never went below the sixties."

"Maybe she just thought it was safer being inside there than being out on the street by herself."

"I guess so. But it sure didn't turn out to be safer for her. To be honest, I don't know how most of them live like that for a single night on the street—much less making it their permanent home."

The most interesting part of the interview came when Wincott revealed that Dora Gayle actually had a savings account with the bank. My reporter got very excited about that—just like I did when I first heard the news. Maybe Dora Gayle wasn't simply some poor bag lady after all. Maybe she had lots of money and secrets about her life she was hiding. Maybe the money in that account was what had gotten her murdered.

But it turned out the bank account was a long dormant one from years earlier with only a few dollars in it. Probably from when she was on some kind of government assistance and still competent enough to open up a savings account. There had been no deposits or withdrawals from it in a very long time.

Did she go to the bank that night in some forlorn hope that she could still withdraw money from that old account of hers to buy coffee or maybe a bottle from the liquor store?

Or just to get off the streets outside for a little while because she thought it was safer there?

Or for some other reason that we knew nothing about, that somehow got her included on that list?

* * *

I already knew a lot about my boss, Brendan Kaiser, too. Or at least I thought I did. His father, Charles Kaiser, had been a successful newspaper publisher and—after he died—Brendan took over the business. But, when Maggie briefed me on his past, there were some real surprises. Especially from when he was younger.

Growing up, Brendan Kaiser showed no indication at all of being the powerful figure he eventually became. The truth is he was kind of a screw-up. Expelled from a series of schools. Picked up by the police for drinking and smoking pot. For more than a year, he drifted from place to place. Los Angeles. San Francisco. France. Italy. Turkey. Japan. He told friends he wanted to experience life.

Brendan's older brother, Charles Jr., was being groomed to go into the family business and take over one day from his father. He had all the credentials. Graduated with honors from Harvard, a star athlete there, president of the student body.

But then Charles Jr. tragically died in a drowning incident off Long Island.

It was a devastating blow to his father. Charles Kaiser Sr. had invested all his hopes and dreams in his oldest son. People said he never really recovered. After Charles Jr.'s death, he tried to get Brendan to join him in the family business. Brendan refused. But that all changed later when Charles Kaiser suffered a massive heart attack and died. His sudden demise left his business empire in chaos. Kaiser had always run it himself, and there was no corporate or executive structure to fill the void of his absence. Only another Kaiser could do that. Brendan reluctantly took over control of his father's business.

He said he would only do it for a short time, but—as the years went by—it became clear Brendan was indeed his father's son. The company grew in ways that even Charles Kaiser Sr. could never have envisioned while he was alive. Brendan Kaiser bought a half dozen television stations, which he turned into a new network. A year later, he bought a giant movie studio and became a force in Hollywood. There was also a book publishing company, a chain of magazines, a worldwide satellite empire, newspapers and local TV stations like Channel 10; plus, popular websites and many other valuable social media properties.

But why was he on the killer's list of so-called "friends"?

Why were any of them?

CHAPTER 9

I SAVED GRACE Mancuso until last because—as the murder victim—she clearly had to be the key to this.

"Grace Mancuso, thirty-three years old, lived alone," Maggie said. "Worked as a stock analyst and broker for a company down on Wall Street called Revson Investments. One of those places that have been in the news recently. They got indicted for helping some big corporations loot people out of their stock options and 401(k) money while a bunch of big shots there made off with all of the money. She didn't go to jail, but some of the people she worked with probably will. Turns out Mancuso walked away with a plea bargain after giving up other people in the company who took part in the rip-off. Many of the victims were senior citizens who lost their life savings over what happened at Revson. That's plenty of suspects who might have wanted Mancuso to die a horrible death."

"Yeah, I figure the company's disgruntled client records are going to make for one long list of suspects," I said. "What about her personal life?"

"She had an ex-boyfriend, a current boyfriend, and apparently a future boyfriend—some guy she told people she had her sights set on."

"Sounds like she was a busy lady."

"Yeah, no specific names of the lovers yet. Still checking on that."

"Next of kin?"

"She's from a little town in Pennsylvania. Came to the city after college and worked her way up on Wall Street. The parents are on their way now to claim the body. Say it's the first time they've ever been here."

"Welcome to New York," I said.

Maggie then went through all the details we knew from the police about her murder.

"Someone made an anonymous call to the police at 12:17 p.m. that day and said there was screaming and other suspicious noises coming from that apartment. The cops sent a patrol car to check it out and eventually found the body. Only problem is that the Medical Examiner's office says Mancuso died at least twelve to eighteen hours earlier. That puts her time of death the night before."

"Which means the caller couldn't have heard her screams then because she was long dead," I said.

"Yes, the police think it was the killer who called."

"Why wait so long? Why call at all? Why not just wait for someone to find her dead?"

"Why leave the note, too?" Maggie shrugged. "The police have lots of questions, Clare. Not many answers yet."

She continued to read from her notes.

"The victim was beaten to death. Badly beaten. She had multiple, massive contusions of the head and body. Struck repeatedly with the statue police found in her apartment—and probably the killer's fists, as well. It was a real mess, and her face—which everyone described as being so beautiful—was almost unrecognizable. It looks like whoever did this was trying to make some kind of a statement.

"The list was handwritten—scrawled in big letters with a pen—on standard white bond paper. There was more of a similar kind of paper found in Mancuso's place, so it appears the killer just picked up a piece of the paper spontaneously and wrote the note and the list of names. In other words, that part of it was probably not pre-mediated. Probably the murder wasn't pre-meditated either—the details make it look like more of an emotional outburst of violence than a methodical planned killing.

"There's still no obvious connection that's turned up between any of the names on the list—either with each other or with Mancuso or with Revson, the company she worked for. The only common link between those five names on the list so far is that they're all around the same age. And Dora Gayle sure doesn't really seem to fit in with the others in any other way.

"There were several sets of fingerprints found in the apartment. Including, of course, Mancuso's own prints. Also, a possible partial set of fingerprints on the paper the list was written on. Again, it doesn't appear that whoever did this plotted it out very much. Unfortunately, none of the prints in the place have turned up any match yet in the law enforcement files."

I nodded. I knew most of this already, but it was always good to lay out all the details of a story like this. Sometimes the individual pieces—the different threads of the narrative—came together in some sort of logical sequence. But not this time. None of it made any sense to the police or to me.

"Anything else?" I asked.

"Yes, the statue that was used to kill her," Maggie said. "There's something about that which doesn't make sense either. Two things about it, actually, that don't make sense. First, a piece of it is missing and can't be found. Where is it? Why would the killer take that—and leave the rest of the statue? Second, everything else in Grace Mancuso's apartment—furniture, clothes, artwork—was supposed to be expensive and classy, a sign of her affluent success on Wall Street. The woman sure seemed like she knew how to live well and spend money. The only thing out of place is the statue. It's a cheap, garish-looking piece of wood that hardly cost anything. No way Grace Mancuso would have ever bought something like that or kept it in her apartment. Which means . . ."

"The killer brought it there," I said.

*   *   *

When we were done with Grace Mancuso, Maggie and I looked back over at the five names on the list—Bill Atwood, Emily Lehrman, Scott Manning, Dora Gayle, and Brendan Kaiser. The five names that seemed to have no obvious connection to each other or to the dead Grace Mancuso. But somehow, they had to be a key to her murder.

"Which one of these five will you go to see first?" Maggie asked me.

"None of them," I said.

"Why not?"

"Like the old saying goes, 'follow the money.'"

Maggie smiled.

"Then you're going first to—"

"Revson Investments, the place where Grace Mancuso worked."

CHAPTER 10

IF REVSON INVESTMENTS was in financial trouble because of the stock scandal, it was doing a nice job of hiding it. The offices took several top floors of a big building near Wall Street. Everything about the place oozed money. Rich leather furniture, plush carpets, expensive paintings on the walls. An attractive woman receptionist greeted visitors with a smile, and soft music played through the halls. Of course, you never knew about a place like this. The bank could be ready to foreclose and they'd still be smiling and assuring the clients everything was all right while the moving vans pulled up.

The CEO of Revson Investments was a man named Vernon Albright. He met me and my video crew in his office, which had a window with a sweeping view of the Hudson River all the way over to New Jersey.

I wasn't sure at first if Albright would talk to me. Or be willing to go on air for an interview. But he had no hesitation about doing either. I got the feeling that Revson was doing its best to put a positive PR spin on all their troubles—and Albright seemed to be the front man for that. He was pretty good at it.

"It was a terrible thing that happened to Grace," Albright said once the interview began, looking at the camera with an expression that combined both gravitas and yet positive vibes for worried Revson investors out there. "We're all still in a state of shock. It's like losing a member of the family. People do die, but for someone to die like that . . . well, it's just terrible."

I told Albright I agreed that Grace Mancuso's death was a terrible thing.

"The police are still trying to find out why someone wanted to kill her," I said. "The most obvious connection is that it had something to do with her work at your company. This would be true in any case, of course. But the possible connections between what happened to her and her job seem even more relevant here because of your recent problems."

Albright nodded. He'd expected the question. And he was ready with an answer.

"I see where you're coming from," he said. "So let me take you through this as simply as I can. Several months ago, I became aware of some . . . well, irregularities . . . in our business practices here. We were informed that federal investigators were looking into a number of questionable business dealings conducted by members of this firm. I, of course, immediately launched my own intensive investigation into the matter. It was eventually discovered that members of the company had taken millions of dollars from investors. There was a number of ways this was done. One involved giving the investors false information about their portfolios. The scenario went like this: The broker was encouraging people to keep investing in certain commodities in order to artificially keep the stock share price high, while he or she was systematically divesting themselves of their own investments in the stock. I call it dubious business practices."

"It's also called fraud," I pointed out.

"Of course, it is," Albright said. "We, of course, condemn any such practices and moved quickly to cooperate with federal and local investigators in the matter. We also encouraged everyone in the firm to be truthful and candid when they were questioned about their knowledge of the matter. Most of the people at Revson are honest and conscientious people. But there's always a few bad apples."

"What about Grace Mancuso?"

"What about her?"

"Was she one of the bad apples?"

"Ms. Mancuso's guilt—or level of knowledge and involvement—was never officially determined during the investigation. She provided information against several of her co-workers that helped greatly in the prosecution. As a result, she was given immunity from any possible criminal charges."

"I imagine the people she gave up weren't too happy about that."

"No, I suppose not."

"What about you?"

"What do you mean?"

"How did the company feel about her actions?"

"As I said, we were pleased that she cooperated with the investigation."

"Pleased enough to let her keep working for you."

"For the time being."

"Meaning?"

Albright cleared his throat nervously.

"Could we stop the cameras and go off the record here, Ms. Carlson?"

"Okay."

I told my video team to stop and asked them to wait for me outside Albright's office.

"May I speak frankly with you about Grace Mancuso?" he said to me once they were gone and I'd established we were off the record now.

"I'd sure like that."

"We didn't sever her relationship with the firm, because it would have sent a bad message to others who might cooperate with the prosecutors. We encouraged her to tell the truth and said there would be no repercussions from us. But, as I'm sure you can understand, it would be difficult for her to have any kind of a future here under the circumstances. So we worked out an arrangement where she would resign quietly in a few months."

"How did she feel about that?"

"She really didn't have any choice. As I said, it was an uncomfortable situation."

I stood up and walked over to the window behind Vernon Albright's desk. From the offices of Revson Investments, you could see the streets of Manhattan below. But you couldn't really see the people. You were so high up here that they looked like ants, running around down below.

Maybe working here gave the people at Revson a different view of the world. They had all this money, all this power—they probably thought they were gods. That they could do anything they wanted with these people's money. They forgot those were real people down there that they were robbing.

Of course, it probably didn't seem like robbery when they did it. This theft was all on computers and electronic files and banking statements. Clean and neat, no violence. But it was robbery, all right. Just the same as the bad guy who walked into a bank or a bodega and announced a stickup. The only difference was the bad guys at Revson couldn't see the people they were robbing.

"I'd like to speak with some of your other employees, Mr. Albright," I said.

"Of course."

"Any suggestions on who could be helpful?"

"I'll give you some names."

He wrote them down on a piece of memo paper. I looked at the names. None of them meant anything to me, but then I didn't expect they would.

Vernon Albright was good. Very good. He'd gotten his whole response to the Revson scandal down perfectly. Maybe even rehearsed it. "We were all shocked, we had no idea, there's always a few bad apples . . ." Albright had used that speech on a lot of people before, and he had it down pat.

There's an old saying in journalism that it isn't always what people tell you, sometimes it's what they don't tell you that matters. Albright had given me a lot of information, but most of it was probably useless. Just like the names on the memo pad that he'd written down. The question was what Albright didn't tell me. And who he didn't want me to talk to in the company.

If I could figure that out, maybe I'd have a lead to what really happened to Grace Mancuso.

CHAPTER 11

AFTER I LEFT Albright's office, I told the video team to go back to the office without me.

"What are you going to do?" one of them asked.

"Walk around the place a bit. See what I can find out."

"What are you looking for?"

"I don't know."

That was the truth. Sometimes you have to let your instincts as a reporter take over. No, I wasn't sure what I was looking for, or even if I was going to find it here at Revson Investments. But I wanted to try. Just stumble around in the dark a bit and open up a few doors at random and see what was there.

I wandered around the Revson offices, questioning various employees and making myself pretty obvious to everyone. I was pretty sure I was the main topic of conversation—a TV reporter asking questions about a murdered woman employee tended to draw a lot of attention. But I didn't really learn anything in the Revson offices.

I'd just about given up when a young woman walked by carrying a pile of file folders and heading toward a small office in the corner. If Vernon Albright's office was a battleship, this one was like a small dinghy. It appeared she didn't rank too high in the

Revson hierarchy. I wouldn't have even given her a second thought except she said softly to me as we passed each other: "Starbucks, two blocks north of here. Twenty minutes." At first, I thought she might be talking to someone else. She didn't even look at me and just kept walking. No one in the office could see we'd made any kind of contact, Which, as it turned out, was her idea.

* * *

Later, sitting with her and drinking coffee, the woman introduced herself as Lisa Kalikow.

"I didn't want to talk in the office," she said. "People are watching. They know I know things about Grace. They don't want me to tell anyone anything. I could lose my job if I do, and I need this job. But Grace was my friend. I want people to know the truth about her. How much did they tell you back there?"

I went through everything Vernon Albright had said. Kalikow didn't say anything until I was finished, but she smiled a few times. Especially at the end where I recounted how Albright had said the company had never determined whether Grace Mancuso was involved in the scandal or not. But that he had encouraged her and all other employees to do the right thing and tell prosecutors anything they knew.

"You don't buy that?" I asked.

"Grace was into the scandal up to her neck," she said. "She was in as deep as any of the ones going to jail. The only reason she didn't was that she went to the authorities when she saw what was happening and made her own deal. The deal was to give up other people in the company to save herself from prosecution. The feds needed her to make their case, so they agreed. Grace always made sure she was protected, even if someone else had to take the heat."

She said it matter of factly, not with any anger. I wondered if she had been fingered by Grace Mancuso in the investigation.

"I thought you were her friend," I said.

"I was."

"You don't sound like it."

"You don't understand Grace. She wasn't like most people. She had no . . . no conscience. I know that sounds terrible, but that's the way Grace was. There was just something missing from her. A human gene or something. Whether something was right or wrong didn't bother her. She was out for herself first. When it came to a moral dilemma like the scandal here, it was an easy decision for her. She bailed out on her friends and took care of herself. That was her one weak point. I guess you'd call it a character flaw."

"That sounds like a pretty big character flaw to me."

Lisa Kalikow shrugged. "We all have character flaws. Hers was just more apparent than others. When it came to money, she was the most cutthroat person I've ever met, and believe me I've run across some real doozies in this business. But I liked Grace. As I said, we were friends. Or at least as good a friend as anyone could be with Grace."

"When I spoke to Albright, he said she was planning on leaving the company in a few months."

Kalikow nodded. "It was made very clear to Grace that she was on the way out. Oh, they couldn't fire her right away—because then it would have looked like she was being punished for cooperating with the investigation. But she would leave in a few months. She couldn't do anything about it. They held all the cards. She was into the whole scandal mess pretty deep."

"How deep?"

"Albright told you it involved Revson giving people false information about their portfolios to artificially raise or lower the prices of certain stocks? Well, that's how it started out. But it got a lot worse. They eventually were actually stealing money out of people's accounts. They told the investors—most of them small time, working folks—that the money was lost in the stock market. Most of these poor people believed it—at least for a while—because they didn't know much about how it all worked. You trust your stockbroker or investment counselor. Big mistake in this case. There were families that were completely wiped out of their life savings or pension accounts."

"Didn't the people at Revson who did this figure they'd eventually get caught?"

"They thought they were too smart, I guess. Or maybe they thought it was worth the risk. They were making a lot of money, and it was so easy for them until it all blew up in their faces."

"And Grace Mancuso was one of those involved?"

"That's right. So she wasn't going to be working here for very long—whether or not she made a deal with the prosecutors to cooperate. She was damaged goods for this place or anybody else in the financial world."

"She had a pretty expensive lifestyle to maintain," I said, thinking of the fancy furnishings and antiques I'd heard about in her apartment. "How was she going to pay for it?"

Lisa Kalikow stared down at her coffee. She tried to pick it up, but her hand was shaking. This was obviously very difficult for her.

"Look, I'm not sure about any of this. But something else happened a few days before she was killed. We went out for drinks after work, and Grace got a bit loose and started talking more than she normally did. Most of it was about work and stuff like that. But then she said this strange thing. Afterward, I thought about it a lot. I was going to ask her what she meant, but I never got the chance."

"What did she say?"

"She told me she had a way to make a lot of money."

"Did she say what that was?"

"No."

"Do you have any idea?"

"My guess is she had something on someone."

"She was blackmailing somebody?"

"That's what it sounded like."

CHAPTER 12

I'VE INTERVIEWED THE families of lots of murder victims over the years. There are usually no surprises for me anymore as a journalist with this kind of thing. The emotions all tend to run pretty much the same. Grief, anger, despair, and—most of all, I suppose—an overwhelming sense of loss. But it was different with Grace Mancuso.

"I suppose I should feel worse," Roger Mancuso said to me when I tracked down him and his wife in New York City, where they'd come to deal with their daughter's murder.

"What do you mean?"

"Grace is dead. I should be devastated. But I'm not. Last night, I ate a great meal at the restaurant in the hotel. I walked around Times Square and looked at the sights. I watched a movie on TV. I enjoyed myself. How can I do that if my daughter is dead?"

"We all grieve in different ways. Sometimes we hide it."

"I'm not hiding anything."

"In a few days or a week ..."

Mancuso shook his head. "You don't understand, Ms. Carlson. I just don't feel anything. Oh, I feel badly that she died. Just like I'd feel badly that any human being died, especially like that. But I don't feel the kind of grief that a father is supposed to feel. She was our daughter, for God's sake. But when I hear about the things she did at that company—the way she stole from people—it's like I'm reading about someone else. Someone I didn't know. I guess I lost my daughter a long time ago. A long time before she died."

We were sitting in a restaurant at the hotel where Roger Mancuso and his wife were staying. His wife was still upstairs. He said she'd be joining us in a few minutes. Mancuso was eating eggs over easy, bacon and home fried potatoes. I just had orange juice and coffee. I never ate much when I was working on a big story. Too much adrenalin or something, I guess.

"Tell me about your daughter."

"Do you mean about her life here in New York?"

"That's fine."

"I don't know much about that."

"Then tell me what you do know."

"All I know is about her growing up in Pennsylvania."

"That's good too."

"Why do you care about that?"

"I care about everything at this point, Mr. Mancuso. I'm trying to put together a picture of your daughter's life in the hopes that it will give us some clues as to how she died."

Grace's story turned out to be a variation of one I'd heard a lot of times before. She'd grown up on a farm in a small town called Brockton. Brockton was outside another small town called DuBois, which was about 100 miles from the Ohio/West Virginia border. Roger Mancuso had run their farm for years. His father and grandfather owned it before him. This was definitely a family from heartland America.

Grace was no typical farmer's daughter though. She was constantly getting in trouble as a young girl and as a teen. Some of it was just normal kid stuff—running around with boys, drinking and smoking, hell-raising. But, when she was sixteen years old, she was arrested for shoplifting. The police found some earrings, a watch, and a necklace in her purse.

"She just wanted them," Mancuso said. "When I asked her why she did it, that was her answer. She just wanted them. There was no remorse, no guilt—the only thing she was upset about was that she'd gotten caught. I looked in her eyes and ... well, that's the first time I realized that I didn't know my own daughter. The first time that I realized I was losing her. It was like there was something missing from her. A conscience. A sense of right and wrong. She didn't have that."

Grace had this one flaw—she had no conscience, her friend at the Revson company had said. Now her father was saying the same thing.

"What happened to her after the arrest?"

"She got off on probation."

"Did she do it again?"

"Not that. But other stuff. Cheating on her SATS. Breaking into a neighbor's house and stealing money. There were other incidents too. I didn't find out about all of them until she left."

"Where did she go?"

"We never knew at first. She just seemed to disappear off the face of the earth for a few years. Then she called one day out of the blue. She needed money. We sent her some, then never heard any more for a long time. By bits and pieces, we later found out how successful she had become. But not from her. We only heard from her when she was in trouble and needed money."

"When was the last time you talked to her?"

"Several weeks ago."

"Tell me about that conversation."

"She said she was going to leave her job. She said she had a lot of bills to pay. She said she needed money in a hurry. She said her financial problems were only temporary, until she figured out a way to make more. She wanted us to take out a loan for her. She wanted us to take out a loan on our farm as the collateral."

"What did you say?"

"Nothing. I was too stunned. She asked me to think about it. She said she really needed the money because she'd had some setbacks in her career."

"What happened after that?"

"She said she'd call back for my answer. But she never did."

"And this conversation with your daughter was how long ago?"

"A month or two."

"Why do you think she never called back?"

"I know why."

"Because she found the money some other way," I said.

Mancuso nodded sadly. "You have to understand my daughter," he said. "That's what she was all about. Money."

Ruth Mancuso came down and joined us. She looked tired and washed out. "I'm sorry I'm late, but I was on the phone making the funeral arrangements back in Pennsylvania," she said. "It's a little complicated, because we don't have her body yet. The Medical Examiner's office here says they can't release it until the inquest is completed."

"So you're going to be burying her back in Pennsylvania?"

"Of course. That's where she's from."

"I thought that maybe since she's been gone so long, you might want to hold the service here where her friends are."

"I have no idea who her friends were."

"She never told you?"

"Grace never confided anything in us," Roger Mancuso said. "Not even as a little girl. That's why we were so confused when she came to us with this last request to use the farm to give her money. We had no idea what was wrong, why she needed it—or what she planned to do next."

"Did you two decide not to give her the money?" I asked them.

Ruth Mancuso looked over at her husband for a second, then just nodded without saying anything. I got the feeling they'd had a lot of discussions about this. How far do you go to save your only child? I wasn't sure about the answer to that one myself.

"When was the last time you talked to your daughter, Mrs. Mancuso?" I asked.

"I can't remember."

There was something hesitant about the way she said it. I picked up on it immediately. She was lying.

"Did you get on the phone during the conversation with your husband about the money?"

"No, I didn't."

"You talked to her after that conversation, didn't you, Mrs. Mancuso?"

She looked flustered for a minute, then gave it up. "Yes . . . yes, I did."

"Ruth!" her husband said in astonishment. "You never told me."

"I had to try, Roger. I couldn't leave it like that between us. I wanted to try and talk to her. Talk with her like a mother and a daughter. I wanted her to tell me the truth for one time in her life."

"But it didn't work?"

"No. She didn't even want to spend any time on the phone with me. She was too busy. Some big meeting she was going to."

"From work?"

"No, it was something else. That's all she would say. She didn't seem to care one way or the other about the farm loan anymore."

"She'd figured out some other way to get the money and she didn't need you anymore," I said.

"Yes."

CHAPTER 13

HOW FAR DO you go to save your only child?

That was the question Roger and Ruth Mancuso said they'd had to deal with even before their daughter's tragic death. They were never sure of the answer. Neither was I.

I remembered something else that Roger Mancuso had told me about his daughter over breakfast: "We lost her a long time ago," he said.

I could sure relate to that.

I took out my cell phone after I left the hotel and called a number I knew all too well from the endless, fruitless calls I'd made to it in the past. Not that I expected any actual response this time either. But I had to make the effort. You always had to make every effort to make things right when it was your own daughter.

"I had to try," Ruth Mancuso had said. "I couldn't leave it like that between us. I wanted to try and talk to her. Talk with her like a mother and a daughter."

I thought about that—and a lot of other things—as I listened to my call ringing the number until someone picked it up on the other end.

"Senator Elliott Grayson's office," a woman said.

"This is Clare Carlson from Channel 10 TV News in New York," I said. "I have to speak to Senator Grayson urgently."

"Is this about a story?"

"Not exactly."

"Well, what is it you need to talk to the senator about?"

"It's a personal matter."

"Then you're calling as a constituent of the senator—"

"Yes, I'm a damn constituent!"

I was a lot more than a constituent of Elliott Grayson. I'd gone out with him. I'd almost slept with him. I'd go head-to-head against him in the biggest story of my life. And, in the end, I'd worked out the secret deal with him to bury the damaging story I had about him—an odorous arrangement that kept me up nights regretting it—in order to get him to lead me to my daughter.

Even now, I find it painful to think about that fateful decision I made months ago, when Grayson was a federal prosecutor running for the Senate.

I'd uncovered something so incredibly damaging about him that it would have been the biggest exclusive of my journalistic career. But Grayson had done his own investigation, too. On me. And he'd discovered the facts about me and Lucy Devlin—that she was the daughter I'd had and then given up for adoption as a nineteen-year-old in college.

That's when he told me the truth about her.

Or at least what he claimed to be the truth.

That Lucy was still really alive.

All grown up now with a family of her own.

And he knew where Lucy was now.

He made a promise to tell me that location and her name and all the rest once the election was over. All I had to do was kill the story I was about to do prior to Election Day. He was ahead in the race, and a scandal could cost him the election. The decision I had to make was a simple trade-off: my story for my daughter.

Well, it wasn't really all that simple.

The arrangement we eventually worked out to accomplish this was a violation of every journalistic ideal I'd lived my life by; an abandonment of the principles I preached to every reporter who worked for me all these years; and a life-changing moment that I still at times wish I could re-live and do over again.

But I've kept my word to Grayson and never told anyone the story. My word is still very important to me. It's pretty much all I have left of my integrity these days, and so I hold onto it desperately—like a drowning person clutches a life saver as the angry seas threaten to swallow them up.

Except Grayson refused to hold up his end of the bargain and tell me any more about Lucy and her fate.

And so we remained in a stalemate.

A stalemate I did not know how to break

All I knew was I had to do everything in my power to find out the truth about Lucy.

"I really need to talk to Senator Grayson immediately," I said now.

"Hold on, Ms. Carlson." The woman put me on hold. I knew the whole routine by now. A few minutes of listening to Muzak, then she'd come back on the phone to tell me he wasn't available to speak to me.

I was right.

"Senator Grayson always likes to hear from his constituents," the woman said when she came back on the line. "But he is unavailable right now. However, I will pass your message on to him."

"And then what?"

"You'll hear back from him if it's a matter he feels he can be of assistance to you in any way."

"Bullshit!"

"What?"

"He's not going to call me back, is he? And you probably didn't even check with him or anyone else about his availability or whatever the hell you call it. I'll bet you just put me on hold, did something else for a minute or two, and then came back on with your little spiel about him being too busy for me. Is that what Elliott Grayson told you to say whenever I called and tried to speak to him?"

The woman sighed.

"Ms. Carlson, you should have gotten the message by now. Senator Grayson does not want to talk to you. He will not talk to you. Ever. So please stop making these pointless calls of yours."

"He has some information that is very important to me," I said. "I'm going to get that information from him one way or another. Tell him."

"Is that a threat?"

"It's a promise."

"Well, it sounds like a threat."

"Take it for whatever it is."

"I could report you to the police . . ."

"You better check with Grayson before you do that," I told her. "Believe me, the last thing he wants is to get the police involved in this thing between him and me. Elliott Grayson has too much to hide."

I hung up the phone.

I hadn't thought I'd get anywhere with the call. Any more than I had with any of the others. Or my repeated efforts to see him at his offices, either here in New York or in Washington. But, like

Ruth Mancuso had said, you just had to try when it came to your own daughter.

You had to try anything.

Whatever it took.

And so I looked back at my cell phone, found the contact information I'd gotten from Janet on Todd Schacter—the scary computer hacker she'd represented—and sent Schacter a message asking for his help.

CHAPTER 14

BRENDAN KAISER SUMMONED me to his office the next morning. Not with Faron this time, just me. Which meant that my original game plan of "no speak, no trouble" wasn't going to work. I decided to be candid, but also discreet, because of the sensitive nature of this story to Kaiser. Unfortunately, being discreet is not exactly one of my strong points.

We had run a story on the newscast the previous night based on my interview with Vernon Albright, the head of Revson, and also Grace Mancuso's parents.

I talked on air about how Channel 10 had learned that Grace Mancuso was not only embroiled in a financial scandal at Revson prior to her death—but also seemed to be desperate for money in her personal life immediately afterward.

We ran some of the on-the-record quotes from Albright about Mancuso's role in the scandal there and her subsequent cooperation with authorities to give up people there in return for a plea deal.

This was followed by video we shot of Grace Mancuso's parents talking about how she had been in some kind of financial distress before her murder.

I then quoted several sources—including Lisa Kalikow, who I did not name—that the Mancuso woman had asked friends and coworkers for money help at that time too, but later told people she'd figured out a way to solve her financial problems.

"You think her murder was all about money?" Kaiser asked after we'd watched a video of the newscast again in his office. "That the financial scandal there and all the ramifications of it were the motive for whoever killed her?"

"Not necessarily, Mr. Kaiser."

"But then why was she killed? And why in the name of God was my name on that list found in her apartment?"

"I haven't the slightest idea."

"Do you know if the police think I'm in any kind of danger from whoever killed her?"

"No idea about that either."

"Well, then are the police for some unfathomable reason considering me as a potential suspect?"

"Same answer."

Kaiser glared at me across his big desk.

"I thought you said you knew what you were doing."

"I don't remember ever saying that."

"People told me that you were the best reporter we had in this building. That's why I put you on this story. To get me some answers."

"If I am the best reporter you've got, Mr. Kaiser, that's because I ask questions—I don't just take things at face value. "

"What kind of questions?"

"There's all sorts of unanswered questions with the Grace Mancuso story," I told him. "Sure, the money thing could be the reason she was killed. Or maybe the fact that she apparently had a very rocky romantic life. But—like you said—and this is the biggest question of all, how in the hell did your name and those other people wind up on that list left next to her body? Everyone from rich and powerful people like you to someone like poor Dora Gayle. Which one of you—or how many of you—was connected somehow to Grace Mancuso? And why? If I can find out the answers to those questions, maybe I can figure the answers to the rest of it too. So why do you think your name was on that list?"

"I don't know," he snapped. "I told you before—I didn't know Mancuso or really know anyone else on that list."

"That's what all the other people on the list say too."

"What does that mean?"

"Someone's lying."

"Who's lying?"

"It could be anyone on the list—even you."

Kaiser stared at me for what seemed like an eternity—as my entire journalistic career flashed before my eyes—but then just shook his head and laughed.

"My God, you've got quite the mouth on you, don't you, Carlson?"

"Thanks, a lot of people have told me that."

"It wasn't a compliment."

"Yeah, they've told me that too."

There was a chart on the wall behind his desk of all the far-flung Kaiser properties. Movie studios, publishing houses, websites, TV stations, and lots of other media properties around the world. This was arguably the most powerful media mogul around right now. And here I was sitting in his office, just him and me. Going head-to-head on this. Holy crap, I thought to myself.

"What are you going to do now?" he asked me.

"Go and personally talk to the other people on that list—just like I'm doing with you—to try to find out what they might possibly know about her or the murder."

"But you just told me that they all have said they don't know anything at all."

"They did."

"Then what do you hope to find out?"

"I won't know until I talk to them."

He smiled.

"You are a pretty good reporter, aren't you?"

"Oh, I've had my moments."

"Winning a Pulitzer is a pretty big moment."

"That was a long time ago," I said.

I sure didn't want to talk about that Pulitzer or the Lucy Devlin story that went with it right now with him.

"And what will you do with the information you find out from these interviews?" he asked.

"Put it on the air."

"Even if it's about me?"

"I guess that's up to you, Mr. Kaiser. You own the station. I just work here."

He nodded.

"Will you come to me first with what you know? Tell me before you broadcast anything? That's all I ask."

I suppose I could have told him that wasn't the way a real reporter worked—a real reporter just reported the facts without censorship or restrictions of any kind, no matter how rich or powerful the subject of the story was. I could have quoted Thomas Jefferson on the importance of a free press and the First Amendment and a lot of other stuff about great reporters I'd admired all my life to him if I wanted, I suppose.

Yep, that's what a real reporter would do.

Except I wasn't a real reporter anymore.

I was just a TV executive now acting the part.

"Absolutely," I told Brendan Kaiser. "I'll report to you first with whatever I find out."

CHAPTER 15

OKAY, THERE WERE five names on the list found next to Grace Mancuso's body. Five names of people who must have had some kind of connection with Mancuso. One of them, Dora Gayle, was dead. I'd already talked to Kaiser. That left three people for me to go interview—Bill Atwood, Emily Lehrman and Scott Manning.

I wasn't sure they'd talk to me, of course. They might be afraid—either of the killer or the publicity from being dragged into a murder case or, most likely, a bit of both. But I was always very good at convincing people that going on the air would be beneficial for them, even when it wasn't. It was time for me to work a bit of that magic again now.

I decided to start with Bill Atwood.

There were three reasons for that:

1) Atwood had been a successful and popular politician for years and he was probably more confident doing media after all his years in Washington and the other public jobs he'd held than anyone else.

2) Atwood had a reputation as a ladies' man—that's what ruined his political career—and it seemed entirely possible to me that he might have had some kind of a sexual relationship with Grace Mancuso.

3) Last, and most importantly in my decision making on who to go see first, Bill Atwood was the only one who agreed to be interviewed on air when I reached out to the three of them. So there was that too.

"Thank you for taking the time to see me," I said to Atwood as we sat in his office at Benson College.

"No problem. I'm just as anxious as anyone to see this resolved and the killer of that woman caught. Having said that, I have no idea why I'm on that list found at the murder scene. I assume the killer just picked my name at random. I'm in the media spotlight a lot, as you know."

I nodded and looked around the office. There were lots of pictures of Atwood on the walls. As a Congressman. Meeting with world leaders. Socializing with celebrities. Even a few shots of him with Presidents. He'd certainly been a powerful guy before the sex scandals ended his career in disgrace.

There was a picture of Atwood's wife and daughter too.

"You have a lovely family," I said. "How old is your daughter?"

"Twenty-one. No, actually, she just turned twenty-two."

"Does she know what she wants to do yet? God, I remember when I was twenty-two. I was still trying to figure all that stuff out."

"Not Miranda. She knows exactly what she wants to do. She's so focused it's scary. She's a senior at Yale, majoring in political science and history. Star athlete on the lacrosse and soccer teams. She wants to work for the government when she graduates. She's already got a job lined up with the State Department when she's finished with school. But what she really wants to do is follow in her old man's footsteps. She wants to be a politician. I'm sure she will be a terrific politician too. Miranda's always been the best at anything she sets out to do. Who knows, she might be our first woman president."

"She sounds like a great girl."

"Yes, she is," Atwood said, looking again at the picture of his family.

I didn't say anything about the turmoil, the arguments, the therapy sessions he and his wife had to send Miranda to because of all the things he'd done that had torn apart his family. I'd read about all that in the stories about his sex scandals. But he did seem to genuinely love his family. And I just wanted to keep him talking about his name appearing on the list at the Mancuso crime scene.

"The police are still trying to figure out if there's some sort of common link between the names on that list," I said. "But what about you, any ideas? Do you know of any possible connection at all between you and the others? I know you've met Brendan Kaiser, the owner of our TV station."

"Just briefly. We're hardly close friends. In fact, the newspapers he owns have been very critical of me in the past on their editorial pages."

"What about Emily Lehrman, the attorney? Have you met her?"

"No, sorry."

"Scott Manning, the NYPD homicide detective?"

"Not that I'm aware of."

"Dora Gayle?"

"The homeless woman. No, I never heard of her before either. Like I said, I'm just as confused by all this as everyone else is."

Atwood seemed fine with going on camera with me to talk about the story. Maybe he figured that going public like this was the best way to prove he had nothing to hide. Maybe he thought it was the best way to hide any secrets he did have. Or maybe he just liked to see himself on the air.

While the video crew was setting up around us, Atwood's secretary came in to put a few things on his desk. She was an attractive brunette, probably in her mid-twenties, wearing a tight-fitting skirt and low-cut blouse. Atwood barely acknowledged her presence as she walked away from him. I could sense some sexual tension there though. I'm very good at spotting sexual tension. It's one of my superpowers. I was pretty sure Atwood and his secretary were having some kind of an affair, no matter how much he professed his love for his family.

We went through it all with the cameras rolling for the on-air interview I would run later on the newscast. It was all pretty much the same things we'd discussed. He didn't know Grace Mancuso when she was alive. He didn't know anything about her death. He didn't know why he was on the list. He didn't really know anyone else on the list. He just hoped police caught the murderer and justice was served.

After we finished, his secretary came back into the room again. This time they weren't so oblivious to each other. I saw her brush the sleeve of her blouse against his face as she put some documents down on his desk. He smiled at her. She smiled back. I had a feeling they were just waiting for me and the video crew to leave so they could jump all over each other. Yes, there was definitely something going on there. For whatever it's worth, I also caught Atwood sneaking a glance or two at me during our conversation—and he commented several times about how attractive I was.

"For someone my age?" I said.

"For any age."

"Well, thank you, I guess."

Yep, Bill Atwood definitely liked to flirt—and probably do a lot more—with women. He was still a player in the sex game. He was not a faithful husband, in the past or now. All of that made Bill Atwood a man who couldn't be trusted.

But it didn't make him a murderer.

*   *   *

Emily Lehrman agreed to see me at her office. But she refused to go on air. Or even be interviewed about the story at all.

"I just want to ask you some questions about the Grace Mancuso murder investigation," I said.

"I answered questions for the police already."

"Yes, well, I have some more questions."

"And I choose not to answer them."

"That makes you look guilty of something. If I go on air and say you refused to comment at all, people are going to think you're hiding something."

Lehrman shook her head. "I'm not a suspect, Ms. Carlson. I'm not even a witness. I'm just somebody you want to question in the hopes of finding out some scrap of information to put on the air and sensationalize. Talking to you does not benefit me in any way, so don't try those tricks on me. I'm a lawyer. A very good lawyer. Don't forget for a second who you're dealing with."

We stared at each other for a few seconds. Emily Lehrman was a formidable looking person. In her fifties, I knew, but she looked younger. Short, brunette hair. Attractive in a way, even though she didn't go out of her way to emphasize it.

"Oh, I know exactly who you are, Ms. Lehrman."

"Have we met?"

"Sort of. A long time ago. When I was a newspaper reporter, I wrote a lot of stories about a bigtime drug dealer named Vincent Gallo. He ran an operation out of Brooklyn that catered to college kids. We spent six months doing an undercover probe and stakeout on him. Did a whole series that should have wound up putting Gallo in jail. He was arrested, but he got himself a good lawyer who got him acquitted. That lawyer was you, Ms. Lehrman."

She shrugged. "I was just doing my job."

"A few months later, a kid named Timmy Ehrhardt died from an overdose from a bad batch of heroin he got from Gallo. Ehrhardt was a straight A student at Brooklyn College. He'd been accepted to medical school. He wanted to be a doctor, he wanted to help people. Instead, he wound up dead in the morgue. He wasn't a bad kid, he wasn't a drug addict. He was just experimenting, trying things out in life the way we all did when we were young. Except he'll never get a chance to get old. If Vincent Gallo had gone to jail, maybe Timmy Ehrhardt would be alive today."

"And you blame me for this?"

"Let's just say I don't like lawyers like you, Ms. Lehrman."

"And I don't like journalists like you."

"Good to know."

"Goodbye, Ms. Carlson."

"I really wish you'd at least consider doing the interview."

"Goodbye."

She glared at me with an icy-cold stare—the same kind of intimidating look she was known for in the courtroom—until I finally made my way out of her office.

Emily Lehrman was one scary lady.

Definitely didn't seem like a very nice person.

But that didn't make her a murderer either.

* * *

I didn't even get to meet with Scott Manning, the NYPD homicide cop. When I tracked him down at his precinct and got him on the phone, he had only two words for my request to meet for an interview. "No way."

I went through my spiel about how it was in his best interests to go public on air with this, but he wasn't buying any of it. Just like Emily Lehrman. Maybe they were both just too smart to fall for it. Or maybe I wasn't as smart as I thought I was. The bottom line was there was still a lot I didn't know about either of them, as well as the other people on the list.

I looked at the list again.

Five names.

No apparent connection with each other or with the victim, Grace Mancuso.

At least according to what they were saying.

But someone must not be telling the truth.

I sure hoped it wasn't Brendan Kaiser.

CHAPTER 16

SCOTT MANNING WORKED out of a police precinct on 67th Street. My ex-husband Sam had spent some time there too, and I knew there was a bar where cops regularly hung out in the neighborhood when their shifts were over. So I stopped in at the bar later that evening in the hopes I could find him.

Manning was sitting at a table by himself at the back of the place. The bartender pointed him out to me. He wasn't what I expected. Good-looking, long curly brown hair—he looked more like a TV cop than a real one. I ordered a drink from the bartender, walked over to Manning's table and sat down across from him.

"Clare Carlson, Channel 10 News," I said. "We talked on the phone before."

"What are you doing here?"

"I still want to interview you."

"I'm not talking to you."

"Actually, you are. We're having a conversation now."

"Go away."

"I just want to ask you a few questions."

"Like I told you before, I have nothing to say to you."

"Yeah, but that was before you saw how cute and adorable I was."

I gave him my best smile. Friendly. Flirtatious. Whatever it took.

"You certainly are tenacious," he said, taking a big drink of what he had in his glass.

"Is that in my favor."

"Not necessarily."

"I've been called worse. What about the interview?"

He laughed now.

"You'd make a pretty good cop."

"I make a pretty good reporter too."

"I can see that."

"So will you talk to me?"

"About what?"

"Grace Mancuso."

"I know absolutely nothing about how my name got on that damn list. That's the truth. You can believe me or not."

"Okay, I believe you."

"Good. Are we done here then?"

"We can still talk."

"About what?"

"Whatever you want."

We wound up spending quite a bit of time—and having more than a few drinks—together. I wasn't exactly sure why I did it. Partly, I suppose, in the hope I'd somehow find out more about him that might help me on the story. But the other reason—and there was no denying it—is I kind of liked Scott Manning. Found him attractive too. It had been a long time since I'd spent time with a man who aroused those kinds of emotions in me.

At one point, I asked him about the departmental charges pending against him over the suspect that went out the window while he was in his and his partner's custody. And about his partner dying of a heart attack after the controversy erupted.

I wasn't sure if he'd talk to me about that either, but he did. He got very emotional talking about his dead partner, Tommy Bratton.

"We were like brothers, me and Tommy. We thought the same way on the street, reacted as if we were one. And, most of all, we trusted each other. I trusted Tommy Bratton with my life, and I knew Tommy felt the same way about me. The thing is, though, the Nazario case brought everything to a head for me. I was already questioning many of the basic decisions I'd based my whole life on. Tommy was my closest friend, the one person I thought I could trust. And then one day he wasn't there anymore."

"What kind of questions?"

"Lots of them. Starting with whether I should have ever been a police officer at all."

"You didn't always want to be a cop?"

"No, I just kind of fell into it when my real dream didn't work out."

"What was your real dream?"

"To be a rock star."

I laughed, but soon found out he wasn't kidding. He told me about coming to New York out of college as a guitar player, joining a band, and performing at clubs in the Village and Lower Manhattan.

"But then I met my wife, Susan, and we got married. I eventually decided I had to get a real job. A friend of mine was taking the police entrance exam and convinced me to go with him. I passed, got in the Police Academy, and the rest is history."

"So you're married?" I said, hoping I didn't let the disappointment show too much.

"Yes and no," he said

"That's not a yes and no question. The answers are either A) yes or B) no."

"Technically, Susan and I are still together. But I moved out after the Nazario business became so messy. There's always been problems between us in the marriage, and all that's happened to me has only exacerbated those problems. Plus, I've had a lot of problems dealing with my youngest son since it all began. He's seventeen, and he used to idolize me and want to become a police officer too. But now he hates me and thinks I'm some kind of a criminal because of the Nazario allegations. He won't even talk to me anymore. I have two older kids who are on their own now, but they're not exactly ecstatic with me either. I just decided to give myself a break from all the family issues for a while, at least until I make some decisions about my own life."

He shook his head.

"For a guy who told you he didn't want to talk, I've done a lot of talking, huh? And all about my own problems. Never even asked you anything about yourself. Guess I've had too much to drink. I'm sorry if I bored you. Listen, I need to get out of here. I have to get up early in the morning."

"Me too."

I stood up. I wasn't sure what to do next.

"This was nice," I said.

My God, that sounded stupid, I thought to myself. Why did I say that?

"Yes, it was."

"I hope everything works out okay for you with the department."

"And I hope you get your big story."

He looked at me across the table, and I suddenly realized he felt as awkward as I did.

"Maybe we could do it again sometime," he said.

"Maybe," I told him.

CHAPTER 17

"LET ME GET this straight," Janet said to me. "The guy is under departmental investigation by the NYPD. He's suspected of killing a man by throwing him out of a window. He may also be involved somehow in the Grace Mancuso murder. And he's married."

"Yes."

"But you still want to go out with him."

"Well, he is awfully cute," I said in my defense.

"Your screening process for men leaves a lot to be desired."

We were sitting in Janet's office, which was in a posh building on Madison Avenue with a view of the Empire State Building. Janet's office was a lot nicer than my office. She had a nice apartment too. And she'd made her marriage and family life work too, which I'd never been able to do. All in all, Janet's life was a lot better than mine. Although I'm sure there had to be some things in my life that were better than hers. I just couldn't quite think of any at the moment.

I'd asked Janet if she could help me find out any more about Emily Lehrman from people she knew in the legal community. Now that I'd talked to Atwood and Manning—plus Kaiser, of course—Lehrman was the one name from the list that I still had a lot of questions about on this story.

"Just to be clear, I've never met Emily Lehrman myself," Janet said to me now. "I don't move in the same kind of world as her or deal with her kind of clients. Everything I'm telling you about her is secondhand. I have no independent confirmation on any of it."

I made a twirling motion with my hand, telling her to hurry up and get on with it.

"Okay, Emily Lehrman. Fifty-three years old. Graduated from Fordham Law School at the top of her class. Worked as a public defender for a while and got very involved in community legal work—fighting greedy landlords and getting involved in all sorts of noble, selfless crusades like that. But at some point, she switched her priorities and began defending top mobsters and drug dealers and high-profile murder suspects. She's very good at it. Very successful in her acquittal rate. And very rich as a result of that."

"I already know all that, Janet," I said impatiently.

"Did you know she had a drug problem?"

"Uh, no."

"It's not anything she's ever gone public about. But a few people who've been around Lehrman in courtrooms and at depositions and stuff say it's a pretty well-known assumption that the woman is addicted—or at least heavily dependent—on a variety of different drugs."

"What kind of drugs?"

"Not heroin or cocaine or anything like that. More sedatives, prescription pain pills, sleeping pills, etcetera. The kinds of things people have when they have trouble functioning on a day-to-day basis—or even sleeping at night. Maybe she has a guilty conscience about all the disreputable people she's represented."

"I didn't think lawyers had consciences," I said.

Janet ignored me and kept talking.

"I think she was married once. A long time ago. Couldn't find any records of it, but people tell me that the guy she was with disappeared from her life at some point. The word around was he took her for a lot of money on his way out the door. Apparently, it was a pretty ugly breakup. No one knows much more about the breakup or her personal life since then. She lives in a big apartment on Park Avenue by herself. Hardly goes out or socializes with anyone. She's kind of a hermit outside the courtroom."

We talked for a while more about Emily Lehrman and the other people on the list at the Grace Mancuso crime scene.

At some point, Janet asked me again about Todd Schacter.

"Did you ever do anything with that contact information I gave you?"

"No," I lied, which was technically true.

I'd never heard back from Schacter.

"That's good. I don't think you should."

"Probably a bad idea," I agreed.

"Speaking of bad ideas, I don't think you should go out with that cop Scott Manning either."

"You're probably right."

"Nothing good can come of it, Clare."

"Nothing good at all," I said.

I stood up to leave.

"So when are you seeing Manning?" she called out after me just before I got to the door.

"Oh, we're going to figure out a night soon to get together."

"Make sure you give me all the blow-by-blow details."

"I'll get back to you on that."

CHAPTER 18

I WAS STILL running the news meeting, which meant I got to make the final decision on what went on the air and how we played it on the evening newscasts.

Now I was pretty sure going into the meeting that I was going to lead with my own story. The interview with Bill Atwood, along with the additional information I'd gotten about Manning and Lehrman. The Atwood interview was a pretty good get, if I do say so myself. Everyone knew Atwood—he certainly was the most popular, recognizable name on the list, even more than Brendan Kaiser—and he'd been involved in scandals before. Whether he had any connection with Grace Mancuso's murder or not, he was the kind of polarizing public personality that could put up good ratings numbers for us. I had run promos about my exclusive interview with him all that day.

But there were other stories happening too—and I listened to the rundown at the meeting.

"The only thing everybody is talking about is the weather," said Wendy Jeffers, the Channel 10 meteorologist. Well, we called her the meteorologist now. It used to be the TV weather girl, but that's politically incorrect. Weather woman didn't work, it sounded like a variation of Wonder Woman. Then we sent her to a couple of night classes about the weather and—presto, she's a meteorologist. "It's only early May, but the temperature is well into the nineties today and heading even higher tomorrow. It's really hot out there."

"How hot is it?" I asked, doing my best classic Johnny Carson/David Letterman impression.

"Well, it's so hot," I said, answering my own question, "that the hookers down in Times Square are offering slurpies today."

Everyone laughed. They always pretty much laughed at my jokes during the news meeting. I like to think that's because they found me funny. Of course, I was the boss too. They probably felt compelled to laugh, funny or not. No problem, I'll take laughs that way. It's nice having the cards stacked in my favor with the audience when I'm doing comedy.

"I'm doing an interview with someone from the National Weather Service," Jeffers said, "about why we might be having so much hot weather this early in the year."

"Plus, we'll do people on the street interviews," Maggie said. "A representative from Con Edison talking about the danger of power outages from so many people keeping their air conditioners on full blast. And an early preview of the state of local beaches for the long, hot summer ahead."

I nodded. Weather stories kind of took care of themselves. It really didn't matter that much what we did

Everyone else went through their list of stories. There was a big fire that destroyed a historic church in the Bronx. A tenant group was planning a massive protest at City Hall against rising rents. Streets were being shut down around the United Nations head-quarters because of an impending summit of international leaders there. And an elderly woman on Staten Island won $25 million in the lottery by playing the numbers from the birthday of her cat.

"Didn't we just do that story?" one editor asked.

"It was a dog last time."

"Jesus, what's next? A hamster wins the damn lottery?"

"If that happens, we'll cover it too," I said with a shrug.

I only had one tricky decision to make. It involved Paul Stafford. Stafford had been the anchor on the Channel 10 News for many years but got pushed out for the younger demographics that Brett and Dani brought to the newscast. He still appeared on air once in a while in a "senior contributor" role.

Not too long ago, Stafford's wife had died. He asked if he could deliver a eulogy for her on the air. He called it: "My Wife—Why I Loved Her." Sure, it was all pretty maudlin, but we figured we owed him that.

"Stafford wants to make another appearance to eulogize his dead wife," Maggie said. "He said he wasn't able to express all his feelings and tell the audience all the wonderful things she had accomplished in her life. He said he needs more time to talk about the years that they spent together."

"Christ, how old was this woman?" someone grunted.

"We already gave him four minutes," another one said.

"What are we gonna call it: "My Wife—Why I Loved Her, Part II?" another editor asked.

I shook my head no

"One wife, one eulogy," I said. "That's my new Channel 10 policy."

* * *

After the news meeting was over, Maggie stayed behind to talk to me more about the Grace Mancuso story. She was already trying to figure out where we went for a follow-up the next night. That's the thing about the news business. No matter how good a story you do, you still have to come up with something else for the next day and the day after that.

"I still like the Revson angle," Maggie said. "The Mancuso woman hurt a lot of people there. First the clients she swindled, then the people at Revson she was prepared to testify against. That makes a pretty good motive for murder."

I thought about the way Grace Mancuso's body had been beaten and pummeled so badly.

"This just seems like it's about more than money," I said. "It feels personal."

"Losing a lot of money can make it very personal," Maggie said. "So can going to jail because she ratted on you."

"My guess is there's something more."

"Like what?"

I thought about it for a second. "'Follow the money' is one saying. But another is 'follow the heart.' That's something an old newspaper editor always preached to me. He said most murders were either about love or money. That's where the answers were, he used to say."

"Money and love?"

"Right. If this isn't about money, maybe it's about love."

"But the cops have already checked out all the men Grace Mancuso was seeing. And so, did we. We looked really hard at the new boyfriend, the old boyfriend, and a few in-between. But they all have alibis or have been cleared by the police. It doesn't look like any of the boyfriends did it."

"We might be looking for the wrong thing."

"What should we be looking for?"

I'd been thinking about this after going through my old notes from the interviews I'd done. I'd come up with an idea. Or at least a new theory. Something that hit me after I re-read my conversations with the various people I'd talked to since I'd started working on the Mancuso story. One interview in particular jumped out at me.

"A girlfriend," I said.

"You think Grace Mancuso liked women too?"

"It's possible."

"But what does that mean?"

"It means we've doubled the number of potential romantic suspects."

Maggie smiled.

"Okay, then how do we find this girlfriend?"

"Maybe we already have," I said.

CHAPTER 19

LISA KALIKOW LIVED in a studio apartment in the Inwood section of Manhattan, about as far north as you can go near the Bronx border. There was a Korean bodega on the first floor of her building. Different neighborhood from Grace Mancuso's apartment. Different worlds.

"What are you doing here?" she asked when she opened the door.

"I have some more questions."

"I'm kind of busy now. Maybe we could do this later somewhere else."

"It won't take long."

I hadn't called her ahead of time for a reason. Sometimes it was good to interview people when they weren't ready for it. That put them off guard, didn't let them prepare their story beforehand. You found out things that way, things they were holding back. I was pretty sure Lisa Kalikow was holding back something.

"Is there any news about who killed Grace?" she asked as we sat in her tiny living room.

"Some."

"Do you think it had to do with the problems at Revson?"

"That's one of the possibilities."

I watched her eyes. She was looking around the room, while at the same time trying to pretend she wasn't. I looked over in the direction where she kept glancing. There was a picture on the wall. A picture of two women on a boat in the water.

I walked over and looked at the picture more closely.

"Is that you?" I asked.

"Yes."

"Vacation?"

"That's right."

"The other woman in the picture looks like Grace Mancuso."

She nodded. "We went white water rafting out West a few months ago."

"Some kind of a group thing from work?"

"No, just the two of us."

"That sounds like fun."

"What do you mean?"

"You must have had a good time. I mean you keep the picture up here on your wall and all . . ."

There were other pictures of the two of them. One at some kind of club, where they both looked a bit smashed. Another at the beach. Grace Mancuso had on a thin two-piece bikini and looked really hot. Not exactly the staid corporate Wall Street look. If Lisa Kalikow knew I was coming, she probably would have taken them down. But they were important to her. They were all she had left of Grace Mancuso. Probably looked at those pictures all the time.

"I'm still trying to find out who Grace Mancuso was seeing romantically at the time she died," I said.

"I don't know much about Grace's personal life," she said.

I looked again at the picture on the wall. "Really? You went on vacation with her. You spent time with her. She must have opened up a little bit about her love life. I mean she was a good-looking woman, right? There had to be lots of boyfriends in her life."

"I wouldn't know," she replied stiffly.

"You have no idea about her boyfriends?"

"Not really."

"Do you have a boyfriend?"

"I don't see what that has to do with anything . . ."

"Were you and Grace Mancuso lovers?" I asked.

Kalikow stared at me, uncertain what to say. Trying to make up her mind whether or not to deny it. I decided to make it easier for her.

"I'm not looking to cause you any problems here," I said softly. "I understand that at a company like Revson, this is probably the kind of thing you'd like to keep quiet. Finance is a very conservative business. Of course, lots of people are out of the closet these days—it's no longer that big a thing. But at Revson, maybe it still is, right? Especially for two women. If people there knew about you, there'd be lesbian remarks behind your back—and you didn't want that. Neither you nor Grace. So you pretended you were friends, but you were really a whole lot more, weren't you?"

"Yes," she said.

"And no one else knew?"

"Grace said we had to keep it a secret."

"How long were you involved with her?"

"Six months or so."

"Was it serious?"

"I loved Grace."

"Did she love you?"

"Grace didn't love anybody."

There it was again. That description of Grace Mancuso as a person with no emotions, no feelings. Even the people who cared about her said that. Did that characteristic play a role in her death? I had to assume that it did.

"Tell me about it."

They had met maybe a year ago, she told me. When Kalikow first started working at Revson. She would see Grace around the office, looking so attractive and so much like a woman on the fast track to success. For a long time, she fantasized about having sex with her. She never thought it would become a reality. But then—about six months ago—Grace asked her to have lunch. Pretty soon they were sleeping together.

"Six months," I said. "That's about the same time as the scandal at Revson erupted, isn't it? Do you think there's a connection?"

"I'm the executive secretary to one of the top legal counsels at Revson. Grace was concerned about what he knew; she needed information. I had information. She used to ask me questions all the time about the investigation, who was cooperating and who wasn't—that sort of thing. I knew what she was doing. She was using me."

"Didn't that bother you?"

"Have you ever been in love?"

"Frequently." I smiled.

"Okay, but were you ever really in love? Mad, passionate love where you can't think about anything else, you just have to be with them—nothing in the world matters except that person. Well, that's the way I felt about Grace. I knew why she was with me, but all I cared about was that she was there. I couldn't live without her. Just the thought of losing her made me crazy. That's why what happened at the end was so difficult."

"You mean her murder?"

"Even before that," she said. "I found out there was someone else Grace was seeing."

"Another woman?"

She shook her head no. "A man."

"She was in love with a man?"

"No. Grace had boyfriends, but she was never in love with anyone. She was using him. Just like she'd used me. This wasn't a real romance, she was stringing this guy along to get something from him. That's what she said when I confronted her about him, and I believed her. She said she was sleeping with him because he was the answer to all of her problems. She was going to make a lot of money off of him. That's what I told you before. I just didn't want to tell you about the rest, about her and me. She told me not to worry, that she didn't feel anything for this guy. It was all business. She said she couldn't wait to see the look on his face when she dropped the bomb on him. She was going to tell him everything and laugh at him. Then she'd make him pay up big to her."

"She was planning to blackmail this person?"

"Yes."

"Did she get the money?"

"I don't know. That was the last time I talked to her."

"When was that?"

"When we were in bed together, not long before she died."

It all made sense. Grace Mancuso needed money. She had some information she could use to blackmail somebody. Along the way, she decided to sleep with him. Not for love. But she had a reason. Maybe to blackmail him even more. Or to find out more information while they were under the sheets. Or maybe she just got off on humiliating him. It was too much for him to take, so he killed her in a rage.

"Do you know who the man was that she was blackmailing?" I asked.

"No, she never said."

"Any idea at all?"

"She said he was very important. That it would blow my mind if I ever found out who he was. That's why she was going to get so much money out of him. He couldn't stand another scandal, she said. Especially one like this."

"Anything else?"

"She said that the guy prided himself on being a real ladies man. Thought he was God's gift to women. That's why she was really looking forward to taking all his money from him and ruining his life."

A ladies' man?

Thought he was God's gift to women?

Couldn't afford another scandal?

That sure sounded a lot like Bill Atwood.

The same Bill Atwood who insisted he never knew Grace Mancuso.

CHAPTER 20

"BRENDAN KAISER LIKES you," Jack Faron said.

"What's not to like?"

"I'm serious. He thinks you're a hard-nosed, bulldog, tenacious, in-your-face journalist who won't stop digging until you get the story. What the hell did you say to Kaiser anyway?"

"We had a very frank and open discussion about the Grace Mancuso story."

"What is the story?"

"I don't know yet, but I think I'm getting closer to finding out."

I went through everything I'd found out about the blackmail angle from Lisa Kalikow.

"I went back to Atwood and asked him again if he had any kind of a relationship with Mancuso."

"And?"

"He said he still didn't know her."

"What did you expect him to say?"

"I had to try." I shrugged.

"It doesn't have to be Atwood she was sleeping with and blackmailing."

"No, it could be anyone," I agreed. "Maybe someone at Revson. That would make a lot of sense too. She had information about the scandal she hadn't turned over to authorities yet—and was going to use it to get big money out of someone there for her silence. Whoever she was getting it from, she expected a big payoff. That's why she told her family and others she'd asked for money that she didn't need it from them anymore."

"And we have no way to determine who that person might be? Atwood or someone else?"

"Not at the moment."

"Or even if the blackmail attempt was the motive for her murder?"

"We don't know anything for certain, Jack."

Faron sighed. "Most of the time in a murder case, there's a shortage of likely suspects or motives. But not here. In the Grace Mancuso murder, we have plenty of possible suspects and motives. Too many."

"But it all boils down to that everything Grace Mancuso did seemed to revolve around sex or money—two of the oldest motives in the world for murder," I pointed out. "We don't know for sure which one got her killed or if—and this is a real possibility too—it was a combination of both that got someone so angry that they beat her to death. All we can do is keep putting these developments on the air each night. Even if we don't know exactly what they mean. Just like we do with any other story."

"Except this isn't like any other story," Faron said.

"Uh, no."

"Kaiser wants to know why his name is on that list and he wants all the answers and he wants this case solved as quickly as possible so he can move on."

"I'm doing the best I can, Jack. I've covered every base I could think of."

"What about the other names on that list?"

"I've talked to them all, even the Lehrman woman—although she wouldn't say much."

"But you're ignoring one name. One person you haven't thought about that much since the Mancuso story started. And still have no possible idea of why she's involved in this. Dora Gayle."

I told you at the beginning that Jack Faron ranked pretty high on my list of TV executives I'd known. Which admittedly wasn't a tough upper tier to crack. But one of the reasons I liked him was that he sometimes actually thought like a journalist, not like an executive producer. I think maybe Faron started out as a journalist before he changed to the business and producing part of the job—and still thought of himself a bit in that role. He always understood everything I did as a journalist. He always supported me as a journalist. And, every once in a while, like now, he even came up with a good idea for me as a journalist.

"This whole thing really started with the Dora Gayle murder," Faron said to me now. "A seemingly meaningless death to us at the time on the streets of New York. Then she turns up on that list with Kaiser and the rest. But you forgot about her. Assumed you knew all about Dora Gayle because you'd already covered that. Except now Dora Gayle doesn't make sense. Her name shouldn't be on that list. She doesn't belong with the others. She's the only one who isn't accomplished or prominent in their field in some way. So why is Dora Gayle's name on that list?"

"Holy crap!" I said in an astonished voice after he was finished.

"You don't think that makes sense?"

"No, it makes a lot of sense."

"Why so surprised then?"

"I didn't think executive producers ever had good ideas."

Faron sighed. "If anything comes of it, just be sure to tell your new best friend Brendan Kaiser where you got the idea."

"Absolutely," I said. "And I'll get right on it, Jack. Go back to the beginning on Dora Gayle. Find out anything more I can about her and try to figure out how she wound up on that list of people at the Grace Mancuso murder apartment. There has to be a connection there that we're missing."

Dora Gayle.

Damn.

The woman who called herself Cinderella might still be the key for me to this story.

CHAPTER 21

I NORMALLY KEEP thinking about a story I'm working on even after I leave the newsroom—going over angles, leads, possible follows, and the like in my mind over dinner, watching TV, or even lying in bed trying to go to sleep.

But tonight, I was thinking about another story—a story I'd covered a long time ago.

The disappearance of eleven-year-old Lucy Devlin.

After tossing and turning for a while, I got out of bed, walked over to the desk area in my apartment, and pulled a scrapbook off the shelf where I kept clippings of all the big stories I'd done as a reporter.

Lucy Devlin was the biggest one, of course. It won me a Pulitzer and lots of journalistic acclaim and helped me have the career that I have today in TV news. I wouldn't be where I am today if it weren't for Lucy Devlin and the way she mysteriously disappeared as an eleven-year-old girl from the streets of Manhattan.

I paged through some of the headlines in the scrapbook: "MISSING: 11-year-old Girl Disappears on Way to School"; "Massive Search for Little Lucy"; "A Mother's Grief: Please Give

Me My Daughter Back"; then, "Hope Dims in Search for Lucy Devlin"; and finally, of course, the most recent headline from last year: "Body in Grave ID'd as Missing Lucy Devlin."

And I read through the articles all over again even though I remembered every fact in them like it was yesterday.

The details of the Lucy Devlin disappearance were heartbreaking. Anne Devlin, Lucy's mother, had put the eleven-year-old girl on a school bus in their posh Gramercy Park neighborhood of Manhattan—but Lucy never showed up in the classroom.

As the city prayed for Lucy's safe return, I filed story after story about the search and the Devlin family's anguish and all the details of the missing little girl's life.

There was a big article in the scrapbook from several months later about me winning the Pulitzer Prize for my Lucy Devlin stories. It quoted the Pulitzer judges as saying: "Clare Carlson's comprehensive—and yet compassionate—coverage of this heartbreaking story sets new standards for extraordinary reporting and dedication to uncovering the truth."

Except I hadn't really told the truth.

Not by a long shot.

I'd kept a lot of secrets about Lucy Devlin to myself.

*　*　*

The biggest secret, of course, was that Lucy Devlin was my own daughter. The one I'd given up at birth as a nineteen-year-old college freshman. Fifteen years later—motivated by some kind of maternal instincts, I guess—I had tracked her down to the family in Manhattan that adopted her. Except I never told them or Lucy who I was.

What I did instead probably doesn't make a lot of sense. But when Lucy disappeared that day on her way to school, I covered the story myself. Without telling anyone about my own connection as Lucy's biological mother.

Then last year—on the fifteenth anniversary of the Lucy Devlin's disappearance—the case exploded all over again.

Anne Devlin came to me with an email that had been sent to her by an anonymous tipster who claimed he'd seen Lucy at a motorcycle gang gathering in New Hampshire just several days after she went missing. And the exploration of that claim led me to Elliott Grayson—who had been a motorcycle gang member—and was then running for the Senate.

As I got closer and closer to determining his role in Lucy's abduction, he used his influence to discover that I was Lucy's biological mother. That's when he revealed to me that Lucy was still alive. He told me he'd share all the details about Lucy and tell me where she was now once the election was over. That's when I agreed not to run my story about him or tell anyone so he could win the Senate seat.

I kept my word on this—and continue to do so—out of some kind of journalistic integrity or whatever.

And now, even if I wanted to change my mind and tell anyone the truth, I would raise all sorts of questions about myself for sitting on the story for so many months.

All I could do was depend on his integrity and honor that he would do the right thing and, at some point, fulfill his promise to tell me Lucy's whereabouts.

The fact that he refused to talk to me, take my calls, or communicate with me in any way seemed to be a pretty good indication that he wasn't going to do the right thing here.

He was, in effect, daring me to try to run the story because he knew I couldn't do that now. If I did, I also would have to reveal the details about the secret deal I'd made with him before Election Day to bury the story in order to help him win his Senate seat. That would destroy my own career, maybe even more than his. And—most importantly of all—I would lose any chance that he might someday reveal to me the truth about where to find Lucy, even if he wasn't prepared to do it now.

Of course, Grayson could also be lying to me about Lucy being alive.

But he was betting that I would not do anything to ruin my chance—no matter how slim—to find out the truth about my daughter.

And he was right about that.

*   *   *

I looked at the contact information again that Janet had given me for Todd Schacter, the computer hacking wizard, and sent him another message saying I needed to talk with him.

He'd never replied to my first message.

But the email hadn't been kicked back as undeliverable—and Janet assured me this was his most recent contact address—so I assumed it got through to him.

I'd just keep barraging him with more requests until he finally relented and talked to me. Just like I did with Emily Lehrman and Scott Manning and all the other people I've dealt with as a reporter in the past. Sooner or later, I would hear from Schacter. Even if it was a no. And, if that happened, then I'd try to figure out something else to do next.

I looked down again at the picture of eleven-year-old Lucy Devlin on the front page of the *Tribune* from the long-ago article that I wrote the day she disappeared.

She would be in her late twenties by now, if she really was alive. Maybe married. Maybe with children of her own. Or maybe she really was dead and my search for her was fruitless.

One way or another, I had to know.

CHAPTER 22

I PUT MAGGIE on the Dora Gayle assignment the next morning. Trying to find some connection—no matter how unlikely—between Dora Gayle and the other people on the Grace Mancuso list. I knew Maggie would be thorough in combing through the homeless woman's past, and she was. She sent reporters again to the park where Dora had lived, the bar and coffee shop where she hung out and panhandled, the bank where she died in the ATM vestibule, and to the neighborhood in Greenwich Village where Dora Gayle grew up a long time ago.

That's when we finally hit pay dirt.

We found someone in Greenwich Village that remembered a lot about the Gayle family. It wasn't easy. Most of her neighbors back then were either dead or moved away. But this old couple lived right next door to her and her parents. Said they'd hear the drunken screams from Dora's parents drinking at night; watched Dora somehow grow up in that situation and eventually head off to college.

They told us they sometimes let young Dora stay there at night when the screaming and drunken behavior of her parents got to be too bad. Dora was such a beautiful and smart girl, they said, and they felt sorry for her having to grow up in that house.

Even after she stopped living at the house to go to NYU, Dora would often come back to visit them instead of her own parents right next door.

The two of them almost became like foster parents to Dora for a while until they lost touch with her later when she disappeared into the descent that eventually wound up with her living on the street as a homeless bag lady.

Dora wrote a lot in those days when they knew her as a young woman, the couple recalled—poetry, journals, and even a diary. She gave them some of these writings to read while she was in college. Most of it had been lost or thrown away over the years since then, but—with prodding from Maggie and her team of reporters—the couple managed to find a few samples.

I read through them now. Much of it was very dark. Gloomy lyrics of despair from songs by people like Leonard Cohen and the same kind of thing from a number of poets—most notably Sylvia Plath, who committed suicide at the age of thirty. Plath was her favorite poet, Dora wrote in one of the journals she kept while at NYU, and then she quoted from a poem that Plath wrote while she herself was in college. The poem was called "Mad Girl's Love Song," and Dora's favorite line was: "I shut my eyes and all the world drops dead."

But then we found a few remaining pages of a diary from Dora Gayle that were totally different in tone—these were written by a woman full of life and hope and love.

In the diary, she talked about finding her Prince Charming. A wonderful man who would take her away from everything bad and they would be happy forever after. "I am Cinderella," she wrote at one point, "and he has put the slipper on my foot. I love him so much."

Cinderella. That's where it came from. Why she thought she was Cinderella still waiting for her Prince Charming. She'd found him once—albeit briefly—when they were young. And she kept hoping he'd come back for her right to the very end.

And I was sad all over again that her life—which once seemed so bright and promising—ended this tragically. Not just on the night of her murder. But long before that when it all began slipping away from her.

I thought too about the strange juxtaposition of the Cinderella fairy tale that she clung to and the dark, depressing outlook on life she got from Sylvia Plath, Leonard Cohen, and the other people she seemed drawn to in her college life.

Or maybe it wasn't so strange.

Maybe we all cling to that dream of the fairy-tale ending where we live happily ever after no matter how many evil stepmothers and stepsisters and other people try to bring us down along the way.

I never imagined I could have truly related to a sad, homeless woman like Dora Gayle when this story started.

But I did.

I felt like I understood her in a way too.

I read some more of the handful of pages we had from her diary:

> *The man I love told me today he has to go away for a while.*
> *But he promised me he will be back.*
> *"What's going to happen to us until then?" I asked.*
> *"It's only for a year."*
> *"A year is a long time."*
> *"It'll go by quickly."*
> *"Then you'll come back to me?"*
> *"Of course, I will."*
> *"And then we'll be together forever . . ."*
> *"Yes, forever and ever."*

He kissed me then. I loved when he kissed me.

"Will you see other girls while you're away?" I asked.

"C'mon . . ."

"I'm serious."

"There's no one for me but you."

"Really?"

"Don't you know that by now?"

It was the answer I'd been hoping for.

"When are you leaving?"

"At the end of the month."

"Promise me you'll spend every minute you can with me before that?"

"I promise."

"I love you," I said, looking into his beautiful eyes and wondering how I was going to spend an entire year without him.

"I love you too," he said.

"I just want to make love to you for the rest of my life."

Then he kissed me again.

My Prince Charming.

The love of my life.

And I knew I would wait for him as long as it took.

That's all there really was from the diary. The other pages must have been lost or thrown away a long time ago. But it intrigued me enough to go looking for more about her time at NYU. Who was the man she was so in love with back then? If I could find that out—even after all this time—maybe he could fill in some of the missing pieces about Dora Gayle.

I learned from NYU that they didn't have yearbooks from that long ago online. But they did keep old print copies of the yearbooks somewhere in the library archives. I took a subway down to the NYU Library on Washington Square and told the woman behind the front desk what I was looking for. It took a while, but she finally came back with an NYU yearbook from Dora Gayle's senior year.

I found four mentions of her in it. One was the same picture she'd posed for that we used in the first story on air we ran. Another was a picture of her—looking just as beautiful—from something called the Poetry Club. And there was also one of her with a group of other students posing at the fountain in the middle of Washington Square Park next to the NYU campus—looking very happy and full of youthful enthusiasm about the future that lay ahead of her.

But it was the last item about Dora Gayle in the yearbook where I found what I was looking for.

There was a page toward the back where seniors were asked about their favorite memories from their college years. Dora Gayle's read: "Reading poetry to my boyfriend, Billy, who is graduating from Princeton and on his way to Oxford. I'm already counting the days until he comes back."

Billy?

Could that be Bill Atwood? Atwood graduated from Princeton. And then went on to study at Oxford as a Rhodes Scholar.

I remembered that now from the research I'd done on him.

Could Bill Atwood really have been Dora Gayle's boyfriend back then at NYU when she was young and beautiful?

And, if he was, why did he lie about it?

CHAPTER 23

I DIDN'T HAVE enough to put this on the air.

Sure, there was circumstantial evidence that Bill Atwood had apparently dated Dora Gayle—as unlikely as that sounded now—when they were both in college. But I needed more confirmation. Dora Gayle was dead and couldn't tell me anything. The only person who knew the truth was Bill Atwood. That meant I had to confront Atwood—just like I had about Grace Mancuso, but this time with more evidence—and get him to admit the long-ago relationship with Dora Gayle.

How did I do that?

Well, I could go to his office again, flash some leg and my come-hither smile and hope he succumbed to my charms. Or I could call him and pretend I knew even more than I did in hopes of getting him to admit to something. But I decided instead that my best option was to confront him with the Dora Gayle questions in a public setting.

We had a show at Channel 10 called *Heads-Up*, where politicians and other public figures were interviewed one-on-one by the host, Josina Bell. The show had won numerous awards and gotten plenty of media acclaim, so a lot of people in the public eye wanted to be on it. I was betting that Bill Atwood—who people said still was eyeing a political comeback—would be one of them.

Josina Bell was an attractive woman—like pretty much everyone else on TV these days—around forty years old. She was African-American, but also had some Hispanic heritage and spoke fluent Spanish—which did wonders for my staff diversity numbers. Josina had also publicly proclaimed herself as a lesbian who avidly supported LBGT causes. So that meant I had hit the trifecta with her—woman, African-American/Hispanic, and gay—as a minority hire. But the best part was Josina Bell was really smart and a really good interviewer. If there was anyone besides myself I'd trust to get Atwood to open up, it was Josina.

I told her now what I wanted her to do.

"In other words, you want me to ambush Atwood on the air in the hope you can get a sensational story out of it?"

"I wouldn't exactly call it an ambush."

"What would you call it?"

"It's more of . . . well, you'd be doing . . . I mean you'd just get him to say if he and Dora Gayle once . . ."

I sighed.

"Okay, it's an ambush."

"I don't do that kind of stuff, Clare. I'm not an 'ambush' journalist. I don't go for cheap sensationalism. This is a serious news show. That's why people watch us, and that's the way I've always hosted it."

"I understand, Josina," I said. "It was just a shot. But I can see why you wouldn't want to do this."

"Oh, I'll do it."

"But you said . . ."

"I don't like Atwood. He's the worst kind of politician—claims to be a liberal who supports minority and women and gay causes, but then lives his life making a mockery of all those high-sounding principles. I know some of the things he's done to women in the past. I don't want to see him in political office again. So I'll do whatever it takes to make sure that never happens. Including this."

* * *

The show went according to plan.

Josina started off by asking some softball questions about Atwood's work at Benson College and the success he'd had there.

He talked about improved curriculums, new construction initiatives to provide better facilities, and his efforts to create a more diverse student body by reaching out to low-income groups and neighborhood high schools. It was his set education speech, all very scripted. The same when she asked him if he had any future political aspirations. "I have been honored to serve the American people for many years in Washington," he said. "If they want me to represent them again in any way, I, of course, would consider that an honor too. But I have a wonderful job at Benson College now. I just want to make the best contribution I can—in whatever way possible—to the people of this city, this state, and this country."

"President Atwood," Josina said at one point, "you've been in the news recently when your name was found on a list of people at the crime scene of a murdered woman named Grace Mancuso. Can you tell us what you know about that?"

Again, his answer was carefully scripted and innocuous.

"I have no idea about that, Josina, and neither do the police. All I can say is my heart goes out to the family of the victim. And I know the NYPD—the finest police department in the world— will come up with some answers and hopefully capture the perpetrator of this tragic event."

"So you never met or heard of Grace Mancuso before her death?"

"I did not."

"And you don't know—or ever had any kind of a relationship with—any of the other names on that list that was found next to Mancuso's body?"

"Not really."

"Brendan Kaiser. Scott Manning. Emily Lehrman. Dora Gayle. Nothing?"

"No."

"Actually, you did know Dora Gayle, didn't you?"

Atwood looked confused, but then shook his head no.

"Are you sure you didn't know her? Know her quite well back at NYU when she was a student there in the eighties?"

"What?"

"President Atwood, weren't you involved in a serious romantic relationship with Dora Gayle then?"

The screen cut to a picture of Dora Gayle from her college yearbook. Looking young and beautiful, with the inscription from the yearbook where she'd written about her boyfriend, Billy, who went to Princeton and now was off to Oxford for a year.

"You went to Princeton, right?"

"Well, yes."

"And then on to Oxford?"

"I did, but . . ."

"And your first name is Bill."

Atwood definitely looked rattled now.

"Are you sure you didn't know Dora Gayle back then? Did you have a romantic relationship with her? And is that why this woman's name might have appeared on this list along with yours?"

"No!"

"No? You never heard of Dora Gayle before this list?"

"I-I . . ."

"Is that what you're claiming on the record as your answer?"

"Well, I suppose I might have known her a long time ago."

"Did you, or didn't you?"

"I'm not sure . . ."

*   *   *

Later, Atwood issued a formal statement through his office, which said:

"After appearing on a television show today, I realized that I did know Dora Gayle—one of the other names on that list found at the Grace Mancuso crime scene—many years ago. And we did have a brief relationship while we were in college. I left soon after for England to pursue my studies at Oxford on a Rhodes Scholarship. I simply had not recognized the woman who died here in the bank vestibule recently as the same person I knew back then. I have now contacted the police and given them this latest information. I hope this clears up the matter and answers any questions."

Well, not all of them.

But I now had a connection between two of the people on the list.

What about the other three?

CHAPTER 24

"I REALLY SHOULDN'T be here with you," I said to Scott Manning.

"I really shouldn't be here with you either."

"You're part of the story I'm trying to cover as an objective reporter."

"And I'm married."

"That probably trumps journalistic integrity," I admitted.

We were sitting in a restaurant on the East Side, not far from his precinct. Manning looked good, even better than I remembered the last time. He was wearing an open collar white sports shirt, a blue corduroy blazer, and designer jeans. I'd fixed myself up a bit for this night too. I still wasn't sure if this was technically a date or not, but it sure was shaping up that way.

"I know your husband, Sam," he said.

"Ex-husband."

"Nice guy."

"Great guy."

"So how come it didn't work out for you two?"

I shrugged. "I don't do marriage well."

I asked him about the police investigation into the Grace Mancuso/Dora Gayle murders to try to keep the conversation on a semi-professional basis.

"How would I know anything about that?" he asked.

"You're a homicide detective."

"Who's on restricted duty and under investigation for the Nazario death."

"So they haven't told you anything about Grace Mancuso?"

"Nope."

"No inside NYPD information of any kind?"

"They barely talk to me these days."

He shrugged when he told me like it didn't matter to him, but I could tell it did. This was the biggest murder investigation in town. He was a homicide detective. And he was being kept completely out of the loop because of the Nazario controversy as well as his own possible involvement in the Mancuso murder because his name was on that list.

"They played around for a while with the idea of giving all of us on the list some kind of special protection, just in case it was a hit list by the killer. But the logistics of doing that were impossible. I mean, how do you guard someone like Brendan Kaiser or Bill Atwood or even the mob attorney twenty-four hours a day? And I'm a police officer. I damn sure don't need anyone babysitting me. From what I understand, they're basically baffled by it all—the murder and the reasons for our names being on that list. I think they're also embarrassed by how you people in the media have been breaking so many of the new developments, instead of them. Like the relationship between Atwood and the Gayle woman."

"I'm not sure how much any of it helps us get to the real answers though," I said. "So Atwood dated Dora Gayle three decades ago— what does that mean? And what possible link could there be between that and you and Kaiser and Lehrman being on that damned list? We're still a long way away from the answers we need."

"It's a piece of the puzzle though," Manning said. "That's how I do an investigation. A piece at a time until the pieces start to make some kind of sense. You're doing a good job. Not as good a job as I could have done if I was working the case, but good enough."

He smiled at me and gave me a big wink as he said that. I smiled back. A flirtatious compliment. This was good. Very good. We talked more about the Mancuso case as we ate our dinner.

At some point, I switched topics and asked Manning more about the status of his marriage.

"You said before you've been married for a long time, right?"

He nodded. "Susan was a cashier at one of the clubs I played at when I was with the band. I flirted with her a few times, and she flirted back. We had a lot of rock groupies chasing after us back then—even if we weren't big stars—who were just looking for a good time. But Susan wasn't like that. She wanted a house and a husband and everything that went with it. She liked the idea of me being a cop, at first. Later, that all changed though.

"We haven't really been happy together in a long time, I suppose. Oh, we put up a good front. We went to neighborhood barbecues and belonged to the PTA and looked just like any other normal suburban couple. I got along with my kids all right until recently. But that all blew up when the Tommy Bratton/Manny Nazario business became front-page news. They're all embarrassed of me. And my youngest, Tim—the seventeen-year-old, who once wanted to follow in my footsteps with the NYPD—now thinks I'm some kind of killer or Nazi or something.

"The dissolution of my marriage was a bit subtler. Over the years, me and Susan just grew further and further apart. I found myself avoiding going home, preferring the company of other cops. 'I'm supposed to be your priority in life,' Susan yelled at me one time. 'But the only priority for you is that partner of yours, Tommy Bratton. Sometimes I think you care about him more than you care about me.' Maybe she was right.

"I'd had a few partners over the years. But of all of them, the only real partner I ever had was Tommy Bratton. We were like brothers, me and Tommy. We thought the same way on the street, reacted as if we were one. And, most of all, we trusted each other. I trusted Tommy Bratton with my life, and I knew Tommy felt the same way about me."

There was an obvious question I needed to ask him.

"Were you telling the truth when you backed up your partner's story about not being there when the suspect went out the window?"

"I told you what I testified."

"Yeah, I know. But I also heard you just talking about how loyal you were to your partner. You seem like a stand-up guy to me. A stand-up guy stands by his partner. He also tells the truth under oath. But what if you have to make a choice between the two—telling the truth and loyalty to your partner? Did you have to make a choice?"

"You expect me to admit to you that I lied under oath?"

"Did you?"

"You're asking as a reporter?"

"No, this is off the record. We're just two people talking here. Even if I did tell someone about the conversation, which I won't, you could deny it. But I'd like to hear the truth. I think what happened to you and your partner is somehow part of the story. Does it have anything to do with this murder case? I can't imagine how. But your name is on that list, and we don't know why. So we have to examine all the possibilities, no matter how far-fetched they might seem. At least that's the way I see it. How about you?"

He didn't say anything, but I plunged ahead with the money question anyway.

"Did your partner push that suspect out the window?" I asked.

"I don't know," Manning said.

"Did you ask him?"

"That last night, before he died, Tommy and I went out drinking after we finished our shift. I wanted to ask him the question. About what really did happen in that squad room. But I didn't. He never brought it up, and I felt uncomfortable raising it. You see, I knew Tommy would tell me the truth when the time was right. I just had to wait for the right moment. I figured there was lots of time."

"But then he died and left you with all these questions? Not just about the case, but about your whole career on the force?"

Manning nodded sadly.

"We all make these decisions in life," Manning said. "We don't think about them very much at the time. But later, looking back from the wisdom of all these years, you realize they were huge, life-forming decisions. I think about that a lot these days. I've had some pretty memorable moments along the way in my police career. Worked on big cases, got promoted to homicide lieutenant, was decorated for bravery in a couple of shootouts."

He was hailed as one of the best homicide investigators in the city, he said—not bragging, just stating it almost without emotion.

"But you know what? The times I remember the best were those early days in New York when I was trying to make it as a musician. Me and the guys in my band. The future seemed so bright back then. And God, we had so much fun.

"My roommate and best pal back then was our lead singer. His name was Dave, but no one called him that. His nickname in the band was Joey, because he loved Joey Ramone and the Ramones. So we always called him Joey. He was from Chicago where he had a girlfriend named Rebecca, but he didn't want to bring her to

New York until we made it big. He was desperately in love with her. Rebecca had long dark hair, almost down to her waist, in the picture of her hung next to his bed. Next to that he had a picture of Joey Ramone standing on the street in front of CBGBs, the punk rock club on the Bowery that was so popular back in the seventies and eighties.

"I remember this one night we were playing at this club in the East Village. It was the night of Game 6 in the 1986 World Series, when the Mets came back from two runs down, two out in the 10th inning to beat the Red Sox and go on to win the World Series. We all assumed the Mets were going to lose. There was a big TV next to the bar, and everyone in the place—even us while we were playing—was watching to see if the Mets could somehow come back from the dead.

"Then Joey suddenly began singing a Ramones song—the famous one with the chorus that goes 'hey, ho, let's go!'—and began chanting that over and over at the Mets on the screen as the rest of us in the band played. Pretty soon, everyone in the place was screaming 'hey, ho, let's go!' And then came three hits, a wild pitch, and Mookie Wilson hit that ground ball through Bill Buckner's legs for the Miracle Mets win.

"God, I'll never forget that. That chanting of 'hey, ho, let's go' and the people there screaming and hugging each other afterward. It was such a special night. That phrase, 'hey, ho, let's go,' sort of became my anthem to make something good happen. Sometimes, years later, I would even do it as a police officer. Mutter 'hey, ho, let's go' to myself before walking into a dangerous situation. It was like my good luck charm, I suppose."

He sighed. "Until my luck ran out with Nazario."

We talked for another few hours that night. It was nice. I liked Scott Manning, even though I still wasn't sure about him or his personal life or his possible involvement in the story. When we left the restaurant, I told him I'd catch a cab home.

"Meaning you're not going to invite me back to your place with you?" he asked

"Uh, no."

"You don't have sex with a guy on a first date, I guess."

"I do sometimes."

"But not with me, that's what you're saying?"

"It's more than that. It's a simple decision whether or not to sleep with someone who you don't really like. But, with you, this kind of decision is a lot tougher."

"Does that mean you like me?"

"Well, you do seem to have some attractive qualities."

Then I kissed him quickly and got into a cab.

Before the cab pulled away though, I rolled down the window and asked Manning: "Do you like to watch TV news?"

"Oh, I'm a real TV news junkie. I can't get enough to of it. Why?"

"Just good to know," I said.

CHAPTER 25

THERE'S NO BETTER feeling in the news business than breaking a big exclusive. Beating out your rivals with a scoop that has everyone talking. It's always been a big adrenalin rush for me, a high almost like sex or booze or drugs for some people. I felt that way when I was a newspaper reporter, and I feel that way now in TV. It still didn't get any better for me than breaking a big exclusive news story.

But there's no worse feeling in the world than when someone else breaks the exclusive instead of you.

Which is what happened on Bill Atwood after his appearance on *Heads-Up*.

A Benson University coed named Sandy Underhill had contacted the producers of a TMZ-like syndicated show called *Inside Scoop*. She said she'd had a torrid love tryst with former Congressman—and now Benson College president—Atwood in a Manhattan hotel room. She said she'd be willing to talk about it on TV for a price. The show, of course, accepted her offer. And why not? Atwood's womanizing had been the subject of countless tabloid stories and gossip items. Now, with his connection to a murder case, he was an even hotter topic.

Maggie and I watched the interview in my office. Sandy Underhill was blond, attractive, and slim—sexy slim—like a model. She said she'd met Atwood one day walking on the college campus and introduced herself to him because she always thought he was so good-looking and charismatic when she watched him on TV as a little girl growing up. She said she told this to him and he asked her if she would be interested in talking about a job as his student researcher. One thing quickly led to another and they wound up in the hotel room, which he rented to stay in the city when working late. But he also admitted to her he used the hotel room for his "entertainment activities."

She talked in the TV interview about how excited and flattered she was to be with the famous Bill Atwood. About his reputation in bed with women.

"'Everyone says you're quite the ladies' man,' I told him when we were in bed. 'And now I know they're right. You are terrific.' I meant it too. He was. Like he'd done it a lot of times before with other women, and he knew just the right buttons to push with me, if you know what I mean."

At one point, Underhill said, she asked him if he cheated a lot on his wife. "He told me 'no,'—and then burst out laughing! He said I shouldn't tell anyone about what we were doing, that it should be our little secret. But I think he knew I'd go right out and tell all my girlfriends I'd slept with Bill Atwood. How could I not? And I got the feeling that didn't bother him too much. He liked the reputation. He even talked about how all the sex stuff wouldn't prevent him from getting back into politics one day.

"He said to me: 'It just adds to the Atwood legend. Being known as a man who likes to bed women doesn't necessarily hurt your political career, sometimes it actually helps it. A lot of voters like that kind of sexual prowess in their leaders. Look at Bill Clinton and John F. Kennedy and Donald Trump. They all played around.'

"He made it clear to me that he was the kind of guy that got laid regularly. And that he even got off a bit on the danger of getting caught. He said the danger factor even made the sex more exciting. Like making love on an airplane or in a public spot."

The most sensational stuff came when the interviewer asked her more about the details of what she and Atwood did in bed.

"Well, like I said, he was really great in bed—but a little weird too."

"What do you mean by weird?"

"He asked me to spank him."

"You spanked Atwood?"

"Yes, that seemed to turn him on."

"Did you spank him like he was being punished for something?"

"That's right. He acted as if he'd done something really bad and needed to be punished for it."

"Did he say what he might have done that was bad?"

"Not really. But, while we were in bed, a story about the Mancuso woman's murder came on TV. The one where his name was on that list found at her apartment. He stopped what we were doing to watch the news—he wanted to hear every word of it. I said it was a shame for a person to die so horribly as she did. He said that sometimes people deserved to die horribly because of things they'd done. He got very agitated. It was scary for a few minutes."

"Did Atwood say he ever knew Mancuso?"

"Yes, pretty much so."

"What else did he say?"

"He said the bitch got what she deserved."

Sandy Underhill looked directly at the camera then. She was clearly enjoying her moment in the limelight.

"Later, when I heard more about his name being on that list in the apartment of the dead woman, I wondered if it might be connected..."

After the interview with Underhill, *Inside Scoop* ran a segment where a reporter and video crew confronted Atwood with the bombshell story as he left a restaurant with his wife and daughter. He pushed past the camera crew and got into a waiting car. So did his wife, with a grim look on her face. But not the daughter—who must be Miranda, the twenty-two-year-old Yale senior he'd talked about with me.

"Get out of our way, you lowlifes!" she screamed at the *Inside Scoop* people. "Leave my father alone! He's a wonderful man, and you people are all disgusting scum!" Then she tried to grab one of the cameras away before her parents dragged her into the car with them. It was all pretty terrific TV.

* * *

"Well, that was fun," Maggie said when the *Inside Scoop* report was over.

"How in the hell did we miss this?" I muttered.

"C'mon, Clare. They must have paid her for that story. That's how *Inside Scoop* gets all these people to talk. They pay them—we don't pay people."

"I think the Underhill woman was ready to talk anyway. Did you see her? She was loving the attention, even more than whatever money they paid her. All it took was someone to find her. They did, we didn't."

"What do we do now?" Maggie asked.

"The only thing you can do after you get beaten by someone else's exclusive."

"Go out and find our own exclusive?"

I nodded.

"Another woman?" she asked.

"Another woman."

"How can you be sure there is one?"

"If Atwood was cheating on his wife with someone like Sandy Underhill," I said, "then he was cheating on her with other women too."

"Maybe one of those other women was Grace Mancuso."

"He did call her a 'bitch,' according to Underhill."

"But Atwood still claims he never knew Mancuso."

"He also said he didn't know Dora Gayle."

CHAPTER 26

THE NAME OF the executive assistant in Bill Atwood's office was Diane Rodgers. I was pretty sure Atwood was having some kind of sexual relationship with her the first time I visited his office. I was even more convinced of it now. All I had to do was figure out a way to get Diane Rodgers to talk about her and Atwood.

I didn't know what that might lead to, but Atwood was definitely shaping up as the person on that list of names who had the most to hide.

Maybe Rodgers could tell us more.

"Diane Rodgers is twenty-three years old, with curly dark hair and a body that makes men drool," Maggie said to me after I asked her to find out whatever she could about the Rodgers woman.

"She flunked out of Benson College the semester before this one, but then suddenly reemerged as an employee in Atwood's office. He gave her the job as his executive assistant over several more qualified applicants, from what I'm told. But I guess she had the type of qualifications he was looking for.

"The people we talked to say she's not very good at typing or taking dictation or even answering the phone or any other of the usual executive assistant duties. But, like I said, she's definitely supposed to be very good to look at in an office—or anywhere else, I guess, for that matter."

"That all makes sense," I said when she was finished. "I sensed a lot of sexual tension between the two of them that day in the office I was there."

"If she's really involved with Atwood, she can't be happy about that Sandy Underhill interview that just aired."

"That's what I'm hoping. She's mad, she's jealous—a woman scorned and all."

"So we think that Atwood was sleeping with Diane Rodgers. Also, with Sandy Underhill, the coed on campus. Maybe even having sex with Grace Mancuso too. And, at the same time all this torrid sex and passion is going on, Atwood's got his wife waiting at home for him."

"Bill Atwood was a very busy guy," I said.

* * *

I staked out the building that evening on the Benson College campus where Atwood had his office. I saw him leaving at one point carrying a briefcase and hurriedly getting into a cab. I wondered if he was rushing off to a meeting or some other sexual tryst somewhere. A few others went in and out of the building afterward until I finally saw Diane Rodgers emerge.

I waited until she was walking across campus and then caught up with her.

"Hi, I met you in Bill Atwood's office the other day," I said when I got her attention.

"You're the TV reporter," she said.

She didn't say it like it was a good thing.

"I'd like to talk to you for a few minutes," I said.

"I have nothing to say."

She turned and began walking away.

"Did you watch the Sandy Underhill interview on TV?" I yelled out. "I imagine that was quite a shock to you. I'll bet Atwood didn't tell you anything about her, huh? Or any of his other women. Don't you figure there's got to be other women out there? I'd bet on it."

She stopped walking, then stood frozen there for a few seconds. When she finally turned around and looked back at me, I could see she was crying.

"Don't let Atwood play you for a fool, Diane," I said. "You need to do the right thing here. The right thing for you."

*　*　*

"He told me he was going to marry me," she said afterward when I took her back to the station. "He said that he had to pretend to be a happily married man for the time being because of his political future. But then he said he would leave his wife and he would be with me all the time."

"Did you believe him?"

"I wanted to," she said with a shrug. "But I've been around men enough to know they always say things like that."

She talked about how she had met him at a seminar on Political Influences for the 21st Century at the college. She didn't really care much about political influences. But she was intrigued by Atwood. He looked so handsome, so distinguished during all that sex scandal stuff on TV—she felt sorry those politicians in Washington were being so mean to him by making him resign. Now she wanted to see him in person.

After the seminar, she stayed around and introduced herself and told him about how much she'd enjoyed his talk. Then they went out for coffee together. They didn't sleep together that night. But they did the next time. That's how she got the job as his assistant. Of course, she wasn't exactly thrilled by all the aspects of their relationship. He said they had to keep it a secret. Not just from his wife, but from everyone else too—the university administrators, his political enemies, the media.

They'd been sleeping together several nights a week for a while now. She hated it when he had to go home to his wife. She wondered what he told his wife about what he was doing and how he explained it. She asked him about it a few times, but he never wanted to talk about his wife. *We have an arrangement*, he would tell her.

"I asked about his daughter once too. He got all emotional that time," Rodgers said. "I could tell he really loved his daughter. I think that's why he and his wife stayed together, for the sake of the daughter. But I kept hoping that one day his wife would be gone and I would be the only woman in his life."

She talked about how devastated she had been when she saw the Sandy Underhill interview about being in the hotel with Atwood. She'd suspected he might be seeing someone besides herself, but now she knew the truth. He was cheating on her as well as his wife. And that hotel—the one where Sandy Underhill said Atwood had taken her for sex—was the same one where Atwood had taken Diane Rodgers many times too. Probably they even had sex in the same room as her and Atwood. That was all really hard for her to take, she said.

"I've been having a lot of trouble sleeping," she told me at one point.

"It's never easy when you find out a man has lied to you," I said sympathetically.

"That's not the reason I'm having trouble sleeping."

"What then?"

"It's something else. Something about the murder of that woman Grace Mancuso. Something I know about Bill and her. I was going to keep it a secret, but not now. I mean, it would be one thing if I thought I was going to become the next Mrs. Atwood. That might make him worth trying to protect. But seeing that woman on TV talking about the two of them, I see everything clearly now. I'm tired of being played for a fool by Bill Atwood."

I waited expectantly, hoping against hope she wouldn't change her mind about telling me what she knew about Atwood that was bothering her. She didn't. A few seconds later, the whole story came pouring out of Diane Rodgers.

"I walked into Bill's office while he was being interviewed by police about his name being found at the apartment of that murdered woman, Grace Mancuso. They asked him if he knew Grace Mancuso. He said no, that he had never met or heard of Grace Mancuso in his life until then.

"It wasn't until later that I remembered. He had gotten a call from a woman a few days earlier. She identified herself and asked to speak to Bill. He wasn't there. I told the woman that and asked her if she wanted to leave a message. The woman said no. She said he was expecting her call and she'd call back later. She never did, at least while I was there. But I left soon afterward, and Bill could have answered his own phone when he came back. Or his voice mail could have picked it up.

"That's what's been keeping me up nights, Ms. Carlson. Thinking about that call. I could be wrong, of course. I didn't write the woman's name down. And it all happened very fast. It's possible that I just confused the name afterward with the one I'd

heard on the TV newscasts. But I don't think that's what happened. No, now that I've thought about it a lot more, I'm sure I
heard the name right.

"The woman who called looking for Bill that day said her name
was Grace Mancuso."

CHAPTER 27

I WAS SITTING in a Starbucks the next morning reading a bunch of texts and online posts about our show the night before—and feeling pretty good about things—when a man I'd never seen before sat down next to me.

"Hello, Clare," he said.

"Do we know each other?"

"Aren't you Clare Carlson?"

"Yes."

"The woman from Channel 10 News?"

"That's right."

"Then we know each other."

He was tall, skinny, and had long, unruly hair. It was hard to tell how old he was. He was one of those people who looked like he could be anywhere from twenty-five to forty-five. The most noticeable thing about him was how nervous he seemed. He kept moving and twitching as he talked, blinking his eyes rapidly and looking around anxiously every few seconds at other people in the place. This guy was really wired. He wasn't drinking any coffee or anything else, which was probably a good thing. Caffeine was the last thing he needed.

"What do you want to talk about?" he asked.

"I have no idea."

"Then why did you reach out to me?"

"Uh, tell me exactly how I reached out to you."

"Don't you know?"

There was more twitching and blinking and looking around the room. Something was making him nervous.

"Goddamit!" I said. "Will you stop answering my questions with more questions? Just sit still for a second and answer me one simple question: Who the hell are you?"

"I'm Todd Schacter," he said.

I stared at him in amazement. I'd been trying to reach this guy for weeks without success. And now he just sits down next to me in a coffee shop.

"How did you know I was here?" I asked.

"Your phone," he said.

I looked down at the phone in my hand.

"You sent me a bunch of messages from it."

"But how . . ."

"It's like a beacon leading me right to you."

I quickly shut off the phone, which was sort of the classic case of shutting the barn door after the horse was gone.

"Janet said you were very good at this sort of stuff."

"I am."

"How good?"

"What do you mean?"

"Do you know more about me than just being able to track my phone?"

He took out a piece of paper and handed it to me. All sorts of information about me was printed on it. My full name, Clare Ellen Carlson. My address. Birth date. Social security number. Mother's maiden name. My job history. Even the account numbers and balances of my bank account and 401(k) account at the station.

"What are you going to do with this?" I asked anxiously.

"Nothing."

"Then why did you search for it all?"

"I figured you' d want proof."

"Proof?"

"To show you how good I am."

"Okay, I'm convinced—you're good."

"So what is it you want me to do?"

I told him. Not all of it, just the part I needed his help on. Which was more than I'd ever told anyone. I didn't like doing that, but I didn't have a lot of other options at this point. I said I was looking for a daughter I'd given up at birth. How she'd grown up as Lucy Devlin for the first eleven years of her life, then disappeared. How I believed she was still alive somewhere. And that one man had the information that might help me find her. That was the information I needed him to get for me.

"Who's the man?" Schacter asked me when I was finished.

"His name is Elliott Grayson."

"The Senator?"

"Yes."

"You want me to hack into a U.S. Senator's computer files?"

"Yes."

"No way!"

"You can't do that?"

"Oh, I can."

"But you won't?"

He shook his head no. The twitching was even worse now. He seemed more stressed out than ever by what I had just asked him to do.

"I barely beat the computer hacking rap that your lawyer friend defended me on," he said. "She was good, and I was lucky. I don't want to press my luck. They're watching me. They've been watching me ever since I walked out of that courtroom a free man. They're probably watching us right now."

"Who's watching?"

"Everyone—the government, prosecutors, all the people out to get me. I'm trying to keep a low profile these days. You're talking about a U.S. Senator here. Hacking into his files? They'd send me to prison for life if they caught me. No thanks."

"I'll pay you whatever you want," I said.

"Doesn't matter."

"What can I do to get you to change your mind . . ." I started to say.

But it was too late.

Schacter had already stood up from the table we were at and was walking away.

A few seconds later, he was walking out the door.

And then he was gone.

Just like my last chance to find Lucy.

CHAPTER 28

BILL ATWOOD CALLED a press conference for the next day after we aired the Diane Rodgers interview. He didn't really have much of a choice. He needed to do something to answer all the questions being asked about him and the Grace Mancuso/Dora Gayle murders now.

A statement from his office said his wife, Nancy, and daughter, Miranda, would appear with him. That was no surprise either. Having the wife and family at your side for an embarrassing moment like this was right out of the disgraced politician's handbook. Elliott Spitzer did it when he was ousted as governor of New York in a call girl scandal—and that even became the premise of the hit TV show *The Good Wife.* Anthony Weiner did it with his wife, Huma, when he admitted to sending X-rated texts to young women as a congressman and afterward. Even Bill Clinton did it with Hillary dutifully supporting him.

I figured it would be the same with Atwood this time.

Except I was wrong.

It started out traditionally enough as Atwood read a prepared statement to the press while his wife and daughter looked on.

"First off, I want to apologize to all of you—but especially to my wife, Nancy, and daughter, Miranda. Two women have come forward in recent days to make sexual allegations against me.

Although many of the details they stated are untrue, I clearly have exhibited unacceptable sexual behavior, which shows I have a continuing problem. And so, I plan to begin receiving treatment for sexual addiction as soon as possible.

"Second, I now acknowledge that I did have a sexual relationship in college with Dora Gayle, one of the names on the list found at the Grace Mancuso crime scene and who is now also dead. I went to college in England after my relationship with Dora Gayle and never saw or talked to her again. I simply did not recognize her name on the list after all this time—or her, given the changes in her appearance and circumstances—until a TV report raised the issue about that long-ago relationship I had with the Gayle woman.

"Finally, and most importantly, I had absolutely nothing to do with the murders of Grace Mancuso or Dora Gayle. To the best of my knowledge, I did not know Grace Mancuso and, as I said, I barely remembered Dora Gayle. I will cooperate with law enforcement authorities in any way I can to aid in the investigation of these cases and capture the perpetrator or perpetrators of these tragic murders.

"Because this is an ongoing police investigation, I can't really elaborate any more about this or answer any questions."

Watching it all unfold, I decided that Bill Atwood had handled the meeting with the media as deftly as he could.

It had all gone according to plan for Atwood.

But then suddenly—and shockingly unexpectedly—everything went off the rails for him.

"Liar!" Nancy Atwood screamed at him as he started to leave the podium where he'd been speaking.

He whirled around in surprise, walked back to the podium, and tried to take her offstage along with him.

But it was now apparent that his wife had an agenda of her own for this public event.

"I want to make my own statement," she said to the stunned reporters. "I want to tell you the truth. Something my husband does not do very often."

The place was in an uproar, the media there putting all of this out live on the air. Atwood tried again to get her to leave the stage with him. But Nancy Atwood just stood there at the microphone with a grim look of determination on her face.

"I thought I had come to terms with my husband's philandering a long time ago. On our honeymoon in Mexico, we made love on our wedding night like any other couple. The next morning, I went into town to do some shopping. When I got back to our room, I found him in bed with the chambermaid. I pretty much knew right then that we were not going to have a traditional marriage.

"But I hung in there and stayed with Bill, through all the embarrassments and affairs over the years. I kept myself busy with charity causes, seminars, speeches, and an endless round of parties and tennis—and pretended not to notice about Bill and all his women. You make your choices in life, and I made mine a long time ago. There were pros and cons in every relationship, whether it came to business or marriage. In the final tally, the pros in our marriage have always outweighed the cons. At least that's what I always thought until now."

She said that on the night Grace Mancuso was murdered her husband came home very late to their home in Tarrytown—a posh suburb north of New York City—and crawled into bed. But she said he slept fitfully, turning and tossing like he was having a nightmare. He began talking in his sleep too.

But it was only one word.

A name.

The name she said her husband was crying out in his nightmare was "Grace."

Later, she told everyone, she heard him get out of bed, leave the house, and get in his car. She followed him in her own car, she said, because she knew something was terribly wrong. So she watched as he drove to the shore of the Hudson River a few miles away, got out of the car, and threw something into the water.

"There's something out there he wanted to hide," she said, looking straight into all the cameras now focused on her. "Something about Grace Mancuso, I just know it. I've put up with so much from this man over the years. But not this. That's why I want everyone to know the truth about my husband."

Atwood had kept trying to get her to leave the stage, but she ignored him and kept talking. There wasn't much he could do. He stood there for a few more moments listening, then walked off the stage while she continued to deliver all the pent-up feelings about him she'd held inside so long.

But the daughter stayed onstage, too—and, at some point, she walked up to the microphone and stood next to her mother.

And at that moment, just when I thought this press conference couldn't get any weirder, it sure did.

"What are you doing?" the daughter, Miranda, screamed at her mother.

"I'm doing what I have to do."

"Why are you doing this to Daddy, you bitch?"

"Miranda . . ."

"You're going to ruin everything!"

"Your father ruined everything a long time ago. It just took me until now to realize that."

"I hate you!" Miranda yelled and then began pummeling her mother with her fists.

The place was in total chaos now.

This was like Big Brother and Jerry Springer and Maury Povich all rolled into one.

The ultimate reality TV show.

Except this really was happening.

And it sure made good TV.

CHAPTER 29

"FROGMEN IN THE water," Cassie O'Neal said on air, standing with a microphone at the shore of the Hudson River. "That's what they called the police unit of expert divers that goes looking for bodies or evidence or anything else connected to a crime case."

She was interviewing the head of the police diving unit, who was standing next to her.

"This must be a very tough job, Commander," she said.

"Trying to find something—possibly something very small—in water like this always is," he said.

"I can imagine," Cassie said to him. "I was scuba diving once down in the Bahamas, and I lost my face mask as I came toward the beach. The water was only about three feet deep. And I pretty much knew where I'd dropped it. But I spent nearly an hour looking for it. I couldn't see underwater, the current kept taking it further away—when I finally found it, the damned thing was maybe twenty feet away already from where I'd started looking. It was pure luck that I found it at all."

This was Cassie at her best. A pretty woman playing dumb and helpless—which wasn't that hard for her to do—who won people over with that persona. The people she interviewed. And the viewers of Channel 10, who seemed to love her, according to all the ratings numbers I saw. Maybe Cassie really did know what she was doing. Maybe she was smarter than all of the rest of us.

"That's what these guys have to do," the commander said. "Only on a much bigger scale. Whatever we're looking for could have moved hundreds of yards away from the original drop point after a few days in the water. Or it could be wedged under a rock. Or it might have broken up and be in pieces. There's all sorts of possibilities, most of them not very good."

He looked out at his men in the water.

"They start in one spot and make a complete search of every square inch within that radius. Then they expand the search a bit wider. They keep doing that until they've been through every place it might be underwater. If it's still there, we'll find it."

Cassie shook her head in astonishment. "I'm glad I don't have your job," she said.

"And this is spring weather too." The commander smiled, looking up at the bright sun in the sky. "Just think what it's like in December."

* * *

We were broadcasting live from the search site in Tarrytown, NY, preempting all the normal Channel 10 daytime programming. So was pretty much every other station in town too and all the cable news channels. There were also all sorts of other people at the scene livestreaming it, blogging and tweeting the search details. This was the media event of the day, and no one wanted to miss a minute of the drama that was being played out here.

A mob of onlookers and curiosity seekers had gathered on the shore and were watching the whole thing too.

One of them was Nancy Atwood.

I guess she wanted to be here for whatever the cops found at the scene she'd pointed them to. For better or worse, she wanted to know the truth about her husband. That's what she said at the press conference, and she was playing it out until the end. We tried to talk to her, of course, but she refused to make any comment to anyone. She simply stood there with a grim, determined look on her face—the same look she'd had at the press conference—as the divers continued to search the water.

I wasn't sure how long the search was going to go on for, or—more importantly—how long Faron would allow me to keep broadcasting live from the scene at the expense of our regular day-time programming.

But, as it turned out, I didn't have to worry about making that decision.

"I think we found something," one of the divers called out from the river. "It's a bag."

All of the media rushed close to find out more.

"Still intact?"

"That's affirmative," the diver said, holding it up for everyone to see.

"What's inside?"

"Looks like a jacket. A man's sports jacket."

"Anything else?"

"Wow, look at this!"

One of the divers held something else up. It was a piece of wood. From a wooden statue.

The same kind of wooden statue used in the murder of Grace Mancuso.

"Good job, guys," the commander said. "Come on home."

* * *

There is often a moment in a case where the evidence all begins to come together in a rush. I had seen it happen a lot of times over the years. You found out one thing, then another, and suddenly it all began to make sense. That was what was happening now.

The jacket the divers found at the bottom of the river—just where Atwood's wife had said he'd gone that night she followed him—was definitely his. Nancy Atwood identified it as the one he was wearing when he left the house that morning. There were blood stains on it. The blood stains were Type O Negative. Grace Mancuso's blood was O Negative. The lab was running further DNA tests.

The piece of wooden statue was a perfect match for the broken piece in the Mancuso woman's apartment. There was blood on it too.

They even had a fingerprint match now. One of the sets of prints found in the apartment turned out to be Bill Atwood's. No question about it—Atwood had been in the apartment, even if he continued to claim he didn't know her. They had proof of that now.

At that moment, Bill Atwood was the top trending topic on social media, along with popular hashtags like #lockhimup and #justicefordoraandgrace. There were still a lot of unanswered questions about both murders. But the evidence was closing in on Atwood from all sides, and the public salivated for more, like a lynch mob with a rope eager to exact quick vengeance.

And the noose for Atwood was getting tighter . . .

CHAPTER 30

"So, the cops think Atwood kills Grace Mancuso, goes back home to Tarrytown—then panics in the middle of the night, gets up, and drives to dump the incriminating evidence in the Hudson River?" Jack Faron asked.

"That's the theory," Maggie said.

We were at the afternoon Channel 10 news meeting. But this was no ordinary news meeting. Faron was there, and he hardly ever came to my news meetings. Even more surprising, Brendan Kaiser was there too, eager to find out every new detail about the case.

I'd gotten a pretty impressive email from Kaiser even before the meeting too. It said: "You've led the way for us on this story all along. Great stuff, Clare! I can see now why so many people told me that you were the best reporter we had. You've made all of us at this station very proud. Congratulations again on breaking this big story for us!"

Yep, he sure was happy. Of course, this made Atwood—not him—the target of the Mancuso murder investigation. I wondered how Kaiser would have reacted if all the information had pointed to him, instead of Atwood.

"Anything that links him directly to the Gayle woman's murder too?" Faron wanted to know now.

"Not yet," Maggie told him. "But we've already established they had a romance in college before he left for a year in England. There has to be a connection between both murders."

"I agree," Kaiser said, speaking for the first time since he'd been at the meeting. "I think that's it then. We have the answers we were looking for. Let's just run with all this at 6 tonight on the newscast. Then we can move on to other stories."

Everyone else in the room nodded in agreement with him, except me.

"There's something still missing here," I said.

"What are you talking about?" Kaiser said.

"Why would Atwood kill Mancuso? What was his motive for murder?"

"She was blackmailing him," Faron said. "You already did the story from the woman at Revson who said Mancuso bragged to her that she was sleeping with—and planned to extort a huge amount of money from—a very important man, a man who had an extremely high profile in the media. A real ladies' man, the woman said Mancuso told her, that she planned to destroy. That has to be Bill Atwood."

"But what did Mancuso have on Atwood that she was using to blackmail for all that money?" I asked.

"Sexy videos?" someone suggested.

"Steamy emails?" another one said.

I shook my head no.

"It still doesn't make sense. Atwood's weathered a lot of sex scandals worse than that. The Underhill woman said he didn't even seem to care if she told anyone about their hotel room romp. That he thought that kind of a reputation just made him even more popular with a lot of voters—like JFK and Bill Clinton and Trump had with their own sex scandals. It wasn't that big a deal to him. No, there has to be another reason Mancuso was black-mailing Atwood. Something else she was holding over him. Something Atwood was afraid enough of her making public for him to resort to murder. I'm just not comfortable until we find out what that is."

"There's always loose ends on every story," Faron pointed out, and he was right.

"Loose ends," I said, "that's the problem. "We still don't know why those other names—including yours, Mr. Kaiser—were on that list. And why Atwood would ever leave a piece of evidence like that list, including his own name, at the scene. And why kill Dora Gayle weeks earlier, who he hadn't seen or heard from in more than thirty years?"

But what I thought didn't really matter a few minutes later, because events dictated what happened next.

"Breaking news!" Maggie shouted, looking down at a text on her phone. "The police just arrested Bill Atwood!"

* * *

In the end, it was Maggie who came up with the final answer we were looking for.

She burst into my office with a big grin on her face, punched her fist triumphantly into the air, and shouted to me: "Yes!"

Being a trained investigative journalist and all, I was pretty sure she'd come up with something.

"We tracked down Dora Gayle's roommate at NYU," Maggie said excitedly. "The woman she shared an apartment with during her senior year of college. She says Dora dropped out of school right before the end of her senior year. Guess the reason she dropped out? Dora Gayle was pregnant!"

"Bill Atwood's baby?"

"Has to be."

I nodded. "Dora used to talk about having a daughter, people said. And about someone taking her baby daughter away. It apparently happened a long time ago and no one ever knew where the daughter was or if she even really existed. So now we know that she did."

"And Atwood murders Gayle to make sure she doesn't reveal this secret from his past," Maggie said.

I made a face. "C'mon, why would he care? Even if he did have a baby with this woman all those years ago when they were in college, so what? Like I said before, Atwood's weathered much worse sex scandals than this. It's interesting, damn interesting. But I'm still not sure what this has to do with any of the rest of it. And what does Grace Mancuso have to do with any of it?"

That's when Maggie hit me with the real blockbuster revelation she'd come up with.

"Dora Gayle's baby would be how old today?" Maggie asked.

I did the math in my head. "A little over thirty, I guess."

"Grace Mancuso was thirty-three."

"But she's from Pennsylvania. We know who her parents are."

"I checked that out. Went back looking for birth records with the Pennsylvania Department of Records and then tried the Mancuso parents again. Guess what I found out? Grace Mancuso was adopted."

"Jesus, are you thinking . . . ?"

"That's right. The Mancusos adopted her the same year Dora Gayle was pregnant with her baby. The baby she said someone took away from her. I found out that the adopted baby the Mancuso family got—the one who grew up to be Grace Mancuso—was from a hospital in New York City. It all fits together, Clare. This could be the link. Why Dora Gayle's name is on that list found in Grace Mancuso's apartment. Because Dora Gayle was her mother. Her biological mother."

"Which means if Bill Atwood was having an affair with Grace Mancuso, he was having sex with his own daughter! Did he know that? Did she know?"

"Oh, I think she knew," Maggie said. "I think it was all deliberate on her part. She found out somehow about Atwood being her biological father. Then she seduced him into bed—which wasn't difficult, given Atwood's penchant for sex with attractive young women—in order to blackmail him once she told him the truth about who she was. Atwood might have survived other sex scandals. But he could never survive this one. If the public found out he was having sex with the woman who was his own daughter, he would be ruined politically and couldn't get elected dog catcher."

"The ultimate sex scandal," I said.

"It was a diabolical plan by Grace Mancuso to shake down the man who was her biological father for big money."

"He was either going to have to pay her off or let her destroy his life and career by going public with the scandalous revelation that he was having a sexual relationship with his own daughter. My God, that would have been devastating news for him to find out when she finally told him what he had done."

"And that must be the reason Atwood killed her," Maggie said.

CHAPTER 31

THERE IS A pretty amazing video of Bill Atwood being interrogated by police after his arrest.

We ran it on Channel 10. But so did all the other TV stations, newspaper websites, cable networks, and pretty much everyone else. The damn thing went viral very quickly. It was a news phenomenon for a while in terms of massive crime coverage. Kind of like O.J., Jodi Arias, and Amanda Knox all rolled into one.

No one ever discovered how the video got out. The NYPD made videos of all their interviews now—in part to protect themselves against possible police brutality or harassment charges—but these videos were only supposed to be used for court or other law enforcement purposes. Except—in this era of instant social media at anyone's fingertips—it's not really that shocking someone got ahold of a copy and blasted it all over YouTube and the rest of the Internet.

Everybody thinks they know everything there is to know about police interrogations. They watch *Law & Order* reruns, and that makes them an instant expert. They know about the good cop-bad cop routine. They know about getting to the guy before he "lawyers up." They know about reading him his rights. They will look at you solemnly and tell you with great authority:

"The interrogation is the most important moment in the prosecution of any criminal case."

These people know nothing about police interrogations.

Over the years, covering cops and the crime beat, I've learned each interrogation was different. You never knew exactly what was going to happen in that little room. Just because a suspect has a high-priced lawyer, it doesn't mean he won't still pour his heart out to the police. Every interrogation has a life of its own.

I remember the big story that taught me that lesson. A college student disappeared on the Upper East Side after a night out on the town. The search for her made the front page for days, until the body turned up in the East River. Beaten, raped, and then drowned, according to the Medical Examiner's report.

The cops' hunt for the killer went nowhere at first. Then they got a break. Someone remembered seeing the girl at a singles bar the night she disappeared. Spotted her leaving with a guy. And, miracle of miracle, remembered the license plate of the car. The problem was the car turned out to belong to a rich kid named Eric Theibold. Theibold's father ran a big corporation, his mother was a patron of the city arts and a major social force. Both of them showed up with their son for the interrogation, bringing with them a lawyer from the top criminal defense firm in town. No way Eric Theibold was going to give anything up in this interrogation, everyone figured.

Except it didn't turn out that way. The kid sat there while his family and his lawyer explained why he wouldn't answer any questions. Then he started talking. By the time he was finished, he'd confessed to the murder of the girl and also to six other unsolved cases involving young girls. It turned out that he hated his mother, and he imagined it was her when he was killing the women. He confessed because he enjoyed the pain it caused his mother to hear this, the psychiatrists' report said later. Go figure.

Then there are the ones you think will be easy but aren't. They picked up a guy once who put a woman tourist into a coma by hitting her in the head with a brick. Six witnesses saw him do it, and his fingerprints were all over the brick. They get the guy in the interrogation room and figure this one's a piece of cake. But he doesn't say a word every time they ask him a question. Just keeps asking for a lawyer. Some legal aid lawyer finally shows up, and it turns out she's an ambitious one—looking to make a name for herself on this case. She confers with him, says he wasn't read his rights properly and demands the charges be thrown out. Eventually they were, on legal technicalities. Later, I asked the lawyer how the guy knew so much about the law. She said he told her he found out by watching a Clint Eastwood movie.

The point is that an interrogation can go either way. It doesn't always matter if the defendant is rich or poor, famous or a nobody.

One thing was for sure though. You get a defendant who wants to talk *and* he doesn't bring a lawyer with him—well, that's the best. You just pull up a chair and listen because you're going to be there awhile. That's what happened with Bill Atwood.

* * *

"You're in a lot of trouble here, Atwood," said the homicide detective in the room, whose name was Marc Briggs.

He didn't call him Congressman or Mr. Atwood or even Bill. He was simply Atwood in here. It was a little thing, but I knew it was intentional on Briggs' part. It helped establish the power dynamic of the interrogation process.

"I understand that," Atwood said nervously. "I've never been arrested before."

"You're not technically arrested yet. You haven't been officially charged with anything at this moment."

"Am I going to be?" he asked, his voice cracking again.

"It doesn't look good. We found your fingerprints at the murder scene, the apartment of a woman you claimed to us you'd never met. We've got your jacket with blood all over it, the same blood type as the victim. We think you threw the bloody jacket into the river the night she was killed. We found a piece of the statue that was used in the murder there too. We've got your assistant telling us the Mancuso woman had called you. And we know that Grace Mancuso had told people she was trying to get money out of somebody who was very important. That she thought she could make this person pay to avoid a scandal. We think that person was you."

"Oh God," Atwood said.

"In addition, we now know that you had a relationship in college with Dora Gayle, one of the other people on the list. You lied about that at first. Dora Gayle is dead too. We have to assume that her death was somehow connected to the Mancuso woman's. You're our leading suspect in that killing too."

Atwood sat slumped in a chair in the stark interrogation room, with the cinder block walls and the one-way glass so people could watch him being questioned without him seeing them. He took a sip from the coffee someone had gotten for him. He didn't look anything like the calm, in-control man that he'd been with me in his office at the college just a few days ago. He looked scared.

"I'd like to cooperate," Atwood said. "I want to clear this up."

"You haven't acted like that. You've lied to us. It's time now to tell the truth."

Atwood took another sip of the coffee. This was the moment you figured he'd ask about a lawyer. "Shouldn't I have some kind of legal representation here?" most of them said about now. Except Atwood never asked for a lawyer. He didn't when they'd come for him at the college. He didn't when they read him his rights. And he didn't now.

"You're right about her trying to get money out of me, Detective. She called me up one day out of the blue. Told me she'd found out about something that happened when I was younger. I have no idea how she knew about it after all this time, but she did. Every detail of what happened. She wanted money to keep quiet. Lots of money."

"And you were willing to pay her?"

"I had no choice. The scandal would have ruined me."

"You're no stranger to scandal, Atwood."

"This was a different kind of scandal," Atwood said simply.

Briggs didn't ask him what he'd done that was so scandalous. Not yet. I understood why. He wanted Atwood to keep talking, keep telling the story his own way.

"Anyway, she wanted a huge amount of money to stay quiet. An outlandish amount of money. Even if I came up with that much money, I was going to have to liquidate it from my accounts. That would take time. I needed to figure out some way to get Grace Mancuso to back off. I set up a meeting with her. I thought maybe I could convince her to change her mind—or at least lower her demands and give me more time. I'd only talked to her on the telephone before. When I saw her, I realized Grace was a real looker. That changed everything. I hoped maybe I could have some fun with her and solve my problem at the same time."

"You started sleeping with her?" Briggs asked.

"Yes."

It wasn't hard to imagine the way he'd figured it. The great Bill Atwood, the man with the magic touch when it came to women. Grace Mancuso falls apart like a starstruck schoolgirl when he hops into bed with her. She forgets all about this extortion plan and loses her heart to him. Another scandal averted. But it hadn't happened that way. I remembered Lisa Kalikow saying how the Mancuso woman was playing the man she was blackmailing. "She was going to throw it in his face when she took the money," Kalikow had said. "She wanted to see the look on his face when she told him."

Was that what had happened on the night Grace Mancuso died?

Is that why Atwood killed her?

"She asked me to come to her place about ten p.m.," Atwood said. "She said she had a big surprise for me. I thought I was going to be able to finally convince her to stop what she was doing to me with the blackmail threat. I wanted to make a deal with her. Reason with her. She was smart, and I was smart. I hoped we could work as a team together and both come out ahead. It wasn't the first time I was able to turn a situation around like that. Besides, she really liked me. She didn't know me when it started, but after she started sleeping with me ... well, I figured things between us were different now.

"When I got to her apartment, the door was open. I went in. That's when I found her. She was lying on her stomach. I tried to turn her over. I just couldn't believe she was dead. Then I saw how badly she'd been beaten. I really freaked out, I guess, and that's when I got her blood on my jacket. And that statue thing ... Christ, it was imbedded in her head. I must have taken it out or it fell when I moved her. I'm not sure. I mean I was in such a panic at that moment.

"I realized how much trouble I was in. I couldn't let anyone know I was there. I couldn't handle the scandal that would explode around me if I were connected to a murder investigation. So I got out of the apartment as fast as I could. I found a cab and had the driver take me all the way up to the Tarrytown train station, where I'd left my car that morning. I realized I had blood on my sports jacket. So, after I went home, I took it off. That's when I found that piece of statue. It had somehow wound up in the pocket of the jacket. I suppose I must have put it there without thinking while I was trying to figure out what to do in the apartment.

"I tried to go to sleep, but I couldn't. Not really. All I kept thinking about was that battered body. I knew I had to get rid of all of it—the sports jacket, the statue, and all the blood. That's why finally I got up in the middle of the night, put it in a bag, drove over to the river, and threw everything into the water. I'm sorry I lied. But I didn't kill that woman. She was already dead when I went into the apartment."

It was a pretty unbelievable story.

But the fact that it was so unbelievable made it almost seem believable.

At least to me.

And there was something else in his timeline of events that didn't fit into the nice, neat package of evidence we'd built up that Atwood was guilty of murder.

He said Mancuso had approached him first with the threat of blackmail for something in his past, then he had slept with her after that in the belief he could win her over in bed. Our theory had been that Mancuso seduced him first to blackmail him later with the shocking information that he'd had sex with his own daughter. These two completely different scenarios of how events unfolded between him and Grace Mancuso simply didn't gibe now.

We'd gone with the theory that Mancuso was his secret love child and that was the explosive secret he had to hide—he'd slept with his own daughter—on the Channel 10 newscast. It had exploded all over the media and social media too with Twitter outrage and overwhelming condemnation of Atwood for committing such a heinous act.

Briggs confronted him with this now.

"Was Grace Mancuso your daughter?" he asked.

"No!"

"Are you sure about that?"

"I only have one daughter."

"There's evidence that Grace Mancuso was the love child of you and Dora Gayle when you were both in college."

"I never had a child with Dora Gayle."

"And Grace Mancuso never told you after the sex you had that she was really your daughter? That she was going to tell people that you'd committed such a taboo act and ruin your political career unless you gave her all the money she wanted?"

"I don't know what you're talking about."

Which left one big question, of course.

"Then what was Grace Mancuso blackmailing you over?" Briggs asked.

Atwood didn't answer for a long time. It was the first time he had stopped talking since the interrogation had begun. But this was one question he clearly did not want to answer, even now.

"You said you wanted to tell the truth."

He nodded glumly.

"I killed someone," he said finally.

"Who?"

"No one you know. It was a long time ago."

"You murdered this person?"

"No, it was an accident."

"Then why would it be so damaging to you?"

"Because someone else went to jail for it."

Bill Atwood broke down completely now and began sobbing uncontrollably.

"It's a guilt I've had to live with all my life. I've done some bad things in my life, but this was the worst. This was the one I could never forget. I've always felt there was somebody—or something—out there waiting for me because of this. Some unfinished business. The ghosts of my past haunting me. I guess I always knew that one day I was going to have to pay for what I did. I've always believed that. No matter how long it took, those ghosts were always out there waiting for me. Do you understand?"

CHAPTER 32

ATWOOD REFUSED TO talk any more about the long-ago murder or accident or whatever it was that Grace Mancuso was using to blackmail him. In fact, every time Briggs brought it up again, Atwood kept sobbing. Eventually, Briggs just focused on Grace Mancuso. That was the main thing they wanted to make sure they had evidence from Atwood on now. The rest they would worry about later

They talked for another several minutes on the video. Atwood continued to insist he had nothing to do with Grace Mancuso's murder and that she was dead when he got to the apartment.

He also seemed genuinely baffled about Dora Gayle. He said he'd dumped her after that romance when he went to England, then hardly ever thought about her again over the years. He said he didn't even remember her name on the list until several days afterward. He said he never knew anything about a child with Dora Gayle, and he had nothing to do with Gayle's murder.

But the case against him was overwhelming.

Atwood was officially charged later that day with the murder of Grace Mancuso. Authorities announced the evidence against him—the fingerprints found in her apartment; the bloodied clothes and part of the statue that had been the murder weapon he'd thrown into the water; and his lies about knowing her—was more than enough to get a conviction.

There was no direct evidence linking him to the Dora Gayle murder yet. But police listed him as the prime suspect and predicted he soon would be charged with that too.

When they brought him out of the station house in handcuffs for the perp walk on the way to being arraigned downtown in Manhattan Criminal Court, it turned into one of the biggest media events ever.

Reporters lined up outside. Microphones were thrust out in the air. TV cameras everywhere. I'd covered a lot of these kinds of things in the past, but I'd never seen a spectacle quite like this one.

"Congressman, did you kill Grace Mancuso?" someone yelled.

"Was she really your daughter?" another reporter asked. "What about Dora Gayle?"

"Do you have anything to say to the people of New York?" a woman with a microphone wanted to know.

Atwood kept looking straight ahead, a stony look on his face—like a man experiencing a nightmare he hoped he would wake up from very soon.

His wife was there in the crowd. So was his daughter, Miranda. She looked sad and confused and stood in a spot far away from her mother. I could only imagine how that relationship was going to play out going forward. Also in the crowd was Diane Rodgers, the Atwood assistant who once thought he might marry her. And Sandy Underhill, the student who'd sold her story of a sex romp with Atwood to the TV show—she was there too, milking in every bit of her fifteen minutes of media fame.

In the end, it was the women that brought him down. There was a kind of irony to that. That's what I was thinking about when it happened.

It was all so quick, and yet I will never forget those horrible few moments—like a modern-day Jack Ruby–Lee Harvey Oswald that played out in public right before all of our very eyes.

She screamed out the words even before the first shots.

"You bastard," she yelled, "I hate you."

There was a gunshot, then another, and after that everything was a blur. Atwood crumbling to the ground. The woman being wrestled to the ground. The gun finally being taken away from her. The cries of horror from the crowd.

"I loved you." The woman with the gun was sobbing. "I loved you so much."

But she wasn't talking to Atwood. She was talking to the dead Grace Mancuso.

"You killed her," Lisa Kalikow cried out at Atwood as he lay on the ground. "You killed the only woman I ever loved. Now you're going to die just like she did."

From somewhere far off, I heard Atwood's last prophetic words from the police interview.

"I've always felt there was somebody—or something—out there waiting for me because of this," he'd said. "Some unfinished business. The ghosts of my past haunting me. I guess I always knew that one day I was going to have to pay for what I did. I've always believed that. No matter how long it took, those ghosts were always out there waiting for me. Do you understand?"

The thing was, I did understand. I knew all about the ghosts. Because I had my own ghosts, too. The ghosts of my own secrets from the past. The ghosts of things from back then that I still had to pay for doing. And now the ghosts that would haunt me forever about Bill Atwood and the role I played in all the events leading up to this tragic ending of his life.

The ghosts were out in full force now, and I was afraid at that instant—even as I watched paramedics working fruitlessly on a dying Bill Atwood as he lay on the street—that the ghosts would be coming after me next.

PART II

FEEDING THE BEAST

CHAPTER 33

THE CASE AGAINST Bill Atwood began falling apart within hours of his death.

The first sign that something was wrong came when Sandy Underhill, the Benson College coed who slept with him and told the story on TV about him calling Grace Mancuso a "little bitch who deserved to die," popped up again in an interview in the *National Enquirer.* In this one, she gave a completely different account of things Atwood supposedly said about Mancuso in the hotel room that day. Under questioning by police, Underhill admitted he'd never mentioned Grace Mancuso. In fact, their hotel room encounter had taken place before Mancuso was even murdered. She said she'd made up the rest of it to make her story seem more sensational. She wanted to be a celebrity.

Then came even more disturbing news. Grace Mancuso was not Bill Atwood's secret daughter. Dora Gayle never had a baby. She was pregnant—apparently with Atwood's child—but she suffered a miscarriage. That, along with being dumped by Atwood—who was partying up a storm with girls in London back then—was apparently too much for her. She dropped out of school and began the long downward spiral that eventually turned her into an alcoholic and a homeless person living on the street.

One doctor who'd treated her said she sometimes talked when she was drinking about being married to a husband named Billy and how they had this beautiful daughter together and lived in this pretty little house—but it was all a delusion. A sad dream that came out of the bottle.

As for Dora's murder, cops picked up a derelict near the park who confessed to the slaying. It turned out she had been talking during one of her delusions about the bank account she still thought she had. This time the delusion cost Dora her life. The guy forced her to the bank ATM that night and then stabbed her to death in a rage when she couldn't produce any money. He said he was sorry he killed her, because she was a nice lady. He also said that he was a secret agent for the CIA, and he asked the arresting officers to notify the President and Joint Chiefs of Staff of his situation.

It got worse after that.

The DNA samples of the blood found on Atwood's clothes matched Grace Mancuso's blood. But that didn't really mean anything anymore. Before he died, Atwood admitted he was in the apartment and gotten her blood on him the night she was murdered. That negated the importance of that evidence, which seemed so crucial just a short time earlier when they found it at the bottom of the Hudson River.

The real jolt though came from the final Medical Examiner's report. It found that the time of death for Grace Mancuso was even earlier than they had first thought, some eighteen hours before police discovered her body—definitely no later than five or six p.m. Atwood had been in meetings at Benson College all that day until six, then attended a fund-raising dinner until after nine. As many as two dozen people had seen him during that time period and could vouch for his whereabouts. He had an alibi. It also bolstered his story that he arrived at the Mancuso woman's apartment sometime after ten p.m.

In addition, the cops found a custodian in the building who remembered seeing Atwood come into the building about that time. Also, they tracked down a cab driver who took him home to Tarrytown. He still had the record of the trip in his cab—pickup at 71st and Madison at 10:35 p.m. for the trip to Tarrytown, NY, which took forty-six minutes. The fare came to $78, plus a $22 tip. The cab driver absolutely identified Bill Atwood as the man who was his fare.

The conclusion was inescapable.

Atwood had been telling the truth.

Yes—Grace Mancuso was blackmailing him, he was sleeping with her, and he did go to her apartment on the night she was murdered.

But he didn't kill her.

Which left us with many unanswered questions.

We still didn't know who murdered Grace Mancuso.

Or why Dora Gayle's name turned up on that list found at the Mancuso crime scene.

Or why any of the other names were there either.

And—even though this didn't seem as relevant now—we never found out what damaging information Grace Mancuso had on Atwood that she was using to blackmail him. "I killed someone . . . it was an accident, but someone else went to jail for it," he said during the police interrogation. But there hadn't been time to get more details then, and now Atwood had taken that secret to the grave with him.

The bottom line of it though was that Dora Gayle's death had nothing to do with the Grace Mancuso murder. Three people were now dead since this had started—Grace Mancuso, Bill

Atwood, and Dora Gayle. It was pretty certain at this point that none of them were killed by the same person. Sometimes a crime mushrooms like that, setting off a chain reaction of dominos falling that no one could have ever predicted. No one else had any other reasonable explanation for the strange confluence of events, including me.

Someone had to take the blame for Atwood's death, of course.

The finger pointing had already started. The Mayor fired his special assistant, the one who'd been working with police on the investigation. The Mayor went on TV to make a public apology for the tragic mistake and subsequent death of Bill Atwood. He said he had received faulty information from the people he had put in charge of the case, and he vowed reforms in the criminal justice system.

Heads were rolling in the police department, too. The police commissioner was critical of everyone, except himself. One deputy commissioner was suspended, another was put on modified duty. They had pushed for prosecution of Atwood too, claiming at the time the case against him seemed ironclad. Both of them blamed homicide detectives on the case for the screwup, saying they'd conducted a sloppy investigation. The detectives claimed it was the police commissioner and the mayor's office that had put pressure on them to arrest Atwood, even though they didn't think there was enough evidence and that the case against Atwood wasn't strong enough.

The media was heavily criticized too for rushing to judgement on Atwood. Everyone from *Inside Scoop* to the New York City tabloids to all of the local TV stations and cable news networks were accused of reckless and irresponsible journalism. Channel 10 had been at the forefront of the Mancuso/Atwood story—so naturally we took the most heat for the tragic outcome.

But you know what?

They were all right in being critical of our actions, especially my own. We had screwed up big-time, and we deserved all the heat we got from that. No one felt worse about it—or more guilty about Atwood's death—than me.

I thought I might even get fired over it. Instead, Faron—and Kaiser too—both supported me and said I'd done nothing more than any of the other journalists covering the case had done. They told me it wasn't my fault that Atwood was now dead. I was grateful for that, even though I wasn't completely sure I agreed with them.

I still have nightmares about Bill Atwood's senseless death—and I fear they will never go away.

Meanwhile, this was all being played out against the backdrop of the funeral for Atwood, which elicited tangled emotions from many people.

At first, there was outrage over his actions. The affair with the dead woman. The other affairs with his assistant and the coed and countless others who had come forward. It seemed like the bill for the web of lies he'd manufactured to the voters and others over the years was finally coming due.

But, amazing enough, this was quickly followed by an out-pouring of sympathy as the case against him for the murders of Grace Mancuso and Dora Gayle collapsed like a house of cards. Sure, he'd played around with a lot of women and he'd lied about it. But that's what a politician does. He'd served his country well in Washington and later as a respected college administrator. Most people felt that was the way he should be remembered, not for the blemishes on his record.

In the end, Atwood got an impressive funeral. Political leaders, celebrities, and just plain everyday people packed the church on

Fifth Avenue where the service was held. There were lines extending for blocks to view his casket.

The most emotional moment of the service came from Atwood's daughter, Miranda, the senior at Yale he'd talked so proudly about to me during that first day in his office. Miranda—with her father's good looks and apparently his gift for oratory too—delivered a moving eulogy, referring to him at one point as "a great man, a great American, and a great father."

Looking at the young woman standing at the podium, I thought again about how much devastation had been caused to the Atwood family and so many others.

Then, at some point while she was talking, Miranda Atwood completely lost her composure. She began crying and couldn't finish the eulogy. They had to lead her back to her seat, and the young woman's sobbing could be heard throughout the rest of the service. At the end, she would break down and throw herself onto her father's coffin.

"A DAUGHTER'S ANGUISH!" the headlines read the next day.

*　*　*

Meanwhile, Lisa Kalikow had no real explanation for shooting Atwood. She just kept saying over and over again how much she loved Grace Mancuso. She said she hadn't gone there with the express intent of shooting him. She heard he was there, she wanted to see the man that had killed Grace—and she just brought the gun along, maybe to scare him or something.

The gun had been given to her by her father a year earlier after she'd been mugged on the subway after leaving work. She'd never fired it before. Even now, she couldn't remember the details of the shooting. When she was told Atwood was innocent, she broke down and cried.

Later that night, she would be hospitalized after a suicide attempt in her jail cell. It was all too much for her to bear. The woman she loved was dead, she'd killed the wrong man, and was going to prison—and the real killer was still out there walking free.

* * *

At some point, I scored an interview with Nancy Atwood about her husband. It was heartbreaking to watch. But it was also pretty amazing TV.

She talked about the good times with Bill Atwood. Meeting him for the first time, falling in love with him, their wedding day, the happy moments they shared and how proud they both always were about their Miranda, who would graduate from Yale.

"I suppose that's why I hung in there so long with Bill, through all the embarrassment and his affairs and the rest. Despite his failings, my husband had a lot of things going for him. He was smart, he was good-looking, he was charming, and he was successful. Most of all, people liked him. I guess I liked the idea of being Mrs. Bill Atwood, and enjoying all the benefits that came with that. And, of course, I always wanted us to stay together for Miranda's sake. Miranda idolized her father. A divorce would have been devastating for her."

She told the story again of deciding to reveal what she knew that led to her husband's arrest and subsequent death.

"I knew he was lying about Grace Mancuso, and I finally decided I had to tell the truth. I was prepared to suffer the consequences of that in terms of losing my marriage. But I didn't realize how much of an impact it would have on my daughter. Miranda won't even speak to me anymore. She hates me for what she said I did to Bill. So I lost my husband and my daughter. I wish sometimes I could go back and change things. Change everything to make it the way it was again. But it's too late for that now."

* * *

Mostly, though, I was back to being a full-time news director again.

The big new project at Channel 10 was to launch a morning newscast, along with our 6 and 11 p.m. shows. That meant hiring a whole new team of perky newscasters for early morning duty. It also meant I probably would start having to get up earlier to oversee our perky new morning team, which I wasn't exactly thrilled about doing. Being perky early in the morning is not one of my strong points.

At the same time, there was a massive new emphasis on trying to create a bigger online presence via social media platforms for our newscasts through an updated Channel 10 app. I understood some of this digital/app stuff, but you had to be like a twenty-five-year-old kid to really grasp it all. So I hired a few twenty-five-year-old kids to run the digital end for me. That's one of the first rules I ever learned about being a TV executive— delegate what you don't know how to do to people who do know how to do it. Careers have been built on this simple premise.

The one constant thing in my life was the news. The news always keeps coming—day after day, week after week, month after month—whatever else changes around it. And filling up a TV newscast over and over was an all-consuming job that never seemed to end.

"Feeding the beast," an editor I worked for once called it. "No matter how much you give it, the beast is always hungry for more."

For a while, the follow-ups on everything that had happened surrounding the Grace Mancuso murder kept the beast at bay. We milked it for everything it was worth. But eventually we just ran out of things to say. And so we began chasing after new stories. There were always new stories out there. New crimes. New scandals. New tragedies and human-interest stories. New celebrity stuff.

That's the other thing about feeding the beast.

The beast always wants something new to eat.

And so eventually everyone forgot—or almost forgot—about Grace Mancuso.

*   *   *

I went out on another date with Scott Manning. Well, sort of.

A few days after our dinner, he asked if he could meet me for coffee. Coffee? That should have been my first sign this was not going to end well. Coffee is a real step down from having dinner together.

When I got there, he announced to me that he was moving back in with his wife.

"Wow, our date was that bad?" I said, trying my best to mask my shock and disappointment.

"The date was great."

"So how exactly did it chase you back to your wife then?"

"Look," he said, "I've made a lot of mistakes with my marriage and my family. I have a son who won't even talk to me. I need to make it all right again. Or I need to at least try to make it right. Do you understand? If it wasn't for Tim, if it wasn't . . ."

I did understand. Nancy Atwood had a daughter she was trying to reestablish a broken relationship with. Scott Manning had a son he wanted back in his life again. Everyone seemed to be reaching out to their children to make up for past mistakes. Everyone except me. I wanted to do that too. But I still had to find my child.

I didn't want to lay anything that heavy on Manning though.

I decided to go the humor route instead.

"Does this have anything to do with being disappointed over me not having sex with you the other night?" I asked.

"Well, it would have been nice. But no."

"How about if I change my mind and say I'll have sex with you now?"

"Tempting, but that doesn't change anything."

"Damn," I said. "Offering up easy sex to you was the best offer I could come up with."

He smiled. But it was a sad sort of smile.

I decided to suspend my comedy routine and just take the high road.

"Good luck," I said. "I really mean that. I hope everything works out for you with your wife and with your son. You deserve that kind of happiness. You're a good guy, I can tell."

"You're a good one too, Clare."

Yeah sure, I thought to myself, but not good enough to keep you from going back to your wife.

* * *

I saw the other cop in my life too. My ex-husband Sam. We ran into each other at a media event I had to go to at Police Headquarters. It was a social reception with a banquet table of food and even a bartender.

"I'll buy you a drink for that first tip you gave me about the list," I said.

"The drinks are free, Clare."

"Uh, I know, that was kind of a joke."

"Oh, right."

He smiled weakly.

"You look good," he said to me.

"So do you, Sam."

Except he didn't. He looked tired and not as attractive as I remembered him in the past. Sam was always good-looking and charming, even if he wasn't quite Scott Manning in the looks and charm department. But I didn't see any of that now, and I wondered idly what I'd seen in him in the past. Maybe it was the comparison with Manning that left him coming up short in the sexual attraction department for me.

I asked him about his wife and baby, just to make some kind of conversation.

"It's exhausting, to be honest with you," he said. "She's busy with the baby all day and night; I hardly get any sleep. Between that and my job, I'm tired and burned out all the time."

"What did you think having a baby was going to be like? You just hand the kid a can opener and a change of clothes every once in a while—and that's it?"

"I don't know. I'm not sure what I expected, or what I want. I'm not sure about anything."

"Are you talking about the marriage?"

"I miss you, Clare," he blurted out. "I miss talking to you like this. Having fun with you. I miss a lot of things about you. Maybe it's not too late. Maybe we could still see each other again sometime and . . . well, you know what I mean."

My God, I thought to myself, he's coming on to me. He's got a new wife and a little kid at home, and he's trying to proposition *me.* Sam finished off his drink and ordered another. I realized at that point he'd probably had quite a bit to drink even before I got there.

"The thing is I sometimes still wonder if I made the right decision," he said. "You and me were so great in the beginning. Maybe I should have stayed with you and tried harder to make it work. Maybe I picked the wrong woman. I guess what I'm saying is I'm not sure I made the right choice; I'm not sure I did the right thing."

"You did the right thing, Sam," I told him.

* * *

"So the guy you wanted to have sex with doesn't want to have sex with you anymore," Janet said to me. "And the guy you don't want to have sex with now suddenly wants to have it again with you. Is that right?"

"Welcome to my life."

"What are you going to do?"

"Evidently not have sex with anyone for a while."

"I'm talking about you and Scott Manning."

"Nothing. He's gone."

"And your ex-husband?"

I shook my head no.

"He's just having buyer's remorse. He's better off with his new wife. He's remembering all the good things about me. If we ever got back together again, he'd remember all the pain-in-the-ass qualities I have too. Believe me, I can be a real pain in the ass to live with."

"No question about it. I can only imagine . . ."

I shot her a glare.

"Besides, I don't want to be a house wrecker."

"Home wrecker."

"Whatever. I've got plenty of other things to feel guilty about without having that on my conscience too."

"You mean you still feel guilty over all the stuff with Bill Atwood and the way he died?"

I hesitated for a second, thinking maybe about telling Janet everything that was bothering me. All about me and Lucy, the daughter I lost a long time ago and somehow needed to find. But I didn't.

"Right," I said. "The Atwood business. That's it."

*   *   *

I was at a dead end on Lucy. I simply didn't know what else to do.

I had even confronted Elliott Grayson about it face-to-face recently. I checked and found out when he was scheduled to visit his office here in New York City. I didn't figure I'd have much luck trying to see him there. But I still remembered where he lived in New York. He'd brought me up there on that long-ago night we went out together. I went back there and staked the place out. It took a while, but I finally found him coming out of the building lobby at around seven a.m.

"We had a deal," I shouted at him.

"I don't know what you're talking about," he said, looking around anxiously and trying to figure out the best way to get away from me.

"I didn't go with my story that might have ruined your Senate bid, and in return you promised to tell me where Lucy was. I never told anyone about what you did. I held up my end of the bargain. Now you need to give me that information."

"I lied to you about Lucy. I don't know anything at all about her."

"I don't believe you."

"Believe whatever you want. Say whatever you want. No one will believe you. And, even if someone did, you'd just be destroying your own career by admitting you buried a story like that for your own personal reasons. You'd be committing professional suicide. It's a gamble on my part, I know. But I'm a gambler, Carlson. I'm betting that you won't destroy yourself just to take me down. Especially because you know that if you do that, you'll lose any chance whatsoever of me telling you at some point in the future whatever I might know—assuming I know anything—about your daughter. So you just have to wait until I decide what to tell you—and when. That's our deal now."

"Don't be too sure about me," I said. But even as I said it, I could hear the lack of conviction in my voice.

"Like I said, I'm a betting man, Carlson. I'm betting that you won't do anything. I think the odds on that are pretty good."

Elliott Grayson walked away from me now. I let me him go. There wasn't much more to say because he was right. I'd lost out on the big story I could have broken about him. And I'd lost out on my chance to finally track down my daughter after all these years.

Damn!

I was running out of options on Lucy.

I was running out of options on a lot of things in my life.

*   *   *

I'm a news junkie at heart. The most important thing in my life has always been the news stories I covered. I really liked the stories. Well, I suppose it was more than that—I needed the stories.

Like a heroin addict looking for the next fix, searching for that next big story had always been the most important thing in my life.

I cut short my honeymoon with husband #1 to go cover a plane crash. I walked out in the middle of an anniversary party with husband #2 to go to the scene of a building collapse. And I drove Sam nuts by reading Twitter news and texting to reporters when we were in bed together, sometimes before or after sex. Okay, that even happened during sex a few times. Hard to believe my marriages didn't work out, huh?

But when I remember wanting and needing and chasing a big story the most was when I was unhappy about something else in my life. I wrapped myself in the safe, protective cocoon of the news so I didn't have to deal with the problem. I simply threw myself into my work as a reporter and shut all the rest of the world out of my mind for a while. That's what I did after all my marriages fell apart. And that's what I wanted to do now after my conversation with Elliott Grayson in order to forget about babies and men and all the rest of it.

I needed a story.

A big story.

And there was one big story still waiting out there for me that needed some kind of closure.

*   *   *

"The Grace Mancuso story is back on," I announced at the next news meeting we held at Channel 10 to go over the story assignments for the reporters.

"Well, it will be once they catch someone for it," Maggie said.

"No one's done a very good job of that so far," Brett said with a laugh.

"Including us," added Dani, drawing a few more giggles from around the room.

I didn't laugh. That surprised a lot of people, I suppose, because I'm always the first one to laugh at news meetings. But I wasn't joking about this. I was deadly serious.

"That's because we were distracted by Atwood," I said. "All of us—the media, the cops, social media—began to focus entirely on him. All the evidence anyone gathered was only looked at from that one perspective—how does this prove Atwood did it? Now we have to go back and look at all the evidence again."

You see, that was the decision I'd made after my confrontation with Elliott Grayson. You could call it a life decision, I guess. I had no control over most of the problems in my life right now. I couldn't do anything about the daughter that was lost to me. Or my failed relationships with Scott Manning and all the other men in my past.

But I could do one thing.

One thing was still under my control.

I could go after the Grace Mancuso story.

I could find out the answers to what really happened to her.

"There's two possible keys to this crime," I said to everyone in the room. "Has been since the very beginning. The scandal at Revson that Grace Mancuso was involved in. And the list of names found at the crime scene. One of those two things is the key to us for finding out what got Grace Mancuso killed. All we have to do is figure out which one it was. We go back and dig into the Revson mess. Find out everything we can find about that scandal—investigators, financial records, interviews with the key participants. See if we can find a suspect there. Second, there's the list. There were five names on that list found at Grace Mancuso's apartment. Two of them are now dead, along with Mancuso herself. That leaves three—Scott Manning, Emily Lehrman, and Brendan Kaiser. Somewhere there has to be a clue there to what this is all about."

"But we already did all that," one editor said.

"Let's do it all again."

"Do you really think we'll find anything?" someone asked.

"Look, there's only one thing to do when you screw up a case as badly as we did," I told everyone in the room.

"What's that?"

I started to answer, but Maggie did it before me.

"We just start all over again at the beginning," she said.

PART III

HEY HO, LET'S GO

CHAPTER 34

"FOLLOW THE MONEY" has been the mantra of every investigative journalist since Bob Woodward and Carl Bernstein said it about the Watergate scandal in *All the President's Men*. Well, sort of said it. Because the real Woodward and Bernstein never actually uttered those words—and the phrase is not mentioned anywhere in their nonfiction book. It was made up for the movie version with Robert Redford and Dustin Hoffman.

But it's still damn good advice for a reporter.

Money usually is, as they say, at the root of all evil.

In this case, the money was at Revson Investments.

So that seemed like the first logical place to go back to looking for answers.

Going over the records of the company's recent scandal, I discovered there were 138 clients of Revson Investments who'd been swindled out of money. Thirteen Revson employees were indicted—mostly due to the testimony of Grace Mancuso, who turned state's evidence and gave them up in return for immunity from prosecution herself.

That made at least 151 possible murder suspects for Grace Mancuso, the way I figured it.

Not even counting, of course, family members and friends of those 151 people who also might have been mad at Mancuso.

I started with the client list first. I obtained a list of all the names of the victims of the scam from the public government documents filed in the courts about the case, and then went through them one by one.

The victims were from all over the country—and ran the gamut of occupations and financial worth. A few were relatively wealthy, but most of them were ordinary working people who'd invested their life savings and retirement money, only to have it all disappear.

Several had already filed lawsuits to recover what was stolen, but that could take years—and a lot of them were too old to ever see any return from that. I could understand how any one of these people might have gotten mad enough to kill Mancuso. It made me mad just thinking about it.

There was a farmer in Nebraska who was going to lose his land because of what had happened. A couple in Arizona who depended on the money to supplement their meager Social Security income. A woman in California who no longer could afford her critically ill husband's medical treatments. "That woman killed my husband," said the man's wife when I got her on the phone.

There were plenty of potential suspects among them too. One disgruntled investor had threatened to burn down the Revson building. Another wanted to punch Vernon Albright, the head of Revson, in the nose. There was even a woman who said she put a curse on the company and everyone in it, sending along a voodoo doll as proof of the evil she had wished upon the people who stole her money.

Most of these were isolated incidents, impulsive acts of anger by people who felt powerless to fight back after having their life savings taken away from them. But some of the victimized Revson investors seemed to be doing more than just venting understandable anger at the company.

One called the Revson offices relentlessly, sometimes forty or fifty times a day. The operators were instructed not to let him talk to anyone, but he went by different names and disguised his voice. Another sent so many faxes that they had to change their number because it clogged up the system. Then there were the emails— thousands of pieces of it sent to the Revson website by one disgruntled investor. First, it was just simple harassment. Then she started sending computer viruses in the attachments that collapsed the entire Revson system on several occasions.

I eventually winnowed down the list to what I considered to be the three leading suspects. Gary Myers, Maryanne Giordanno, and Joseph Ortega.

Gary Myers was a construction foreman from Dublin, Tennessee. He and his wife invested about $210,000 of their life savings with Revson. The money was supposed to be for their two daughters' college education. Myers was furious and made all sorts of threats when he found out that the money was gone

Maryanne Giordanno worked as a nurse in Berkeley, California. Her husband had leukemia. They needed the money to pay for his medical bills. But when they went to draw it out of the account, they discovered it was gone. Because they couldn't pay, the treatments were put off. Her husband died. She was the one who had clogged up the Revson computers on several occasions with harassing emails and computer viruses. Anyone who would go to that amount of trouble might be capable of murder too.

A man in the Bronx named Joseph Ortega had invested a total of $351,000 in Revson over the years. Most of it 401(k) and IRA money, his life savings for retirement. He was fifty-nine years old, and he planned to buy a condo in Florida to retire before he was sixty-five, he had said on his financial application. The money was all gone now, along with his dream for a comfortable life in Florida. He had threatened to burn down the Revson building.

There was a lot of anger like that, and I thought again about how Grace Mancuso's body had been battered beyond recognition even after death.

That made it even more likely that her death could have something to do with what had happened at Revson.

But I still had absolutely no idea how or why or what that was.

Or how it might possibly be connected to the other names on the list found next to Mancuso's body.

Then there were the people at Revson who were probably going to jail because of her testimony against them. Most of them wouldn't talk to me when I reached them, on the advice of their lawyers. But I tracked down the lead prosecutor on the case, an assistant U.S. Attorney named Karen Fenton.

"They were all really mad at Mancuso," Fenton said.

"How mad?"

"When we first brought them all in for questioning, we offered everyone the same deal. The first one who agreed to cooperate with us would get a get-out-of-jail-free card. No prison time in return for a plea bargain. The rest of them all turned it down. I guess they figured they could get out of it somehow if they all stuck together. But Mancuso went for the deal. She gave us chapter and verse on all of them, and now they're going to jail for a long time."

"That sounds like they'd be awfully upset with her."

"The funny thing is that after we made the deal with Grace, we suspected she was the real ring leader of the whole thing. I think she planned it, recruited the others to help her—and then hung them out to dry when the shit hit the fan. Doesn't seem fair, does it? But we wanted to get convictions in this, and her testimony was the only way to do it. So we let her walk."

"What happens to your case now that she's dead?"

"Well, we've still got her sworn testimony, which we'll introduce in court. But it isn't quite the same as having your key witness testifying on the stand. So I guess you could say her death helps the indicted people, which probably makes them pretty happy. Not to mention the people she swindled. I guess they're happy too."

"That's a lot of suspects," I said. "A lot of people happy to have her dead."

"Hey, maybe it's like that old Agatha Christie book. *Murder on the Orient Express*. The one where all the suspects get together to all kill one person they hated. They each stab him individually, so they can each get revenge for what he did to them. What if that's what happened here? All thirteen of these people we indicted because of her, maybe the 138 swindled investors too—they all get together for this one murder." Fenton sighed. "I guess that doesn't make much sense, huh?"

"Why not?" I told her. "It makes as much sense as anything else about this case."

Of course, Grace Mancuso's murder didn't necessarily have to be about the Revson financial scandal.

The reason for it could have been personal.

Mancuso was having a lesbian affair with Lisa Kalikow. She was having another affair with Bill Atwood at the same time she was blackmailing him. She was involved with one guy and had just broken off a relationship with another. While I was digging into the Revson story, I even heard rumors that she was sleeping with Vernon Albright, the head of the beleaguered company.

Yep, Grace Mancuso had sure been a busy girl.

Embezzlement.

Blackmail.

Promiscuity.

But which one had gotten her killed?

CHAPTER 35

THE BEST WAY for a reporter to find out the truth is to figure out who's lying.

Sure, that sounds like a fairly simple journalistic principle, and it has served me well in the past on other confusing stories.

The trick is you have to catch someone in a lie.

Well, I knew Bill Atwood had lied—but he was dead and out of the picture now.

Same with Dora Gayle—she was gone too.

That left three names from the list: Emily Lehrman, Scott Manning, and Brendan Kaiser. If Bill Atwood had lied about his connection to Grace Mancuso that got his name on that list found at the murder scene, then maybe one of the others lied too. Or all of them. I sure hoped it wasn't Brendan Kaiser that was lying though. Pointing the finger of guilt at your boss as a potential murderer is generally not a smart career move.

I painstakingly went through the notes of my interviews with all of them and the stories they had told after their names turned up on that list. In Scott Manning's case, it was more than just an interview. He had given me a lot of information about him and his background in the bar and the restaurant the night we went out together. I checked and re-checked every fact that they gave out to me and the rest of the media since the story began. I wasn't exactly sure what I was looking for. Some kind of discrepancy, I guess. Something that didn't quite ring true. Except I couldn't find anything.

I thought some more about the three surviving people from that list. Manning, Kaiser, and Lehrman. If one of them was hiding something—or at least not telling the whole truth—my best guess was it might be Lehrman. She was the only one who'd refused to talk to me for the story.

Why was that?

Maybe because there was something she didn't want me to find out.

I had no idea what that was, of course—but I decided to pretend I did.

I was going to run a bluff on Emily Lehrman.

* * *

I tracked Lehrman down in a courtroom near Foley Square, where she was working her legal magic on a judge and jury—cross-examining a young police officer who had arrested her client.

The client was a mobster named Tony Rinaldi, who'd been busted for running a numbers operation. The cop had stumbled onto it while he was responding to a disturbing the peace complaint. He'd taken Rinaldi into custody, confiscated the money, and found all the betting slips.

The only problem was he violated Rinaldi's constitutional rights about a dozen times. He might have gotten away with it if the person he arrested couldn't afford a good lawyer. Rinaldi hired the best. He got Emily Lehrman.

As I watched her expertly and brutally taking apart the young cop on the stand, I thought again about how she'd once been a public defender dedicated to seeking justice for the poor and downtrodden—instead of representing mobsters, drug lords, and wealthy white-collar criminals like now.

What changed her?

Of course, none of this had anything to do with me or why I was there.

When the court session was over and the case against the mobster Rinaldi dismissed, I confronted her in the corridor outside.

"Doesn't your conscience ever bother you about doing stuff like that?" I asked, pointing over to Rinaldi who was accepting congratulations for beating the court rap.

"A simple hello would suffice."

"Hello, Ms. Lehrman."

"What are you doing here?"

"I have another question for you about Grace Mancuso."

She stared at me with the same calm, cool expression she had on her face when she was in the courtroom cross-examining the cop. If I'd shaken her up at all with my appearance there, she hadn't shown it so far.

"Well?" she said finally. "What's your question?"

"What would you say if I told you that your phone number was found by police going through Grace Mancuso's call log?"

"What would my number be doing in her phone records?"

"That's what I'm asking you."

She looked at me blankly. No reaction at all. She was good. Very good.

"Was my phone number really found in Grace Mancuso's records?"

"I didn't say that."

She shook her head sadly. "But you hoped it might rattle me, and I might say something to confirm it or say something else damaging. My God, that's the oldest courtroom trick in the book. I'd heard you had a reputation as a pretty smart journalist. I guess I overestimated you."

"So that's your official—on the record—reply to my question?"

"What is it you want from me?"

"I want you to talk about how your name might have wound up on that list at the Grace Mancuso crime scene!"

She turned and began to walk away.

"I have one more question for you. It's not about the Mancuso murder. I read up on all your background. You used to be a whole different kind of lawyer, a whole different kind of person. You worked with the homeless, tenants getting evicted and clients like that who couldn't afford to pay you much money. Then suddenly you became a high-priced attorney for a completely different kind of clientele. I'm just curious. Why?"

"I decided I was wasting my time being a do-gooder."

"What took you so long?" I asked.

"Sometimes it takes a while to see the obvious."

For just a second or two, I thought she actually might open up to me. That I had gotten through the cold attorney exterior of hers to reach the real Emily Lehrman. The one who used to represent the poor and the downtrodden instead of drug czars and mob bosses. The real person, not the high-powered attorney.

But then she put her lawyer face back on, the same way she did in the courtroom.

"I don't have to talk to you at all," Emily Lehrman said, walking away from me and out of the building.

CHAPTER 36

"THERE HAS TO be some reason Emily Lehrman was on that list that we're all missing," I told Janet. "Same with the other names on it. The connection is there somewhere, we just have to find it. And find out if someone—or maybe all of the people on that list—are hiding something from us."

"Logical," Janet said.

"That means I need to go back and ask some hard questions to Scott Manning, the NYPD detective I was—and still am, truth be told—hoping to have some kind of a personal relationship with."

"Tricky."

"And then I need to do the same with Brendan Kaiser, the man who's worth about a jillion dollars and also happens to own the television station that I work for."

"Even trickier."

I'd called Janet after the encounter with Emily Lehrman to ask her advice about Lehrman and a lot of other stuff I didn't have answers for. It turned out that she was in another courtroom nearby and agreed to meet me after that case was over. Now we were sitting on a park bench near Foley Square talking about it all. Actually, I was doing most of the talking. I pointed that out to her.

"It sure would be nice if you could give me more than one- or two-word answers, Janet," I said. "This isn't Twitter, you know. There's no limit on the amount of characters you can use."

"What do you want me to tell you?"

"What did any of these people do to make them wind up on that list next to Grace Mancuso's body? Who murdered Mancuso? Why was she killed? What could the homeless Dora Gayle possibly have to do with any of it? Or Bill Atwood, for that matter? Answers to all—or any—of these questions would work for me."

"Look, Clare, I deal in facts in my job just like you do. But sometimes, when all the facts aren't available, I have to put together a likely scenario of events and why I think they happened. That's what you need to do here.

"Let's take the cop first. Scott Manning. How would he have ever come in contact with Mancuso? Well, maybe he arrested her for something. And then one thing led to another and—well, I know you don't want to hear this—they had some kind of romantic relationship. That seems to be par for the course with Mancuso. She slept around a lot. Why not with Manning, the cop?

"Then there's Brendan Kaiser, your boss. Same scenario here. Kaiser had a whole lot of business interests which could have put him in contact with Revson. Maybe he was sleeping with her too. I understand he's got a wife and kids and big house. But maybe he's tempted by Mancuso and he winds up in bed with her.

"And, last but not least, Lehrman. Why does she not even want to talk to you about Mancuso? Like I said, she's a strange lady. Very high profile in her public persona, but totally secret about her personal life."

"You think the motive for Mancuso's murder will turn out to be about something personal?"

Janet shrugged. "Who knows? I mean, it's hard to dismiss the timing of the Revson scandal. Mancuso gets murdered when she's right in the middle of all that—cheating people and sending others to jail by ratting them out for the same things she'd been doing. That's a pretty good motive too. Any indication any of these people on the list ever had anything to do with her at Revson or with the scandal?"

"Duh, I never thought of that," I said sarcastically. "Of course, I went through them all. Checked and re-checked, looking for any possible connection to any of the names from the list. But there was nothing."

"Maybe her murder was about love then. Or what about maybe some combination of love and money? Someone she stole money from and also had some kind of sexual relationship with. It could have been the people on that list. And someone—God knows who or why—left that note behind as a clue for everyone to follow."

"But what about Dora Gayle?" I pointed out. "She had no money and she sure as hell didn't have a romantic relationship with Mancuso."

"Dora Gayle doesn't seem to fit into either category," Janet admitted.

"And even Atwood, who had a romantic relationship of some kind with Mancuso, didn't have anything to do with her company's finances. The only money connection between him and Mancuso seems to be her demands for blackmail. Damn, every angle I try leads nowhere."

Janet sighed. "I don't understand why you're even still working on this. Everyone else—the police, the rest of the media, the public—have pretty much forgotten about it and moved on. Even your own boss probably doesn't care anymore. But you won't let go. You're like a dog with a bone that won't give it up no matter what. No matter how many times everyone tries to get you to change your mind. My God, Clare, you are the most stubborn person in the world. Do you disagree with that?"

"I prefer determined."

Janet stared at me.

"Dedicated journalist?"

More staring.

"Okay, I am stubborn," I said.

Janet said she had to get back to her office. I needed to get back to mine too in time for the afternoon news conference. But I still wanted an answer from her.

"Will you see if you can find out anything more for me about Emily Lehrman, Janet?" I asked as we walked toward the subway.

"No."

"Why not?"

"I don't have time to do your work for you."

"Okay, I understand."

"Good."

"Just get back to me as soon as you can with whatever you find out."

CHAPTER 37

I DECIDED TO confront Manning before I tried Brendan Kaiser. The way I figured it, if things went badly—and the people from the list got mad at me for asking them all these questions—it would be a lot easier for me to find a new potential love interest than a new job. As you can see, I had this all pretty well thought out.

My plan also called for me to be totally professional about it with Manning. Which meant I didn't want to call him at home. No matter how this turned out, the last thing I wanted was an awkward conversation with his wife if she answered. Of course, calling him at home wasn't really an option anyway because he had never given me his home phone. Or his personal cell number. The only way I knew how to reach him was through the precinct where he worked.

Manning was sitting at a small desk in the corner of the squad room, away from the other detectives, when I walked in. He seemed to be working at something. But, when I got closer, I saw that he was just filling in blanks on a crossword puzzle from the *Times* that morning.

"What are you doing here?" he asked when he saw me. Not like he was upset about it, just surprised.

"It's professional," I said.

"Well, if you're looking for a cop, better talk to one of the other guys in this squad room. I'm on the bench. Suspended. Removed from active duty. This is how I spend my time instead," he said, looking down at the crossword puzzle on his desk. "Sometimes, just to switch things up a bit, I do the Jumble Words in the *Daily News* too."

"I was hoping your suspension might be ended by now."

"Oh, it's worse. Before, I was on what they called limited duty. But then the political pressure began building in the department with all sorts of groups up in arms about police brutality and profiling of minorities and all the damn rest of it. So they needed to make an example of somebody. That's me. I'm completely deskbound now. I still get paid, but they won't let me do anything at all."

I felt badly about that. My instincts told me Manning was a good cop at heart, despite whatever he might have or might not have done to back up his dead partner. But that wasn't why I was here.

"I want to ask you some more questions about Grace Mancuso," I said.

"Go ask the detectives in homicide who are actually working on that case."

"I did. They don't have any new leads. And I don't think they're looking very hard for any either after all this time."

Manning shrugged. "That's the way it is with murder cases. Especially big, high-profile ones. They never go off the books. But, after a while, they slip down the ladder in priority to the more recent cases. There's a lot of murders in this town."

"It's still a priority for me. I'm trying to do another big story about it for the station. I'm looking for answers."

"Why come to me?"

"Your name was found on that list next to Grace Mancuso's body."

"Like I told you before, I have no idea why. No one ever figured out a reason for that list either."

"That's why I'm trying to find out now."

I told Manning I wanted him to go through everything about himself for me again. His career on the force. His personal life. And anything else he could think of to tell me. I said there had to be a clue in that somehow, which connected him and the others on the list to the murder case. I said I was going to keep digging until I found out what that was.

I did not tell him that I hoped he'd eventually leave his wife again; or that I wished now I'd taken him up on his offer to come back to my apartment for sex that first night; or that I was fantasizing right now about jumping his bones. Like I said, I was totally professional this time.

He talked about it all again. His past and his present career on the force. His troubled marriage. His estrangement from his son, which he felt was in large part because of his police work. Coming to New York as a young man with the dream of being a rock star, then abandoning that for a job on the NYPD once he got married. Even repeating the story about the "hey, ho, let's go" expression he always said to himself whenever he went into any tense or dangerous situation, which had come from his old band mate while they were watching the Mets win the World Series a long time ago. None of it meant anything to him or to me in terms of what was happening now.

"What are you going to do next?" he asked when we were finished.

"Go back and do this with the other people on the list. My boss, Brendan Kaiser. And Emily Lehrman, if she'll even talk to me again. Someone has to have some sort of connection with the Mancuso death. That's the only thing that makes sense for what's happening here."

Manning nodded. Then he hit me with a question that floored me.

"Need some help?"

"With what?"

"Your story. I'm a pretty good investigator, you know. I've solved a few murder cases in my time. But I don't get to solve many murders or any other kinds of crimes these days. To tell you the truth, this thing has been bothering me ever since it started, the same as you. I don't like the idea of my name being dragged into this by someone. I want to know who did it and why. Maybe I could work with you."

"What would the NYPD think about that?"

"Well, they just want me out of their sight right now. They don't even care if I show up for work here or not. But I do anyway. Out of habit, I guess. Old habits die hard. At least this way I'd be doing something useful with my time. And who knows, we might even find out some useful information. What do you say?"

I hesitated before answering.

"You could turn out to be a suspect in the Grace Mancuso murder," I finally pointed out.

"Do you really think I had anything to do with that?"

"No, I don't."

He smiled.

"It would have to be on a totally professional basis," I said

"I wouldn't have it any other way."

"And you'd be willing to spend your time investigating this case with me?"

"What else do I have to do?" he said, looking down at the cross-word puzzle in front of him. "I'm looking for answers to this case. Just like you. I'm a helluva homicide detective, Carlson. And, from everything I've seen and heard, you're a helluva journalist. Together I'd say we could make a pretty good team on this. What do you say?"

A pretty good team.

Me and Manning.

I liked the sound of that.

"Hey, ho, let's go," I told him.

CHAPTER 38

"WHY ARE YOU doing this story again?" Brendan Kaiser wanted to know.

"Look, Mr. Kaiser, you asked me when this started to cover the story personally. That you wanted me to put my journalistic reputation as a top reporter—my Pulitzer Prize–winning background—on the line to come up with the answers to why your name was on that list found next to Grace Mancuso's body. And the answers to who killed her and why. I didn't do that. I made some mistakes, but so did everyone else along the way. Now no one seems to want to talk about the Grace Mancuso story anymore. I do. I'm not giving up. I still want to know why your name—and those others too—were dragged into this. Don't you?"

It was a nice little speech, and I'd spent a good deal of time rehearsing it before I'd come to see Kaiser again. Not that I probably needed to rehearse it. Playing the dedicated journalist searching for truth was a role that came easy for me because I really believed in it. I just wasn't sure how dedicated Kaiser was to finding out the truth anymore.

I had another little follow-up speech ready to go about how if I had to quit Channel 10 to pursue this story elsewhere, I was prepared to do that. Except I wasn't sure I wanted to go down that road. At least, not yet.

As it turned out, I didn't have to make the decision.

"Okay," Kaiser said when I was finished talking.

"Okay, what?"

"I'll help you in any way I can."

"Really?"

"Just tell me what you need from me."

"Wow!"

"You're surprised?"

"I just assumed that most media moguls wouldn't want to open up a Pandora's Box of a story like this again that drags them into a murder investigation—they'd want it to quietly go away."

"How many media moguls have you known in your life, Ms. Carlson?"

"Uh, you're the first."

"I guess you were misinformed." He smiled.

I told him the same things I'd said to Manning. That I wanted Kaiser to go through everything he could about the details of his past and his career in the hopes that something there might be a clue to his involvement with that list. I said there had to be a connection between the five names on the list, and the only way I knew to find it was to go through every bit of information about all five lives looking for the link between them all.

"Why are you so interested in me talking about my past?" Kaiser asked. "What could my past life have to do with any of this?"

"Because the only connection we have so far between any of the people on the list—Bill Atwood and Dora Gayle—happened a long time ago while they were both in college. Maybe there's something in your past too that could link you to other names on the list. Something that could help us make some sort of sense out of the meaning of the list. So just tell me everything about yourself."

"Everything?"

"I want to hear about the entire life of Brendan Kaiser."

"What exactly is it you're looking for?"

"I haven't the slightest idea."

I figured there were two ways this could go. Brendan Kaiser could fake it and talk superficially about his life without revealing too much. Or he could open up completely to me about every-thing—his entire life, his feelings, his emotions—all of it in a search for answers. I think he started out trying to do the first option but wound up doing the second.

He talked about growing up in New York City during the eighties just like a lot of other kids back then—smoking pot, watching MTV, and partying a lot. His brother, Charles, was the heir apparent to take over his father's business one day—but Brendan had no interest in that. He wanted to travel, he wanted to enjoy life, and—most of all, he said to me—"I didn't want to be like my father."

"I had absolutely no interest in growing up to be Charles Kaiser's heir," he recalled. "I just wanted to be Brendan Kaiser."

Charles Jr. was clearly the favorite son as the anointed successor to his father, while Brendan was an embarrassment to him.

"'What's wrong with you, Brendan?' my father would say to me," Kaiser told me now. "'Your brother graduated magna cum laude. Your brother is already working for me in the company. Your brother has goals and ideas and a plan for his life. Why can't you be more like Charles? He's got a plan for his life all figured out. You don't have the slightest idea.'"

But then one day his brother, Charles Jr., was gone, killed in a drowning accident near the family's summer house on Long Island.

"I was in Europe when it happened," Kaiser said. "Traveling around the world and really enjoying myself. But, of course, I had to go back home when my brother died so unexpectedly. My father was devastated. Not only over the loss of a son, but even more—I always believed—because he'd lost his heir for the business he cared about so much. Now someone else would have to take Charles' place. And I—with all my faults and weaknesses—was the only choice he had for the role. But I still didn't want that kind of a life for myself, still didn't want to wind up like my father. So I told him no, I wasn't going to work for him. I started partying hard instead in New York City—partly because it was fun and partly, I suppose, because I knew it pissed my old man off. But then he died suddenly of a heart attack. I was the only person left to take over the business for the family. I told myself that I'd just do it temporarily—until we could get someone else to put in charge—but I wound up staying in the job myself."

He then went through the years afterward—the explosive growth of the Kaiser empire as he acquired more and more properties; the dramatic expansion into TV, movies, books, the Internet, and all sorts of social media that went far beyond anything Kaiser's own father could have ever envisioned.

Now he was worth an incredibly obscene amount of money and was recognized as one of the most powerful media figures in the world—rivaling the Hearsts, the Murdochs, the Newhouses, and all the other names from the past.

"I never wanted to be my father." Brendan Kaiser smiled sadly. "And look at me now . . ."

CHAPTER 39

WHEN I GOT back to the newsroom, I told Jack Faron my plan for revisiting the Grace Mancuso story in a big way.

"We run interviews on air with Brendan Kaiser, Scott Manning, and hopefully even Emily Lehrman—if she'll ever talk to me. Otherwise, we tell the viewers all about her and her background. All the stuff about how she used to represent little people, but now all her clients are big money cases—many of them mobsters and drug lords. About her hermit-like personal life. Everything we can find out about Emily Lehrman. We take a new look at her and all the other names on that list to try to figure out the connection that got them there. Talk about their lives, their past—everything about them. We even dig more into the backgrounds of both dead people too—Bill Atwood and Dora Gayle—for possible answers."

I told him highlights I'd found out so far about all of them.

I told him the details about my confrontation with Emily Lehrman and my conversation with Manning.

I did not tell him that I had already discussed all this with Brendan Kaiser, which was kind of sneaky—I suppose—on my part.

"No way," Faron said when I was finished talking. "Bad, bad idea. No one wants to go back and hear about an old story—there's too many good stories that are better for us to do, ratings-wise. More importantly, you don't know what you're looking for or what you might find out about these people. Especially with Kaiser. For Christ's sakes, Clare, the idea of you looking into his past more on the air is filled with potential booby traps and big dangers for us. I'm not going to let you do it. I know you're stubborn, I know you're dogged about a story, and I know you like to argue whenever decisions of mine don't go your way. But there is simply no way I'm going to let you do this. You're my news editor. Act like a news editor. Go back out there and spend your time putting out the best newscast we can every night. Forget about the Grace Mancuso story unless there's an arrest or some other big development. Is that all clear? And nothing you can say will get me to change my mind about this."

"I've already discussed it with Kaiser and he thinks we should do it," I said.

Faron sighed.

"Okay, Jack," I said, "I know I shouldn't have gone over your head to Kaiser without talking to you first. And I know I should have told you he was on board with the idea before I asked you about it. But, if I'd done it that way, we never could have gotten to that great little speech you just gave me. About acting like a real news editor and all the rest. It was quite stirring. One of your best."

Sometimes I go too far with people. I wondered if I'd done that with Faron. He was one of my supporters at the station, but right now he was just staring at me with a blank expression on his face. I couldn't tell if he was mad at me or not. Actually, I was pretty sure he was mad at me. The question was how mad?

"Don't ever do that to me again," he said.

"I won't."

"I'm serious, Clare."

"Understood."

"Imagine how you'd feel if Maggie or one of your people who worked for you came to me for a decision instead of going through you. Your damn head would explode. That's the way I feel right now about what you did."

"I'm sorry, Jack. I really am."

He nodded. It seemed like the worst was over. Or at least I hoped it was.

"Have you thought about the possible negative consequences of what you're doing?" he asked.

"You mean the drop in ratings if we don't break something big and just rehash a lot of old news to the viewers?"

"Worse than low ratings."

"What's worse than low ratings?"

"Losing all of our jobs. Have you considered the possibility that there might be a reason Brendan Kaiser's name was on that list? And if we reveal that reason—no matter all the highfalutin things you say about journalistic integrity or whatever—it could turn into a nightmare for us. Think about it, Clare: What do you do if you find out something really bad about Brendan Kaiser?"

"I don't know," I said.

"But you're still willing to jeopardize your career as a TV executive here to find out?"

"I'm a journalist at heart, Jack—not a TV executive. I have to find out the truth."

Just before I left his office, Faron asked me one more question.

"If Kaiser hadn't agreed to do this—if he'd said no, just the way I did at first—you would have just kept working on this story anyway, wouldn't you?"

"Have we met?" I asked.

* * *

I talked to Maggie next, taking her through what was going on and all the new information I'd found out.

I also told her Manning would be working with us now on the story.

"The cop on the list?" she asked.

"That's right."

"The one you went out with?"

"Not really relevant here, but yes."

"What exactly is he going to do?"

"Help us investigate."

"I already have our own investigative people working hard on this."

"Now you have one more."

"You just went ahead and did this without talking to me first?"

"I didn't think you'd mind, Maggie."

"You could have asked me and found out."

"Sorry."

"Are you still seeing this guy?"

"No."

"You have no personal feelings about him whatsoever?"

"He's married, Maggie."

"That's not answering my question."

"Maggie, just try to do the best you can with him on our team."

"Whatever you say," she snapped and stalked out of my office.

Jeez, now she was mad at me too—just like Faron.

My two favorite people in the office.

I was just making friends all over the place today.

* * *

The idea was to tape the interviews with Kaiser and Manning over the next day or so. At the same time, we'd begin digging deeper into the backgrounds of Atwood and Dora Gayle for more stuff to put on the air about the two dead names on that list. And try to pinpoint how their long-ago romance might have played a role in including them in this murder story all these years later. That left Lehrman. I was trying to decide on the best way to approach her again when my phone rang. It was Janet.

"What the hell did you say to Lehrman anyway, Clare?"

"What do you mean?"

"No one's seen her around the courthouse since then. Same with her apartment, no sign of her there either. I just found out why. She's in Connecticut. Admitted to Silver Oaks."

"What's that?"

"It's a drug rehab. Apparently, Emily Lehrman almost died from an overdose."

CHAPTER 40

I FOUND LEHRMAN sitting in a sunroom for patients on the second floor, looking out a window at the beautiful view of the lush Connecticut landscape. Flowers, trees, grass, and even a small stream running through the back. Of course, she didn't have to let me in, didn't even have to confirm for me that she was there. All the patient records were confidential. But she had told the people at the front desk to send me up once she found out I was there.

"Why did you agree to see me?" I asked her now.

"I don't have that many friends that come here to visit me."

"I'm a reporter, I'm not exactly a friend of yours."

"But you're here. No one else is. I guess you're the closest thing to a friend I've got at the moment."

She looked tired. The ice-cold professional exterior was gone now, replaced by something more real, more open, and more humane.

"What happened?" I asked her.

"I took too many drugs."

"Intentionally?"

She shook her head.

"No, I didn't try to kill myself, if that's what you're asking."

"Then why?"

"All that stuff you asked me about my life and career choices . . . I told you I didn't have to answer any of your questions about it, and I didn't. But I do have to answer to myself. And so, after that day you confronted me in the courthouse, I began thinking about what I had become. I guess I didn't like those answers."

"Drugs aren't the answer either."

"Oh, they have been for me in the past. They've helped me get through a lot of personal crises like this. But not this time. This time I just took too many or the wrong kind or something. And that's how I wound up here."

I stayed there for a long time with Emily Lehrman that day, comforting her and talking with her about the near-death experience she'd gone through. At some point, I told her about my interviews with Kaiser and Manning that I was going to put on the air, and I asked if she'd do the same kind of interview. I told her I needed to hear everything about her past and her entire life, just like what I'd done with the others from the list. And I said that included talking about the sudden career shift years earlier that changed her from a dedicated attorney fighting for the poor and defenseless, to a high-powered mouthpiece for drug lords and mob bosses. Of course, she asked me how any of this about her past could possibly have anything to do with the Grace Mancuso murder or why she was on that list in Mancuso's apartment. I told her the same thing I'd told the others. I didn't know either, but the Dora Gayle/Bill Atwood connection had been more than thirty years ago—so maybe that was true for her and the rest of them too. I said I just wanted to accumulate all the information I could and see where it led me.

To my surprise, she agreed to do the interview.

Whatever had happened, her brush with death from the overdose had turned her into a different person.

A real person.

I was finally talking to the real Emily Lehrman.

And finding out a whole lot about her and the person she used to be.

"When I was younger, I was a romantic at heart," she told me at one point when I asked her about those long-ago days. "I believed in love. And I thought I found my love. His name was Terry Antum. God, Terry was drop-dead gorgeous. He had long blond hair that he pulled into a ponytail in the back, big blue eyes. He was a dropout from Columbia University where he'd helped lead a strike against military recruiters on campus that had shut down the school. After that, he'd gone on to organize protests at another college over demolishing low-income housing to make room for more university construction. I was representing the threatened tenants, and that's when I met—and fell in love with—Terry.

"We lived together in a loft downtown. We never got married. We told each other we didn't need a marriage license or a ring to verify our love. That our love was stronger than any marriage vows. What we shared was a bond that was so deep and so full of integrity and significance that nothing could ever tear us apart. It was all so glorious and fulfilling and exciting."

"Sounds perfect," I said.

"Yeah, doesn't it? It was also all bullshit."

She shook her head sadly.

"I should have known from the arguments we began having. Mostly, they were about money. For Terry, money was a necessary part of the social activist movement. He would organize protests or actions just to raise money to support their causes. It seemed to me at some point that money had become more important to him than even the social causes we were working for. Terry was always talking about money, plotting ways to get it and spending freely whatever he obtained. For me, this presented a moral dilemma. If the money took precedence over the social causes we were trying to improve, were we still idealists or were we becoming part of the problem?"

The answer to that when it came, she told me, was very clear. Lehrman said she turned on the television one day to see a news report about a bank robbery in New Canaan, Connecticut. A group of robbers, dressed in ski masks and carrying automatic weapons, had burst into the bank, stolen several hundred thousand dollars, and fled in a panel truck. A guard tried to stop them. One of the robbers shot him dead. There was another shootout on the Connecticut Turnpike a short time later, and police killed three of them.

A few hours later, Terry stumbled in—dazed, disoriented, and panicky. He said the police were after him, and he needed to get out of the country right away. He said the bank robbery was supposed to be a political statement for social justice, but it all went wrong. They hadn't even gotten the money. It was lost in the shootout. Now he had to get away or he'd go to jail for the rest of his life.

"He told me he needed money to run. I went to the bank and drew out everything I had. My savings, money we'd collected for political causes. I gave it all to Terry. He promised he'd call me later when he got settled somewhere else, and we'd meet up again. I kissed him goodbye at the door. The next day I found out there'd been a wild police chase in Massachusetts. State troopers had tried to pull over a car, then followed it at ninety miles per hour until the driver lost control. It crashed through a guardrail, rolled down a cliff alongside the road, and burst into flames below. When the cops got there, they discovered the charred bodies of two people in the car. One of them was later identified as Terry Antum.

"I wasn't sure how I felt about Terry in the months afterward. I mourned his death, of course. But I couldn't come to grips with some of the things he had done, such as taking part in the bank robbery where that guard died. Whatever his motivation, that was murder—pure and simple. So what did that say about me? If I was wrong about Terry, how could I be sure I was right about anything else I once believed in so fervently? I tried throwing myself into my work, but it wasn't the same. I was no longer sure I was on high moral ground, and I didn't know how to deal with that.

"Then, a few years later, I went to Montreal for a conference on affordable housing for the poor. While I was walking through the lobby of the hotel, I saw him. Terry Antum. My Terry. He had dark hair now, the ponytail was gone, and he had a beard. But the eyes were the same. I'd recognize him anywhere, even if he was supposed to be dead. I followed him to a mansion on the outskirts of town. I found out it belonged to a man named Lawrence Redmon who had come to Montreal a few years earlier, saying he was retired after making a lot of money in the computer industry. But that was a lie, of course. Lawrence Redmon was really Terry Antum. And the money had come from that bank heist. Somehow, he'd faked his own death and gotten away with all the loot. With my life savings, too, as an added bonus. I never knew exactly how he did it. The only way to find out would have been to talk to him. And I couldn't do that. Couldn't face the reality of what had happened. I just went back to New York, told no one what I'd found out, and tried to get on with my life."

She walked over to the window in the room and looked down at the trees and flowers in the beautiful green landscape below.

"Terry took something more valuable than money from me. I'd lost my idealism. I'd lost my moral bearings. I'd lost my trust in people's inherent good. Anyway, that's when I decided to start representing different kinds of clients. People who wouldn't disappoint me. I had no false illusions about them, nothing to lose in an emotional sense. Does that make sense to you?"

"Was it that he broke your heart or that he stole the money that bothered you the most?"

"It was the betrayal," she said. "The overall betrayal of my trust. I didn't think I could ever trust anyone again. From then on, I devoted myself completely to my career, no matter what it took or who I had to work for or what I had to do. I made the money my priority. Life was so much simpler for me that way. Or so I thought until this happened."

I felt sorry for Emily Lehrman. I really did. And I felt badly that my conversation with her had played such a role in pushing her to this point. I wanted to say something to make up for doing that. I wanted to say something to make her feel better.

But there was one big question I still had to ask her.

"Did you know Grace Mancuso at all or do you know any reason why your name is on that list?"

Lehrman shook her head no. "I never heard of her until then. That's the truth. You have to believe me about that."

"I believe you," I said.

CHAPTER 41

WHEN I'M WORKING on a big story like this, a lot of other stuff in my life seems to fall into place too. My personal and professional lives have always been intertwined that way. A big story always makes everything better for me.

So, even as I continued to pursue the Mancuso story, I decided to keep pushing on the other big issue in my life that I simply couldn't drop: the search for information about my daughter, Lucy.

Which was how I found myself walking into an Internet cafe on the Upper West Side to look for someone.

I spotted him sitting in the back, drinking coffee and staring at the screen of a laptop in front of him—his fingers pressing keys rapidly as he worked on something.

"Hello, Todd," I said, slipping into the seat next to him.

Todd Schacter looked up, startled.

"What are you doing here?"

"I want to talk to you again."

"How—how did you find me?"

"That computer of yours leaves fingerprints, Todd. Just like you told me. All I had to do was download your IPO, access your Internet provider for all your personal and security information, then it was easy to open up a LocateMe app in your name to search for myself—which really was you, of course—and obtain your exact location in the Cloud."

"That's all gibberish," Schacter said. "What you said doesn't make any sense."

"Yeah, I know."

"Then how did you find me?"

"I got your address from Janet, staked out your building, and then followed you here. Old-school methods."

"Why didn't you just knock on my door?"

"I thought it would be better to confront you in a public place, and besides . . ."

"You wanted to surprise me in a coffee shop the same way I surprised you. Payback, huh?"

"I thought it was a nice touch," I admitted

He closed the laptop computer in front of him so I couldn't see what he was working on. That was okay with me. I didn't really care. I was only interested in one thing with this man.

"Now that you've found me, what do you want?" Schacter asked.

"Same thing as last time we talked."

"I told you then that I'm not breaking into a U.S. Senator's computer records. Too risky if I get caught. There's nothing you can say or do that will get me to change my mind. I don't want to take a chance on going to jail. And hacking into a federal government file like that—especially one belonging to a Senator—would very easily put me behind bars."

"I have another idea."

"Does it still involve Grayson?"

"No, this has nothing to do with him or his files."

I'd come up with the idea in the midst of chasing all the Grace Mancuso stuff. I'd been assuming all along that the only way to find out information about Lucy was from Grayson's files. But there was another possible way.

I took out a printout and handed it to Schacter. It was the original email someone had sent Anne Devlin—Lucy Devlin's adoptive mother—last year claiming to have seen Lucy at the motorcycle conference in New Hampshire with Grayson. It had been signed "Concerned Citizen" and sent from a Hotmail account.

"Could you track down who sent this email?" I asked him now.

I didn't tell him why. I didn't tell him that I still held out the long shot hope that maybe Lucy herself had sent this original email. That she had somehow reached out from the past to alert us she was still alive. I didn't tell Schacter that—if all this were true—he could lead me directly to Lucy this way.

"It would be very difficult," he said. "Not much information here."

"I know."

"Most people couldn't do this."

"That's why I came to the best."

"And no government files are involved at all?"

"Right."

He nodded. I was getting to him. I figured it was the appeal to his ego. Telling people they're the best at what they do tends to make them like you and be on your side.

"How much would it cost?" I asked.

"I don't care about money."

"Everyone cares about money."

"I know you might find this hard to believe, but I do what I do for the challenge of it. I love a good challenge. I've never hacked into any computer file to steal money or people's identity or any of the other stuff you always hear about. I do it just to prove I can do it."

"So will you do this for me?"

He looked down at the printout I'd given him. The email from CONCERNED CITIZEN that might have—just possibly—come from Lucy herself and could lead me back to her after all this time.

"Why not?" Schacter shrugged. "Like I said, I love a good challenge."

CHAPTER 42

"It's the news at 6 with the Channel 10 News Team: Brett Wolff and Dani Blaine at the anchor desk, Steve Stratton with Sports, and Wendy Jeffers with your up-to-date weather forecast. If you want to know what's happening—you want it fast and you want it accurate—Channel 10 has got you covered!"

"And now here's Brett and Dani":

BRETT: Good evening. The city's schoolteachers are talking strike again, there's been a tragic hit-and-run accident in the Bronx, the Yankees open a big four-game series with the Red Sox tonight, and there's some nasty weather headed our way.

DANI: But first, we open with an exclusive look at one of the city's most baffling murder cases in recent years, the death of Wall Street executive Grace Mancuso—who was found beaten to death in her Upper East Side apartment earlier this month. Our own news director—Pulitzer Prize-winning journalist Clare Carlson—has the story.

ME: Who brutally murdered Grace Mancuso? Who left behind a note with five names on it next to her body? What do those five people named on the list—ranging from prominent people in New York to a homeless woman—have to do with the crime or the reason for it or any other possible link? Those are the questions that have baffled police—and all New Yorkers—since the Mancuso murder happened. We don't have all the answers, but Channel 10 has uncovered new details, which we will now share with you in this in-depth report . . .

*　*　*

I'd gotten all three of them—Kaiser, Manning, and Lehrman—to sit down for on-air interviews. I tried to milk it for the most dramatic impact, saying it was the first in-depth interviews with the people whose names were on the Grace Mancuso list. And I said it seemed clear that these three people—as well as Bill Atwood and Dora Gayle—must have some connection to what happened, no matter how improbable that seemed. I talked about the Revson scandal too and how the angry investors and Revson employees had been victimized in different ways by Mancuso during the scandal.

I'd heavily promoted the whole thing during our daytime program, and I ran pictures of a sexy Grace Mancuso during the report too—so I figured the whole thing would get us some pretty good ratings.

Of course, the truth was it wasn't really news at all. It was just an accumulation of facts and interviews wrapped up in a pretty nice on-air package. I hadn't uncovered anything that substantially changed—or helped break open—the Grace Mancuso murder case or any of the rest of it. But it was all I had, so I went with it.

The actual on-air interviews with Kaiser, Lehrman, and Manning had been taped without me by Maggie and the other reporters, after I set it all up. Me, I still had to do my other news editor job. And the production team had to do a rush job on those interviews to get them ready for the newscast. So I didn't know exactly what everyone had to say when I actually went on the air.

I watched it all now during the broadcast, just like our viewers were doing. It was pretty interesting stuff, I decided. Even if we weren't breaking any new ground on the crime itself, the back stories of everyone on the list—told in their own interviews, at least for the surviving ones—gave the story real depth and drama.

Brendan Kaiser was the last of the three. It was kinda amazing to see this mega-rich mogul—mostly known in the past for his ruthless business dealings and acquisitions—coming across in the interview as a real person. Just like that day in his office with me, he talked about growing up in New York City during the turbulent 1980s. About all the fun and good times he had as a young man back then. About his brother, Charles, dying in the drowning accident. And the death of his father from a heart attack afterward. Then how he took over his father's business and turned it into the media empire it was today.

But, most passionately of all, Kaiser talked about those long-ago memories of a carefree life when he was a young man in New York—before all the events that irrevocably changed his life.

"I still remember some of those summer nights. Hanging out in Washington Square Park. On Bleecker Street. Down in the East Village. There were so many great things to do, so much great music, so many great people to meet. I could lose myself in that world for a few hours—who I was and what my father wanted me to be. I could just be me. That was a long time ago, but I look back now and miss those days sometimes.

"The East Village was my favorite place. So many memories. Like the night the Mets came back from the dead with a miracle rally in the 10th inning to beat the Red Sox in Game 6 of the World Series. What a great night to be a New Yorker! A lot of people here still remember where they were when that 10th inning was happening, and I sure do too. I was in a place called the Domino Club on St. Mark's Place and they had the game on TV behind the bar. Well, when that Mets comeback happened, everyone in the place gathered around the screen to watch. And when Bill Buckner booted that ground ball from Mookie Wilson—and Ray Knight came home with the winning run—the place just exploded. I'll never forget that . . ."

My God! I thought to myself.

I sat there staring at the image of Brendan Kaiser on the studio monitor in front of me—and playing over and over in my head what he'd just said.

A journalist doesn't always know what he or she is going to find by digging deep into a story. Sometimes the answers are evident, but other times you're never quite sure what you're looking for until you find it. That's what had happened here. I'd just begun digging in the hopes I might find out something.

Something that made sense of all this.

Game 6 of the 1986 World Series was it.

It was the one thing that linked two of the people on that list—Kaiser and Manning.

They'd both watched that historic game at a club in the East Village that night.

And, I was willing to bet, the rest of them did too.

This had to be the connection.

CHAPTER 43

I CALLED EMILY Lehrman at Silver Oaks, where she was still a patient.

"Do you remember what you were doing during Game 6 of the 1986 World Series?" I asked her. "Mets vs. Red Sox. The moment when Bill Buckner booted the ground ball from Mookie Wilson that let the Mets come back for a miracle victory and go on to win the World Series?"

"Why would you ask me something like that?"

"Do you know what you were doing that night, Ms. Lehrman?" I repeated.

I didn't want to tell her any more yet; I wanted her to tell me.

"As a matter of fact, I do remember. It was a very memorable night. Terry—the guy I told you about—and I had gone out to some clubs in the East Village that night. The last one we stopped at had the game on TV. We watched the ending along with all the people there. There was a band playing and people were cheering and hugging each other. I remember someone taking a picture of a bunch of us at one point celebrating with people we didn't even know. It was very exciting."

"Was it at the Domino Club?"

"I don't remember after all these years."

"Okay, do you know if it might have been on St. Mark's Place?"

"Yes, it was. That's a very unique street in the Village, and I'd never been there before that night. And, now that I think about it, the Domino Club sounds right. That definitely could have been it. But what is this all about?"

I told her as much as I knew, then I called Scott Manning at the precinct and went through it all with him. He'd seen Kaiser on the newscast and already come to the same conclusion as I had.

"All three of you were in that same club in the East Village that night," I said, as he confirmed it had been the Domino Club with him too. "We can't know for sure about Bill Atwood and Dora Gayle because they're dead, but I'm willing to bet they both were there too. That's the connection between everyone on that list."

"One night from more than thirty years ago? But why?"

"Something significant must have happened there that night."

"Like what?"

"That's what I'm asking you. You were there."

"I have no idea what it could be."

"We have to find out. Let's assume all five of you were at the same place in 1986. Now those same five people turn up on a list found in Grace Mancuso's apartment. We don't know how or why, but the seeds of Grace Mancuso's death must have been planted a long time ago. Down on St. Mark's Place back on that night more than thirty years ago. That means what I need to do now is . . ."

"I'll meet you down there," Manning said.

"Huh?"

"You're going to St. Mark's Place to look for answers, right?"

"Yes."

"I can help. I want to work with you on it. And I know a lot about investigating and asking questions. Just like you do. Plus,

I still have my detective's shield. That might help open some doors too."

*   *   *

St. Mark's Place was one part of the city that hadn't changed that much over the years. It somehow remained frozen in time, at least to outward appearances. Much of it bore remnants of its heyday in the late sixties, where it became a gathering place for hippies and all the rest. Today, the block that stretches between Second and Third Avenues was still littered with tattoo parlors, T-shirt shops, and even a few old record stores. The kids who hung out there didn't seem all that much different than they did in the past either. Their hair was shorter and their clothes different, but they were still rebels of their own generation.

The building that used to house the Domino Club—the place where they had all been that night—was a big white three-story structure, about midway down the block. It wasn't the Domino Club now. That had closed years ago.

"Yes, this is the place," Manning said as we stood in front of it.

"Wonder what happened to it since 1986?"

The building was empty except for paint cans, lumber, and construction equipment lying around. We found out from people in the neighborhood that it was a restaurant for a long time after the club closed, then a community recreation center and later a welfare center headquarters. Now it was about to be renovated into apartments.

"I remember the club," one store owner who'd been on the block back then told us. "It was very noisy. Lot of music and drinking, some drugs too. Of course, that wasn't unusual for St. Mark's Place. I think the club shut down sometime in the early nineties."

"Do you remember who the owner was?" I asked, looking for any kind of a lead to someone else who might have been there that night in 1986.

"Sure, Bob Geraci. I knew him pretty well. Nice guy. We kept in touch for a while after he left the city."

I looked at Manning, and he looked back at me. Bob Geraci. All we had to do was find him. He could be the key to all this; he could have some answers. Or so we thought.

"Do you still know how to reach Geraci?"

"Oh, he's dead."

Damn!

"He died about ten years ago. No, maybe more like fifteen. He had lung cancer. Never smoked a day in his life either. Isn't that ironic? Bob never smoked, he ate health food, he worked out—and he's dead and buried."

"Did he have any family?" Manning asked

"Well, his wife is still alive, I believe."

"Any idea how we can find her?"

"They moved to a retirement community somewhere in North Carolina. As far as I know, she's still there. I'll see if I can find the number for you."

The number still worked, and a short time later I was standing in front of the old club site with Manning and talking to Mrs. Geraci on my cell phone.

"An apartment house now, you say?" she said when I told her what happened to the building. "My, my, I wish we hadn't sold it. It probably would be worth a lot more money now. But that was a long time ago."

She talked for a while about the old days, but none of it was really relevant to what we were looking for. She didn't remember anything about that night back in 1986 when the Mets won the classic game or the five names from the list or anything else that might help. This was turning into another dead end. Then I remembered something. Emily Lehrman said someone was taking pictures there that night. Sure, it was a long shot after all these years, but it was worth asking. A picture—if it somehow still existed—might be a key to all this.

"Do you remember anyone who took pictures at your husband's club back then?"

"Marcus Dupree," she said immediately. "It must have been Marcus. He was the one always taking pictures there. He was kind of strange, but nice. He photographed everything that happened in the club. Night after night, he was there. He had quite a portfolio of pictures back then. The bands. The people who showed up. The whole East Village scene in the eighties. That was such a wonderful time for Bob and me and the rest of us too."

I let her go on for a while. She was just an old lady, probably lonely and happy to have anyone to talk to.

"Do you have any idea what happened to Marcus Dupree after the Domino Club closed?"

"Of course. Marcus ran a camera store."

"Where?"

"On St. Mark's Place. Just across the street from the old club."

Standing there now talking to her on my cell phone, I looked around. Sure enough, across the street—right behind where Scott Manning was standing—there was a sign that said: "Dupree Photography."

"Everyone always told Marcus he should move away from the neighborhood," Mrs. Geraci was saying. "That it wasn't the same as it used to be. But he said that was where he belonged. He loved St. Mark's Place. He said to me it was a special place."

Jeez, Dupree might be the key to this whole case. He could have the answers. All I had to do was get off the phone from this woman.

"Thank you very much, Mrs. Geraci. You've been a big, big help . . ."

"It's a shame about poor Marcus. The way he went so young."

"He's dead?"

"Yes, he passed away a few years before my husband. We even went back to New York for the funeral."

CHAPTER 44

AFTER I HUNG up, I told Manning what Mrs. Geraci had said. Then we walked across the street to the photo store. So why was the name of Dupree on the sign even though Dupree was long dead? It looked old and battered. Maybe the new owners thought it was too expensive to replace. Or people in the neighborhood knew the name so well it didn't make sense to change it.

Manning pushed open the door and we went inside. There were pictures all over the walls, many of them years old. They showed New York City over several decades. There was a picture of the building of the World Trade Center in the early seventies. Then scenes from the big New York City blackout a few years later. But most of the pictures were from the eighties where it appeared Dupree had become the most consumed with chronicling the events of the city, especially in the East Village where he lived and worked.

A man from the store saw us looking at the photos and came over.

"Are these for sale?" I asked.

"Everything in the store is for sale," he said. "These, plus many others we don't have room to show out here."

"Did you take these?" Manning asked, pointing to some eighties shots of places in the East Village then.

"No, my father did. He was quite obsessed about keeping a visual record of the New York City he knew and loved." He gestured toward all the pictures displayed around the store. "This is a result of that obsession."

"Was your father Marcus Dupree?" I asked

"That's right. I'm his son, Jonathan. Did you two know my father?"

"He and I might have met once," Manning said. "That's what we're trying to find out. It would have been a long time ago."

"Where?"

"The Domino Club."

Manning looked over at the pictures from the eighties in the East Village years ago.

"You told us there were more pictures besides these," Manning said to Dupree. "More from this era here—the eighties? In the East Village?"

"Sure, lots of them. My father kept everything he did. He was fanatical about it. I've never had the strength to throw any of them away either. They seemed to mean so much to him. Besides, you never know when they might be worth something. Do you want to buy one?"

"Where are the rest of the pictures?" I asked. "In the back of the store?"

"No, there's not enough room. My father had a loft on Allen Street. We used to live there, and he eventually turned it into a storeroom for his work. Everything's there."

We told him what we were looking for. Pictures from the Domino Club on the night of October 25, 1986. The night of

Game 6 of the World Series when the Mets came back to beat the Red Sox and go on to later win the Series. We said we wanted to go through all of his father's files looking for it.

"I don't have time to do something like that," Dupree told us, realizing now we probably weren't regular customers who were actually going to buy anything from his store.

"I'm afraid we must insist," Manning said.

"Look, if you want to buy something, go ahead and do it. Otherwise, you'll have to leave."

"We're not leaving until we see all those pictures," Manning said.

"I'm going to have to call the police then."

"Don't bother."

Manning took out his NYPD detective's shield and showed it to Dupree.

"Now take us to the rest of the pictures."

Working with a cop—even one like Manning who probably didn't even have the right to be flashing his NYPD credentials to anyone at the moment—sure made things a lot easier.

Dupree kept protesting about how long a search was going to take him until we got to the storage place on Allen Street, but Manning ignored him. Dupree was right about one thing though. There was a huge amount of pictures stored there inside the Allen Street location. There were boxes and boxes of stuff piled up all over. Some had specific dates on them. Others seemed alphabetized by names or locations—or sometimes both. But a lot of it didn't seem organized in any way at all.

"My father had a very . . . well, unusual filing system," Dupree said. "I've come to understand some of it over the years, but it's still difficult. What's the date you're looking for again?"

"October 25, 1986."

Dupree shook his head. "I hope you're getting paid overtime, Lieutenant. We could be here for a while."

He climbed up a ladder and began taking stuff off the shelves. There were thousands of pictures in all sorts of different boxes. Manning and I split them up, each of us going through every picture to eliminate it from consideration.

It took an hour and a half. We finally found what we were looking for. A folder labeled: "Domino Club." We opened it and pictures came tumbling out.

There were lots of shots that showed people dancing and drinking and having fun at the club. The pictures all had dates stamped on them. We found several from the night of October 25, 1986. Manning and I looked through them excitedly. One of them was a picture of Manning's band playing that night, which showed him onstage. Another picture was of the scene around a big television set with the crowds gathered to watch the end of the classic World Series game that night.

Then I found another picture of Manning. A young Scott Manning standing with his arm around a girl at the bar, apparently during a break in the band's performance and maybe after the music had ended. She had shortly cut cropped hair—almost a crew cut—and was dressed in leather and adorned with tattoos on all arms and other visible body parts.

"Wow, that's me and Jennifer!" he yelled out when he saw the photo.

"Not your wife, I guess."

"Nah, that was before I married Susan. Jennifer—Jennifer Hartley was her name—she was just a punk rocker groupie that hung out at a lot of our band gigs. I guess she was there that night too. I honestly don't remember that picture being taken. But I'd probably had a lot to drink by then."

He did look a bit wasted in the photo. But what really mattered is that we now knew that Dupree had taken pictures there that night. Of course, this picture didn't tell us anything we didn't already know about any of the others from the list being there.

But, if Manning had now showed up in two pictures from that night, maybe there were more.

We were almost through everything else in the file when we found it. Another picture of Manning. But the woman named Jennifer Hartley wasn't in this picture. It was Manning and four other people. On the back of the photo, someone had written an address: "207 Avenue C, Apt. 2G."

I stared at the five people in the picture. Bill Atwood. Emily Lehrman. Brendan Kaiser. Dora Gayle. Scott Manning.

They'd all been at the Domino Club that long-ago night.

Marcus Dupree had taken their pictures.

And now this was somebody's blueprint for murder.

CHAPTER 45

"WHAT DOES ANY of this have to do with the killing of Grace Mancuso?" Manning asked.

"I was hoping you might know."

He and I were sitting outside at a rooftop bar in Gramercy Park, with the lights of Manhattan below us. We had decided we needed a drink to help sort things out after the shock of seeing the picture in Dupree's file. Both of us were drinking beer—he had a Michelob and I had a bottle of Corona. The beer was ice cold, and it felt like the perfect thing to be drinking on a hot summer night like this.

The setting was perfect for a beautiful date.

Except this wasn't a date.

It was just a business meeting.

That's what I kept telling myself anyway, while my mind was racing to try to put together the pieces of what we'd found out into some logical scenario.

Manning looked down now at the photo of him and the four others that we'd brought with us.

"My God, I was so young then," he said. "Did I really look like that once?"

They all looked different. Manning, Emily Lehrman, Bill Atwood, Brendan Kaiser, and, of course, most of all, Dora Gayle.

Bill Atwood and Dora were obviously together. He had his arm around her in the picture, and she was looking at him adoringly. Dora looked so beautiful in the photo, and I still had trouble accepting the fact this was the same woman who'd become a sad, tragic homeless person on the streets of New York. "I'm Cinderella," she had told people. "I'm waiting for my prince to take me away so we can live happily ever after." She had found her prince, but he turned out not to be a prince at all. Atwood had run off to chase other women and build a great life for himself, leaving Dora behind reeling into a downward spiral that she never recovered from until she finally died. Damn. So much for believing in fairy tales.

Kaiser was just a kid, all decked out in trendy, hip-at-the-time clothes and sporting an eighties-style haircut. Emily Lehrman looked pretty and was dressed very sexily; completely different than the conservative business suits she wore to court. She had on a denim miniskirt, a T-shirt that said "Impeach Reagan," and what looked like go-go boots. Manning was a good-looking kid in the picture too, and he had changed the least—despite his amazement at the way he looked back then. As far as I was concerned, he still looked really good. But then I was a bit prejudiced because I was eager to jump his bones.

"Somehow this picture got to whoever killed Grace Mancuso and wrote that note," I said. "Marcus Dupree, the photographer, is long dead. His son said it was never distributed in any way, as far as he knew. So how did the killer get it?"

"The photographer gave it to one of the five of us. That person kept it all these years. That's the only logical explanation."

"Did you get a copy of the picture?"

"No."

"Neither did Lehrman and Kaiser. At least, that's what they say. I checked before I came here. They don't remember anything at all about getting a picture from that night. Of course, I don't know about Atwood and Gayle."

I turned over the picture and read the writing on the back again. An address: "207 Avenue C, Apt. 2G."

"That address is our only lead," I said.

"Except it wasn't the address of any of Dupree's places or the club."

"And we checked this address after we left the photo shop and discovered it was now just another big new apartment building. Whatever it was in 1986 is long gone."

"So we have a lead that really isn't a lead."

I looked down again at the lights of New York City below us. New York City always looked beautiful from way above—like sitting in this place or coming in on a plane at LaGuardia or Kennedy Airport. You saw all the beauty of New York, but none of the ugliness that went with the place.

"What are you going to do next with all this?" Manning asked me.

"Go on the air with it. Tell everyone about the picture with all five names on the list that we found. We may not be sure exactly what it means, but it's the link we've been looking for. That's a big story. And a big break in the investigation for you and the police too."

"Yeah, well . . ."

"You're going to pass on to the department everything we found out, right?"

"I'm not sure. They're going to jump all over me if I do that for getting involved in an active murder investigation when I'm supposed to be on limited duty, or whatever the hell it is I'm on."

"What if I just broke it on air then so the police could pick it up from there. I'd leave you out of it."

"Except they'd go back and interview Dupree. Who'd tell them about the cop who showed him the detective's shield to convince him to go look for the picture."

"Oh, right."

"I'm probably going to be in big trouble no matter what I do."

"I'm sorry."

He shrugged. "I was in big trouble before. A bit more won't make a whole lot of difference to me at this point."

I got the feeling he was talking about more than just his police career when he talked about the trouble in his life. I was on my third beer and had a bit of a buzz going. So I asked him about the state of his marriage right now. Hey. I'm an investigative journalist—I always want to know the facts.

"We're together," he said.

"How's that going?"

"Day-to-day."

"What about your relationship with your son?"

"That's day-to-day too."

"But you're going to keep trying to make it work?"

"I think I owe it to them."

I was debating whether or not to ask more questions on the topic, but it turned out I didn't have to. He knew where I was headed with this.

"Look, Clare, I like you. I like you a lot. And I'm very attracted to you. If the situation were different, I'd really want something to happen between us. But I can't do that. I can't cheat on my wife and family when I'm trying to make things right again for the things I've done wrong in the past. That's just the kind of person I am. I hope you understand."

"Of course I do."

But I was disappointed. I tried my best not to let that show as we talked some more. About his wife and son. About his situation with the NYPD. And, most of all, about the Grace Mancuso story and everything that went with it. Going through everything over and over in hopes of stumbling across something—anything—that we'd missed.

It was just before we were getting ready to leave when Manning suddenly picked up the picture again. I thought maybe he remembered something about one of the five people in it. But he didn't even look at that, just turned it over and stared at the address on the back again.

"I think I know what this is," he said. "Or was."

"You recognize the address?"

"It seemed familiar to me when we checked it out before, but I couldn't place it then. Figured it was just some place I'd been before on a case I'd worked on. But it wasn't a case that brought me there. I went there before I joined the force. I think that same night. It was Jennifer, that woman you saw in the other picture at the club with me."

"What about her?"

"This is where she lived."

CHAPTER 46

I WENT WITH the story the next night on our newscast.

Sure, I didn't have the whole story yet. And, in a perfect world, it's always best to have the whole story before you go with it. But journalism, especially TV journalism, is rarely a perfect world. I now knew there was a picture from more than thirty years ago of the five people whose names were found on that mysterious list next to Grace Mancuso's body. That was news. Good enough for me.

And so there I was back on the air again, talking to the Channel 10 audience:

> ME: There are shocking new developments in the baffling Grace Mancuso murder case. Channel 10 News has exclusively obtained a picture taken at an East Village club more than thirty years ago which clearly shows five people together that night—the same five people whose names were left on a list next to the Mancuso woman's body.

The picture went up on the screen of Bill Atwood, Dora Gayle, Emily Lehrman, Scott Manning, and Brendan Kaiser. I'd told the production people to freeze it there while I talked:

> ME: This picture was taken on October 25, 1986—the night the New York Mets made a miraculous comeback

from two runs down, two out in the 10th inning of World Series Game 6 with the Red Sox—and the Mets then went on to win the World Series.

All five of these people were together at this spot in the East Village when that happened.

What does this have to do with the murder of Grace Mancuso, who would have been a baby when this picture was taken?

Was there any further connection between all five of them beyond this seemingly random encounter?

Why did someone leave all five names at the Mancuso crime scene?

All of these are questions that still have to be answered.

But Channel 10 has turned the picture over to NYPD homicide investigators who say it's the first real break in the case since Grace Mancuso's body was discovered in her East Side apartment several weeks ago.

And, of course, two of the people in the picture, Bill Atwood and Dora Gayle, have died in tragic crimes not directly related to the Mancuso murder—but which could still be a part of the overall puzzle.

Channel 10 News will continue to stay on top of developments in this fast-moving story . . .

* * *

I did not say anything about Jennifer Hartley or the address on the back of the picture or the fact that Manning had recognized that as the place where Jennifer Hartley lived in the East Village back then.

I'd considered it.

Thought about making a public appeal for her to come forward.

That would have been the easiest way to track her down after all this time.

But it also meant everyone else in the media would have the same information—and the same story—that we did. I preferred to keep the Jennifer Hartley information secret until we could find her ourselves and get her to tell us her story exclusively.

Now all we had to do was find her.

I explained the dilemma to everyone at the first news meeting we did after my broadcast.

"My God, that was a long time ago," Brett Wolff said.

"She could be dead," Dani said.

"Probably married and living under a different name," Brett added.

"It's going to be awfully hard to find her," Dani agreed.

"She also is the one person—our only real lead here—who might have some answers for all this," I pointed out.

I turned to Maggie, who hadn't said anything yet. Which was unusual for Maggie. I figured she was still mad at me for working with Manning on the story without telling her. I was right.

"What do you think, Maggie?" I asked.

"Can you tell me again exactly how you got the information about the Jennifer Hartley woman being the person who lived at the East Village address on the back of the picture?"

"Someone told me."

"Someone who?"

"Someone who had knowledge of her back then."

"Someone in the picture?"

"Well, yes."

"Scott Manning?"

"That's right."

Maggie sighed.

"Problem?" I asked, knowing full well there was one.

"I really don't like the idea of this Manning guy being involved in the story with you like this."

"He's a trained investigator, an NYPD homicide detective."

"He's also a potential murder suspect."

"I really don't think—"

"Clare, those five names on that list are the best potential murder suspects we have for the Grace Mancuso killing. You know that as well as I do. And two of them are dead. That leaves three—Emily Lehrman, Brendan Kaiser, and Scott Manning."

"God, I hope it's not Kaiser," someone muttered.

"Did she just call our owner a murder suspect?" someone else asked.

"I think she said 'potential' murder suspect," I said.

"Still not good."

I glared at Maggie. I was kinda mad at her now. Mad for being so critical of me using Manning on the story. Mad for bringing it up in a public meeting this way. And, most of all, mad because I knew she was right. Manning did still have to be considered a potential suspect. All of them on the list did.

But I needed Maggie more than ever now.

"Can you find Jennifer Hartley?" I asked her.

"Sure."

"Just like that?"

"We have that address in the East Village. If she lived there, there will be a trail of all her forwarding and subsequent addresses. Even if she changed her name or the way she looked or anything else. All we have to do is follow that trail, and we'll find Jennifer Hartley—whoever she is and wherever she is today."

"How can you be so certain?"

"I might not be a hotshot like Scott Manning, but I'm a pretty good trained investigator too."

CHAPTER 47

JENNIFER HARTLEY HAD come a long way from the short-haired, tattooed punk rocker she was in the 1980s.

We tracked her through a series of addresses until we got to the one she lived at now—a big house, a mansion really, in Greenwich, Connecticut. She'd married a man named Zach Monroe, who developed some kind of computer super-chip that made him rich and gave her a life of leisure.

Jennifer Hartley—now Jennifer Monroe—met us in front of the house as we drove up the long driveway. She had long, perfectly coiffured hair now. Wearing an expensive-looking, fashionable sundress and sandals. She had garden tools in her hand, and it looked like she'd been working on a lavish bed of flowers near the front door. She put them down now and walked over to us.

Manning had called ahead to tell her that we were coming but wasn't specific about the reason—just saying the visit was about "police business." There were some awkward introductions and then an equally awkward hug between her and Manning. The kind of hug you see when two people used to know each other really well in another life but were complete strangers now.

"It's been a long time," Jennifer said to him.

"More than thirty years."

"You look good, Scott."

"You, too, Jennifer. But different. A lot different . . ."

She smiled.

"Let's go inside and talk," she said.

* * *

"I'm still not sure exactly what this is about," she said as we sat in her living room. "You told me on the phone that it all had something to do with a night we spent at a club in the East Village."

"That night seems to be the link to a murder case."

She shook her head. She was confused.

"How? Who was murdered?"

"A woman named Grace Mancuso," I said. "A stockbroker who lived on the Upper East Side of New York. Does that name mean anything to you?"

"I read about it in the papers and saw it on TV. But she was in her thirties, right? What does this have to do with a night we spent out at a club when she was barely born?"

Manning and I went through everything we knew about the picture from that long-ago night at the Domino Club and finding her address on the back.

"Do you have the picture?" Manning asked.

"If I do, does that mean I'm some kind of suspect?"

"Of course not."

"Maybe I should call my lawyer before I talk to you anymore."

She said it casually, and I wasn't sure at first if it was a joke or not. But then she laughed.

"I had the picture," she said. "I had both shots. The one of just you and me, then you with the other people that night. I don't have them anymore. I threw them away."

"When?"

"Several months later, I guess. I found them one day. I was moving out of the East Village place, and they brought back too many memories. I had a bit of a crush on you back then, Scott. Don't know if you were aware of that or not. I guess I was into my rock groupie phase, and you were so cute when you played onstage with your band. Anyway, then I found out from someone that you'd quit the band, enrolled at the police academy, and were engaged to be married. I didn't like that Scott Manning. I was mad at him for taking away the cool guy onstage I used to know. It felt good at the time, although now it seems kind of silly what I did. It was just a couple of pictures, you know. Pictures of you and me and some other people out for a night in the city. Of course, I had no idea this might one day wind up as possible evidence in a murder case. Do you think that one of the people in the other picture with you is the killer?"

"Not necessarily. Two of them are already dead. And one of the deaths was by someone for a completely different reason."

"So why is it so important?"

"I think there's something about that night that could tell us who killed Grace Mancuso . . . and why."

* * *

A short time later, she walked us to the door and then out to our car. She gave Manning another awkward hug, and they said their goodbyes.

"I sure wish I'd kept that picture of you and the other four from that night you're looking for," Jennifer said.

"Me too."

"I guess you wish you'd kept yours, too."

"Huh?"

"Your copy of the picture. You threw it away too, right?"

"I never had the picture."

She stared at him.

"I ordered two copies of both pictures from that night," she said. "I asked the photographer to send them to me afterward. He sent one copy for me, and another one for you. He said I should send them on to wherever you lived. It took me a while, but that's what I did. I mailed it to you."

"When?"

"Quite a while later, I'm not sure how long. I found them in a drawer one day. The picture of you and the picture with the four other people. I realized I'd never told you I had the pictures and figured you might want them. But I hadn't talked to you in a while at that point. Your band had broken up. So I just mailed both pictures to you. I was always surprised I never heard anything back from you."

"I never got any pictures."

"Well, they didn't come back, so . . ."

"Where did you send them?"

"To your apartment then. The place on Sullivan Street. I was there once and had written down the address."

"I moved out of there after I quit the band and enrolled in the Police Academy."

"Then the pictures should have been forwarded to you," I pointed out to him. "Or else sent back to you, Jennifer."

"Unless . . ."

"Unless it wound up in someone else's hands."

"Who?" Jennifer asked.

I didn't have an answer for that. Neither did Manning. I had been hoping this would all end somehow once we tracked down

Jennifer Hartley. That she would have some answers. But it didn't work out that way. Jennifer Hartley wasn't the answer to all this, just another piece of the puzzle. The killer was still out there somewhere, and I didn't have the slightest idea who that was.

CHAPTER 48

"THE GOOD NEWS is we found Jennifer Hartley," I told Jack Faron. "Tracked her down to her house now in Connecticut. She did get that picture sent to her, just like we thought. And I got an exclusive interview."

"Okay, what's the bad news?"

"She doesn't know anything."

I sat in Faron's office and ran through all the highlights of the conversation with Hartley, including the part about the copy of the picture with the five people she'd sent to Scott Manning—but that somehow disappeared.

"But there was another copy of that picture," Faron said, his voice getting more excited now. "That means it could still be out there. And there's a possibility—a good chance—that this picture is in the hands of the person who killed Grace Mancuso and left that list of the names of the people in the picture. For whatever reason. So we just go with that. Play it up big. Get the Hartley woman interview on air too, talking about the mystery of the picture and the events of that night and all the rest. Clare, that sounds like a terrific story to me."

"Wait a minute—aren't you the guy who didn't even think this even was a story anymore?"

"That was before."

"Before what?"

"Before this."

He picked up some papers and slid them across the desk to me.

"It's our latest overnight rating report."

"Yippee!"

"I know how much you love reading ratings book numbers."

"More than life itself."

"These include the overnights for our last show. You got a monster rating number for this story. Some of that probably came from all the promo we did during the day for it, but the numbers kept going up even during your segment. Nobody was turning it off. You struck ratings gold on this one, Clare."

I looked through the numbers quickly. It didn't take long to see what Faron was saying. Big numbers everywhere, including all the key demographics. There are some stories that just seem to strike a chord with the viewing audience. The emergence of the long-ago picture and its connection to the Grace Mancuso murder seemed to have done it. But there was something else in the numbers too. Everyone suddenly cared about Dora Gayle now. The connection between all the money from the Revson scandal and all the other powerful and important people on that list with her seemed so incongruous that people desperately wanted to learn more and find out the reason a homeless woman was a part of this story.

I remembered now how crazy it seemed to everyone to do a big on-air piece in the beginning about Dora Gayle and her seemingly meaningless death. That was a murder that could never draw big numbers, people said. You covered murders by the numbers on TV news. The all-important rating numbers. And there was a formula that you followed in deciding what murders to put on the newscast. Dora Gayle had proved just how flawed that method was. A good story is a good story.

"Tell me about Scott Manning," Faron said now.

"What about him?"

"Why he seems to be working with you on this story."

Damn. Did Maggie go to Faron with a complaint? I doubted that. Not her style. She was the "in-your-face" confrontational type, not the "behind your back" type. But everyone in that news meeting had heard what she said about Manning. And it had no doubt become a hot topic in office gossip. A newsroom is a small place, so it wouldn't have taken long for the news to get to Faron.

"Are you sleeping with him?" Faron asked.

"How could you even ask me a question like that?"

Faron just stared at me.

"I'm not sleeping with him, Jack."

"Are you planning on sleeping with him in the future?"

"I don't really plan these things out."

"Probably not a good idea to do anything like that. At least until we get some more answers on this story. And make sure this Manning isn't involved in any way we're not aware of yet. That would be bad news if we were employing him in some capacity and he turned out to be guilty of something here, maybe even murder. Bad for you. Bad for me. And bad for the station."

"I'll do my best to control my sexual urges," I said.

"Just let me know if anything changes in your personal relationship with Manning."

"You'll be the first person I tell, Jack."

* * *

We talked about the next story we were doing. I'd go on the air with the Jennifer Hartley picture stuff. That was easy. The trickier element was how to keep the story going after that.

It was Faron who came up with the plan we finally decided on. I probably would have thought of it eventually too. But I was a little rattled by all the Manning talk. So maybe I was not exactly at the top of my game right at the moment.

"Everyone wants to hear more about Dora Gayle," he said, pointing again to the ratings numbers.

"But we've already told her story."

"Let's tell it again."

"We already did that too. Not much left about Dora Gayle's life to say in this story."

"Then let's tell a different Dora Gayle story. Go back and compare her life to all the money and power and influence of the others—the victim, Grace Mancuso, and the other people on that list. Keep asking the question over and over again. What does a sad, tragic homeless woman have to do with any of this? Show the picture again and again of her as a young, beautiful woman at the club in the East Village in that picture—and then the way she looked and lived now. It would be powerful stuff."

He was right. Dora Gayle. And I suddenly came up with the perfect way to show how Dora Gayle just didn't fit into the facts we knew about this story.

"Revson," I said.

"What about it?"

"Of all the things that seem strange about Dora Gayle—the facts of the story that just don't make sense with her involvement—the strangest is the Revson financial scandal."

"You still think there's some kind of bizarre connection between Dora Gayle and Revson?"

"There has to be a connection between all of it. Dora Gayle. The other people on the list. Mancuso. The mess at Revson. It's the only way any of this makes any kind of sense."

"But what could possibly be the connection between a thirtysomething-years-old picture and a homeless woman in it to a financial scandal and murder happening now?"

"Let's go back to Revson and ask them," I said.

CHAPTER 49

Todd Schacter was standing in front of my apartment building when I got home that night.

That was a surprise. I hadn't heard from him since our last encounter in the coffee shop. I sort of assumed that he'd forgotten about me or decided not to do what I asked him or he'd failed at it and was afraid to admit that.

But here he was waiting for me.

"Let's talk," Schacter said when I approached him.

No hello, no pleasantries of any kind.

"Sure, want to come upstairs to my place?"

"No."

"I'm pretty tired, it's been a long day. I'd be a lot more comfortable there. I could make you a drink—I know I sure could use one."

"No," he repeated.

"Why not?"

He pointed toward the lobby of my building. There was a doorman letting people in and out.

"There might be a security camera in there."

"There's no security camera in my building."

"How do you know that?"

"Well, I've never seen one."

"The best security cameras are the ones that no one is aware of."

"Do you spend your whole life worrying that any place you go might somehow catch you on a hidden security camera?"

"Yes."

Damn, this guy was a weird dude.

He asked me to start walking with him. So that's what we did. We began walking down the street away from my building. He said that was the best way to make sure that no one was watching or listening to us from any recording devices. I remembered how John Gotti, the old New York City crime boss, always held his meetings like that. Walking down the street of New York with his lieutenants to make sure the FBI wasn't listening in on them. I told that to Schacter now.

"It's a very effective method to avoid detection," Schacter said.

"Yeah, well, they finally did catch Gotti on tape, and he went away to prison for the rest of his life."

"I'm smarter than he was."

He reached into his pocket, pulled out a large manila envelope, and handed it to me.

"The information you're looking for is in there."

"About the email?"

"Yes."

"You know who sent the original email about Lucy Devlin that I told you about?"

He nodded.

"It's all in there. Her name. Address. Date of the email. Where she sent it from."

"She?"

"It was sent by a woman."

"Any idea how old this woman is?"

"Of course."

"Mid-twenties?"

"That's right."

The same age Lucy would be. I tried to let the enormity of what he was saying sink into me for a few seconds.

"How can you be sure this is the right person?" I finally asked. "I mean, I didn't give you a whole lot to work with, I realize that. Are you absolutely sure this woman is the one who sent the original email?"

"I'm sure."

"How sure?"

"I double-checked it with another source of information."

"What do you mean?"

"Her email appeared in another computer file I was able to breach at the same time."

"Who?"

"Senator Elliott Grayson."

"Holy crap!" I said.

"That was kinda my reaction too," Schacter said, and he gave me the closest thing to a smile that I'd ever seen from him.

"But you said you were afraid to go into Grayson's computer files."

"I changed my mind."

"Why?"

"Like I said, I still like a good challenge."

And then he was gone.

Walking away from me down the street like he'd never been here at all.

* * *

I went upstairs to my apartment, poured myself a big drink, and opened the envelope Schacter had given me.

It was all there, just like he'd said.

The email had been sent from a Hotmail address in Winchester, Virginia. Schacter had tracked the owner of the account to a house there that belonged to a man named Gregory Nesbitt. He lived there with his wife, Linda, and his daughter, Audrey. Linda Nesbitt was twenty-seven years old, which is the exact age Lucy would be if she were alive. For whatever it was worth, I noted that Linda's first name also began with an "L"—just like Lucy—which might make sense for someone to do if they were choosing a new name for themselves. Their daughter, Audrey, was eight years old and a third-grader.

The Elliott Grayson file information confirmed it was the same person who had been in touch with him, just like Schacter had said.

There was a series of email exchanges between Grayson and the same email address. The contents of the messages had been deleted, probably by Grayson. But Schacter was still able to track the IPO number Grayson had communicated with—and it was the same one as the original email about Lucy in New Hampshire.

I read through all the other information in the file Schacter had given me, then got up and poured myself another big drink.

I sat there for a long time in my apartment thinking about what I knew now.

Well, I knew who sent the original email.

And I knew that person could be—in all probability really was—Lucy Devlin, the daughter I had been searching for so long.

I knew too that all I had to do was to go to Winchester, knock on the door of her house, and maybe get answers to all of the questions that had been haunting me for so many years.

Yep, that was all I had to do, all right.

I finished my drink, closed the file, and put it away in a drawer.

There would be plenty of time for me to deal with it later.

But now, I had a big story to work on right here.

And so I tried to put any thoughts about Lucy Devlin out of my mind—just like I'd done so many times in the past—and think about what I was going to say and do the next day when I went back to Revson.

CHAPTER 50

VERNON ALBRIGHT SEEMED different this time.

The CEO of the Revson Securities firm had worked hard that first day I was there to put on a good face for the media—to show how compassionate and concerned he was about the death of an employee and the possible link to the Revson scandal.

Now, as I sat in Albright's office again, he seemed more cocky, more self-assured. I picked up the sense that he wasn't worried as much about the Grace Mancuso murder anymore. He'd probably gone through a tough time with the scandal and the murder, but now the worst was over. Things were getting back to normal for him, and he was going to survive this without a scratch. Guys like Albright usually did.

"I understand you've made some progress on Grace's murder," he said, glancing down at his watch in a not so subtle sign that his interest in finding out who killed his employee was limited now. "I saw your piece about the picture of those five people from the list. It sounds like that's the way to go in looking for Grace's killer."

"Certainly seems like a strong possibility."

"And then there have been those messy revelations about Grace's love life. The affairs with men. And women too. My goodness, a lot of those people she was involved with certainly had a motive to kill her, didn't they?"

"There's a number of leads still being pursued," I said.

"Do any of them seem promising?"

"Well, that's why I'm here, Mr. Albright."

I took out the two pictures we had of Dora Gayle—the one of her looking young and beautiful in college, and the other off the documentary as a homeless woman living on the streets.

"Do you know her?" I asked Albright.

"Well, I know who she is from the stories you and others have done about her."

"Did you ever meet her?"

"Of course not."

"So she never came here to Revson for any reason?"

"Why would someone like that have anything to do with us here at Revson?"

"That's what I'm trying to figure out. Of course, there shouldn't be any connection between this homeless woman and a place like Revson. But what if there was? That might help explain a lot of things."

"I can't imagine any possible connection to Revson." He pushed the two pictures of her back to me across his desk. As if just looking at a person like Dora Gayle was terribly distasteful to him.

"Okay, then I want to talk to you a bit more about the scandal here and the repercussions from it."

"I don't understand," Albright said. "I thought everyone believed now this must have had something to do with that list of people from the eighties that was on the list in Grace's apartment. The people in that picture you found."

"That's the operative theory."

"So why are you still asking me these questions about what happened at Revson?"

I shrugged. "The idea that Mancuso was involved in a scandal here, that she ripped off hundreds of investors and then turned state's evidence against some of the other people here . . . well, that's a pretty good motive for murder. Maybe we've been trying too hard, making this case too complicated. Maybe the answer is right here where she worked."

Albright didn't look at his watch this time. He was not happy about this line of conversation. Yep, he'd definitely assumed the focus of the police investigation was shifting away from Revson, not toward it. But he was too good, too cool to let me see his anxiety. He nodded solemnly as if I were talking to him about opening up a new brokerage account.

"You think that one of our disgruntled investors could have killed her?"

"That's certainly a possibility."

"And the other?" he asked, even though he knew the answer.

"Someone at the company who thought she knew too much."

Albright nodded solemnly. He didn't even flinch. This guy was good.

"I can't even imagine that," he said. "But, like I said before, there's always a few bad apples in every company. I want to help you and the authorities, to do anything I can to find any of them here at Revson. You have my solemn word on that, Ms. Carlson."

That's when I knew. I just knew. Albright was involved in the scandal. Maybe he found out about what was going on but didn't do anything. Maybe he helped plan it. Maybe he was the brains behind it, the one who put the whole scam together. If so, he probably insulated himself with layers of protection so that the other people involved—like Grace Mancuso—didn't even know about him.

But now, if someone dug too deeply and didn't accept the "just a few bad apples theory," they might eventually get to him.

Is that what happened to Grace Mancuso?

Had she found out?

Had she tried to blackmail him just like she did with Atwood?

Had he murdered Mancuso to keep her quiet?

But, even as I was thinking it, I knew that was unlikely. Albright wasn't the type of guy to kill someone like Grace Mancuso. He would have used his money and his power and his influence to buy her off. Besides, I remembered what the killer had done to Grace Mancuso's body. This was a crime of passion. There was no passion about Vernon Albright.

Still, the guy was dirty. I was sure of that. If not this scandal, then another one. I wondered how many people Albright had stolen money from over the years while maintaining the image of corporate respectability. The more I thought about it, with Albright sitting there smiling smugly at me from behind the big desk, the madder I got. There were people who had died here. Dora Gayle first. Then Grace Mancuso and Bill Atwood. Lisa Kalikow was going to spend the rest of her life in prison for a moment of violent passion. Lives had been ruined, but not Albright's life. Not yet anyway. But I couldn't worry about that now. I needed this guy to get more information.

"Let's forget about Dora Gayle and the people on the list for a minute," I said. "Focus instead on the idea that it could have been a disgruntled Revson investor who lost money—and blamed Mancuso enough to kill her. It's a long list of people, but we've narrowed down the list to several leading suspects. I'd like to run through them with you and see if any of them strike a chord of recognition."

"Of course."

I took out four folders I'd gotten from Maggie. They included pictures and information on Gary Myers, Maryanne Giordanno, and Joseph Ortega, the most obvious cases of disgruntled investors we'd discussed earlier. The fourth file was for a man named David Zachary from Chicago. Maggie had gotten this information from the Revson security people, who reported it to the police. They said Zachary had caused a big scene there not long ago, demanding to see Grace Mancuso. The incident—with Zachary's picture—had been captured by security cameras.

"First, we have Gary Myers, a construction foreman from Dublin, Tennessee," I told Albright now, showing him the picture of Myers.

Albright shook his head no. "I've never seen him before," he said. "There were, as I'm sure you would expect, many angry investors in the days when all this came out. But this man . . . well, I don't remember anything about him that would make him stand out from any of the others."

I showed him a second photo. Maryanne Giordanno. Another shake of his head from Albright. "I know about the case. It was one of Grace's accounts. I know the woman's husband died, and she couldn't afford proper medical treatment at the end. Terrible, just a horrible tragedy. But I don't know anything personally about this woman. I never saw her, never heard from her—don't know that she even had any firsthand contact with Grace before her death. Much of this stuff would be handled by lower-level employees. That's probably who she was talking to. Not Grace. And certainly not me."

I took out the third photo. The one of Joseph Ortega from the Bronx. Albright shook his head no again.

I sighed and showed him the last photograph. The security camera shot of David Zachary, the one who'd shown up at the Revson building. This time there was a look of recognition on Albright's face.

"Do you know him?"

"Yes, I saw this man. He caused a loud disturbance in the lobby. Demanding to see the person in charge of the company. I decided it was best under the circumstances to humor him, before we called the police or anything."

"What happened?"

"He wanted to talk to Grace Mancuso."

"What did you tell him?"

"That he couldn't see her."

"What did he do then?"

"He got very upset—but eventually he left."

I nodded. "Do you have any idea how much money he lost with Grace Mancuso in the investment scam?"

"That's the strange thing. We checked on that afterward. It turned out he hadn't put any money at all into our company. There was no record of him anywhere. He was never one of Grace's clients. He was never one of our investors."

"So why was he so upset?"

"I have no idea."

* * *

Back at the office, I went over everything with Maggie and her team of reporters. I invited Manning to the meeting too. Since he was supposed to be working on the story with us, I wanted to hear his thoughts and opinions. But I figured his presence wouldn't go over well with Maggie, and I was sure right.

"I'm Detective Scott Manning," he said when I introduced them. "I'm—"

"I know who you are."

"I'm just interested in doing anything I can to help."

"I don't see how you can help us on this story."

Manning looked confused. "Did Clare tell you what she and I discussed for my role here?"

"Yes, she did. And I told her I thought it was a very bad idea."

At least she wasn't a hypocrite.

"Clare's my boss," Maggie said now. "I have to do whatever she decides. Even if that decision is stupid like this one."

I thought it might really get ugly, but Manning just smiled at Maggie. "Well, I'm glad we got that all straightened out," he said.

We went through everything about the story again. The things we did know, the things we didn't know, and the things we didn't even know if we should know or not. The list of names. The old picture from the East Village. The Revson scandal. Grace Mancuso's torrid love life along with her blackmail and scheming for money. Had we missed something? We must have, but for the life of me I couldn't figure out what it might be. Neither could anyone else in the room.

When we got to the Revson angle, I told everyone about my meeting with Albright. My suspicion that he was somehow involved in the scandal. His "just one bad apple" excuse. But I also said how I felt that whatever he did—or didn't do—with the Revson scandal, I did not see any reason to think he was actually involved with Grace Mancuso's murder.

Finally, I went through the list of suspects from Maggie that I'd run through with him to see if there was any possible link to Revson.

There was a computer in the conference room where we were meeting, and Maggie—sitting at a computer—would project on a wall screen the images of whatever we were discussing.

She did that now with the four people connected with Revson that I'd shown to Albright:

Grey Myers.

Maryanne Giordanno.

Joseph Ortega.

David Zachary.

"Oh, my God!" Manning suddenly yelled out.

"What's wrong?" I said.

"That last guy! David Zachary!"

"What about him?"

"That's Joey! He used to be in my band—the one who called himself Joey because he idolized Joey Ramone! He was my roommate! He was my best friend!"

PART IV

CINDERELLA—AND OTHER FAIRY TALES

CHAPTER 51

DAVID ZACHARY WAS a high school music teacher in a suburb of Chicago.

I found a number for him, called, and got his wife who said he wasn't home. I told her I was a TV journalist in New York City and I wanted to interview him for a story. I didn't say specifically what the story was. I figured I'd see where this conversation went first.

Scott Manning and Maggie were in my office, and I put it all on a speakerphone so they could jump in when needed.

"Did your husband ever mention the name Grace Mancuso to you?" I asked Mrs. Zachary.

"No. Who is she?"

"An investment banker here in New York."

"Dave hasn't been in New York in years."

"Have you ever had any business dealings with a company called Revson?"

"Never heard of them."

"They're a big investment firm in New York."

"We don't have any investments in New York. What is this about anyway?"

"I really need to speak with your husband, Mrs. Zachary," I said, trying to make it sound as casual as possible.

"I told you that David's not here."

"Where is he?"

"I don't know."

I assumed at first—wrongly, as it turned out—she might be lying, trying to cover for her husband.

"You must have some idea of his whereabouts or when he'll be home, Mrs. Zachary. I really can't believe . . ."

"My husband has terminal cancer," she said. "A malignant brain tumor. It was diagnosed a few months ago. He doesn't have a lot of time left. Three months, maybe six at the most. He still has some good days and bad days, but they're mostly bad now. The doctors said there was nothing they could do."

I glanced over at Manning who had a stunned look on his face. It must have been a double shock for him about Zachary, I realized. First, he finds out that his old friend might be involved in this somehow. Then he learns that the friend is dying.

"Mrs. Zachary, my name is Scott Manning," he said now. "I'm a detective with the New York City Police Department. But I'm also an old friend of your husband. I'm sure he must have mentioned my name to you over the years."

"What was your name again?"

"Scott Manning."

"No, I don't recall anything."

There was a moment or two of silence on the line, and I was afraid maybe we'd lost the connection with Mrs. Zachary. Or she'd hung up. But she was still there. Maggie jumped in to ask if she could tell us any more about her husband's disappearance.

"He just left," Mrs. Zachary said. "He's done this a few times in the past month or two, ever since he got the bad news from the doctor. There were a lot of loose ends he needed to tie up, that's what he told me. Before he died is what he meant, even though he didn't say it. He just said there were things he needed to make right. Whenever he went away before this, he came back. Until this time. He left a few weeks ago, and I haven't heard anything from him since. David's not well. I'm very worried about him. That's why I finally reported him missing to the police. I don't think they took me very seriously though. Do you think you can talk to them, Detective?"

We got a cop named Kowalski on the phone at the Chicago police precinct where Mrs. Zachary had filed the missing person report.

"There's not much to tell you," Kowalski said. "You know the routine. We get hundreds of missing person reports in here. Most of them don't want to be found. Runaway kids, husbands skipping out on their wives, businessmen trying to avoid debt collectors—there's no violence, no crime. We just don't have the manpower to really check them all out. We go through the motions, and maybe every once in a while, we get lucky and stumble on the missing loved one. It happens. Of course, I could also win the Illinois lottery tomorrow. But I don't count on either one."

"David Zachary falls into this category?" Manning asked.

"He got bad news from the doctor. That's enough to send anybody over the edge. So he takes off into the night. Maybe he kills himself. Maybe he just turns up dead somewhere. Maybe he shows up back at his wife's door tomorrow with flowers and candy for her. Like I said, the guy's not breaking any laws so there's a limit to what we can do."

"David Zachary could be a murder suspect in New York," Manning told him.

"No kidding? Who's the victim?"

"An investment broker. A woman named Grace Mancuso. She worked for Revson, the company that's in a big financial scandal."

"Oh, right. I saw something about that on one of the cable news channels. You think this could be your guy?"

"Maybe."

"Did he lose a lot of money to her in that scam?"

"None that we know of."

"So what's this Zachary guy's motive?"

"That's what I'm trying to find out. Tell me whatever you know about him."

Kowalski put the phone down for a few minutes and went looking for David Zachary's missing person file.

"There's no sign of any violent behavior in his past," the Chicago cop said when he came back on the line. "He seems pretty clean. A teacher for more than thirty years. Taught high school music classes and was a faculty advisor for the school's marching band at football games and stuff like that. Been married to the same woman the whole time. No kids, a house, a couple of cars—all very average."

I asked if he could tell us again about what he had learned about the events leading up to his disappearance.

"That's the damnedest thing about it," Kowalski said. "There doesn't seem to have been any one thing that was the catalyst for him leaving. Nothing that makes sense anyway. His wife said Zachary was simply watching TV one night and he got very agitated. He kept mumbling to himself, pacing around furiously, and saying some things that didn't make any sense to her."

"Did she tell you what he was watching?"

"It was a news show about some murder in New York."

Christ, it was all coming together now. This was the link we'd been looking for. Zachary was the key. Except it didn't quite make sense. If Zachary was watching a news show about Grace Mancuso's murder *before* he disappeared, then maybe he wasn't the one who had killed her.

"Was the news show he was watching about the Grace Mancuso murder?" Manning asked.

"Nah, I would have remembered that when you mentioned her name to me earlier. This was no big high-profile case. Just the death of some homeless woman in New York."

"Dora Gayle?" I asked

"Yes, that was her name. He's watching this news show about the Dora Gayle woman's death, and that's when he got very worked up. Told his wife 'Cinderella is dead' at one point, even though she had no idea what he was talking about. She figured it was just the brain tumor that was doing it. Weird, huh?"

Dora Gayle.

She'd been there from the start of this story, hovering around the edges even though neither I nor anyone else could figure out what she might possibly have to do with all the events that happened.

And now she was back in a big way.

Dora Gayle was the key to it all.

But how?

And why?

CHAPTER 52

MANNING AND I flew to Chicago the next day.

Manning was still having a lot of trouble dealing with the developments about his old friend Dave Zachary. And not just because of his possible involvement in the Grace Mancuso murder, he told me on the flight there.

"The thing is the Dave Zachary I knew was a dreamer, a visionary, a man who always wanted to strive for great things," he said. "He wanted to make a real mark in the music industry, even more than I ever did. I was happy just playing gigs and working in the clubs. He liked that, too. That's why he idolized the Ramones, because he wanted to emulate their whole punk rock act persona. He called himself Joey, after Joey Ramone—the Ramones' lead singer.

"But he wanted even more than that. Dave—or Joey, as he wanted to be called back then—aspired to be like Dylan or Springsteen. He began talking about us getting a record contract and becoming music superstars—and, most of all, about writing great music and meaningful lyrics that could change the world. He really believed that, too. I remember once we were listening to one of Springsteen's big songs, "Born to Run," and he told me that someday he would write something even better.

"He always aimed for the top; he wanted the best in everything. Same with women. The rest of us would run around with whatever women we could find. But he had his girlfriend Rebecca back in Chicago. She was the most beautiful woman I'd ever seen. He had a picture of her above his bed in our apartment and talked about bringing her to New York as soon as he made enough money to support them both.

"Rebecca was just drop-dead gorgeous. She looked a lot like Chrissie Hynde of The Pretenders back then. I told that to him once, and he said: 'In Chrissie's dreams; Rebecca is better looking.' I heard later he eventually did go back to Chicago and marry Rebecca after I moved out of the apartment. I always wanted to meet Rebecca. I guess I'll finally get my chance now when we get to their house.

"He and I lost touch after I joined the NYPD. I tried reaching out to him a few times, but he never got back to me. I figured he was mad at me because I quit the band. I was never exactly sure what happened to him after that, but I always figured it would be something great. I sure as hell didn't expect to find out he was a high school music teacher all his life. I guess I just find it all a bit confusing."

* * *

That confusion wasn't eased when we got to Zachary's address. It was a nondescript one in a suburban community about fifteen miles from O'Hare Airport.

"My God, the Joey I knew would have laughed about a house like this," Manning muttered. "'Matchbox houses', he called them, like from the Pete Seeger song. 'All those ordinary people living in their ordinary matchbox houses living their ordinary lives,' he'd say contemptuously."

His wife was a lot different than the gorgeous portrait of the Chrissie Hynde look-alike Manning had remembered too. That beautiful Rebecca had morphed over the years into a matronly looking woman with gray hair and wearing a shapeless house dress. She led us into the living room.

We told her everything now about the murder of Grace Mancuso. About Dave Zachary's confrontation with the security people at Revson when he showed up and demanded to see her. We asked Mrs. Zachary again if she could think of any connection between her husband and the Mancuso woman. She said she couldn't. She seemed confused and scared.

I tried to calm her down by asking her some innocuous questions about her and her husband.

She talked about their life together since. She worked as a receptionist in a doctor's office, sang in the church choir, and she and Dave enjoyed gardening together on weekends. She said it had been a good marriage, a good life. There had been no children. They'd tried, but she was unable to conceive so they'd just accepted that as God's will.

"Dave was a fine teacher. He worked with a lot of young people over the years. Turning them on to the pleasures of playing and composing and listening to good music. Many times, we'd get letters or emails from former students, thanking him for everything he'd done to help them become better people. Many of them went on to become successful musicians and music teachers themselves. Dave always felt he played at least a part in that. I think that gave him real satisfaction."

"When did he get sick?" I asked.

"He found out about the cancer several months ago. He hadn't been feeling well for a while. Run down, headaches, trouble sleeping. I finally convinced him to go to the doctor. I figured they'd just give him some antibiotics or vitamins to get him back to normal. But instead the doctors said Dave had a brain tumor. It was malignant, and there was nothing they could do. There were times after that when he was his old self. Then he'd just lose it so much he couldn't remember what year it was, who was president, or even the school where he used to teach.

"The doctor told us this was natural with the progression of the disease. Of course, we knew it was only going to get worse. I thought he'd be depressed. But it was never like that. The illness—the death sentence from the doctor—almost seemed to give him new life, a heightened sense of urgency. He said he wanted to make use of the little time he had left. He said he needed to take care of a lot of things before he was gone.

"Anyway, that's kind of what Dave seemed to be doing now. He was going back in his life, making amends. Like he was settling up the final bill. He started spending a lot of time going over old stuff in the house—pictures, reports cards, letters—that sort of thing. He began reaching out to people he hadn't talked to in a long time—friends, coworkers, former students. Like I said, I guess he was putting his affairs in order."

"Could we see some of the stuff you're talking about?" I asked.

"Sure, if you think it will help."

She led us down to the basement. There was a trunk in the corner. She opened it up. It was filled with scrapbooks, school papers, honors, and awards—the memories of a lifetime.

"He spent hours down here after he got sick," Mrs. Zachary said. "I asked him once what he was doing. He said he was looking for answers. Answers about his life. He kept talking about the things he needed to make right before he died. I was his wife. I thought I understood him, I thought I understood what was going through his mind. But I realize now that I didn't understand. I still don't."

She went back upstairs, while Manning and I went through the stuff in the box. A few minutes later, we found what we were looking for.

It was the picture.

The same picture.

The one of the five people from that long-ago night at a club in the East Village.

It wasn't hard to figure out what must have happened. Jennifer Hartley had sent it to Manning at the last address she had for him. Except he wasn't living there anymore. Zachary was the only one at the apartment now. Zachary got the picture and for some reason held onto it all this time.

Except this picture looked different than the one we'd found in the East Village photographer's studio.

Dave Zachary had put a black X in magic marker over the faces of all five of them—Bill Atwood, Dora Gayle, Brendan Kaiser, Emily Lehrman, and Manning, too.

On the back of the photo, written in faded ink, it said:

"FIVE FACES OF OUR YOUNG GENERATION ON A MEMORABLE NIGHT IN NEW YORK CITY; 1) My best friend and my roommate—who's going to help me to make meaningful social statements with my music; 2) a law student who's dedicated to donating her skills to help the poor gain affordable housing and decent lives; 3) a Rhodes Scholar who wants to be the kind of politician that one day we'll be proud of like we used to be back with John F. Kennedy; 4) the son of a ruthless newspaper baron who has decided to be a different kind of man than his father; and 5) a lovely, brilliant young woman who understands the beauty of words and poetry.

It was dated 1986, presumably when he'd gotten the picture mailed to him from Jennifer Hartley that was meant for Manning.

Underneath, there were more words in fresher ink that obviously had been written by Zachary much more recently.

"We all had such high hopes for the future back then. And look how we all turned out. A dirty politician, a dirty lawyer, a dirty cop, a corporate moneygrubber, and a waste of a woman's life. And, of course, me. What was the point of it all? Where did we lose our way? There's only one thing I can still do to make it right . . ."

Manning stared at the picture and the words. "Jeez, Dave Zachary never stopped being a dreamer," he said. "He remembered Dora Gayle from the picture that night and realized what had happened to her since then. So he went back and looked at the lives of the rest of us from that picture too. Then, in his confused and rapidly declining state of mind, it was all too much to take for him. Something snapped. He then went on some crazy mission before he dies that involves all of us in whatever delusion he's under."

That all made some weird kind of sense to me too.

Except, I couldn't get the thought out of my head that we were still missing something.

What did Grace Mancuso have to do with any of this?

If Zachary had no investment money he'd lost in the Revson fraud scandal, then why would he murder her?

And the Mancuso woman wasn't just murdered. She was brutally beaten and killed. The fury, the anger, the excess of it all. This was a crime of passion the medical examiner had said. Did that sound like Dave Zachary? Not the Dave Zachary Manning and his wife knew. Besides, Zachary had no history of violence. For most of his life, he was a mild-mannered schoolteacher. This was completely out of character for him.

I looked down again at the black Xs drawn over the faces of Manning and the four others.

Was Dave Zachary out to kill the people in that picture because they had disappointed him? Disappointed him by the way they'd lived their lives?

Maybe.

But he hadn't come after any of them.

Instead he murdered Grace Mancuso.

Why?

And what was he planning next?

* * *

Upstairs, there was an uncomfortable moment before we left. Both Manning and I wanted to offer some words of assurance to Mrs. Zachary, but what could we say? That we'd find her husband somewhere. When that happened, he'd be arrested for murder. Then it would be a race to see if he died of a brain tumor before they convicted him. No, there was going to be no happy ending to the Dave Zachary story.

"Dave used to talk about you a lot," Manning said to her now, still trying to make some kind of innocuous conversation before we left.

"When did he talk to you about me?"

"When we lived together in New York back in 1986."

She looked confused. "I didn't meet Dave until after he came back from New York."

"Aren't you Rebecca?"

"No, my name is Maureen."

"Dave always talked about somebody named Rebecca. And he went back to Chicago and he married Rebecca."

"Oh, she was his first wife. She left him. It was a very messy business. It hurt Dave very badly. I always thought he never really got over losing Rebecca. Oh, he loved me. But I always thought he still carried a torch for that Rebecca. God knows why."

Damn.

This wasn't Rebecca.

Rebecca was still out there somewhere.

And Dave Zachary was trying to tie up all the loose ends from his past before he died.

"Do you have any idea how we might find Rebecca?" I asked.

CHAPTER 53

HER NAME WAS Rebecca Steffani and she lived in a fancy two-story Tudor house in a posh Chicago neighborhood. It was only about twenty minutes away from Dave Zachary's house, but it might as well have been in another world.

I Googled her before we went there and also had Maggie do some checking back at the office for any information about Rebecca Steffani. To my surprise, there was a lot about her.

She had been married for many years to a man named Anthony Steffani. He was ostensibly a building and plumbing contractor. But, for much of the past two decades, he had also been at the top of the Chicago police department's list of crime bosses. Tony the Tongue Steffani they called him. That's because legend has it that he once cut out the tongue of a stoolie in his organization. A story like that, whether true or not, tends to cement your reputation as a tough guy. He ran a massive prostitution, drugs, and gambling operation on the south side of Chicago.

Then, a few years ago, he'd been shot to death while having lunch at his favorite Italian restaurant. Since then, Rebecca had been living the good life as a mob widow. She was part of the city's night club crowd, she dated a rich lawyer who'd defended her husband before he was shot, and, in general, didn't seem that heartbroken ol' Tony was gone.

There was even some speculation she might have had something to do with setting him up that fateful day he had his last lunch, supposedly because she had heard he might try to divorce her. She was still an attractive woman. Big, bouffant hairdo. Tight Capri pants. Low-cut sweater. Think the *Mob Wives* reality TV show, and you had Rebecca Steffani.

"Yeah, Dave came here a few weeks ago," she told Manning and me as we sat in her house. "I hadn't even thought about him in years. The putz began talking about all the good times we had. Good times? I don't remember why I was even with him in the first place, but I sure remembered why I dumped him."

"Why?" I asked.

"He was a loser."

"How was he a loser?"

"He wound up spending his whole life as a schoolteacher, for crissakes. Who the hell wants to be a schoolteacher? Or be married to one?"

"His wife said he got a great deal of satisfaction out of working with young people."

"Oh, right," she snorted. "Well, satisfaction doesn't pay the mortgage."

Sitting there now and talking to Rebecca Steffani, I suddenly suspected that she really might have had something to do with her husband's death. Maybe she used him for years to get what she wanted—this house, nice clothes, fancy cars. And then, when it looked like he wasn't going to be of any use to her anymore, she got rid of him. No way the cops would probably ever prove that. But my instincts told me that this woman would probably do anything—even murder—to get what she wanted.

The question was whether she was always like this. Did she get hard and mean and greedy as she got older? Or had she always been this way, and the young Dave Zachary was just too blinded by love to notice?

"Dave's missing," Manning said.

"So I heard."

"He's also sick. That's one of the reasons we're trying to find him. It could be a life or death situation."

Rebecca Steffani shrugged. "Nothing to do with me," she said.

I thought again about how much in love Manning had said Zachary was once with this woman. How he used to describe her as a goddess, the love of his life. Maybe he was just deluding himself the whole time. Maybe we all are. Maybe there's no such thing as love. Maybe it's all just an illusion, a moment in time that we make up in our head—and that's then gone as fast as it came.

"What did Dave Zachary say to you?" I asked.

"Most of it didn't make a lot of sense. He kept talking about looking back on his life, trying to make sense out of a lot of things, right the wrongs he'd done to people over the years. He said he wanted to see something that told him he'd left the world a better place after he was gone. Crap like that. It was like listening to a bad Dr. Phil show. To be honest, I was bored silly. I just wanted to get him out of here."

"What happened then?"

"He finally asked me what happened between us. So I told him. I gave it to him straight. I said I was nineteen years old, and I thought I was in love with him. But the truth is I never really was. I think I just thought it was kind of cool to be with a rock musician at the time. It gave me a kind of stature, if you know what I mean. It was fun to tell people that. Of course, then I got pregnant with his friggin' kid. That was no fun. But hey, that was forever ago. I didn't understand why he was making such a big deal about it now."

"You had a kid with Dave?" Manning asked

"Yeah, the asshole knocked me up."

"I knew Dave really well back then. He talked about you all the time. He never said you were pregnant."

"That's because he didn't know. I didn't tell him until after he got back to Chicago after those months he spent in New York trying to start his music career."

"What happened then? Didn't he want to be a father to the child? Wasn't he in contact with your child over the years? He never had any children with his second wife, so he must have tried . . ."

She shook her head. "There was no child."

"You lost the baby?"

"No, I had the baby. A baby girl. I wanted to get an abortion, but my parents—I was still living with them at the time—wouldn't let me. They believed in all that religious crap about sanctity of life or whatever. They made me go through the whole friggin' pregnancy ordeal. I finally gave birth to the damn baby girl. I never saw her though. Gave her up for adoption as soon as she was born. I told Dave that after he got back from New York. He was gone for months—trying to get his big break in the music world, as he put it—so he never found out until he moved back to Chicago. He was very upset. Said I had no right to do that without telling him. I said that I was young and didn't want to be tied down with a baby or a damn family. I told him if he really loved me, he'd just have to accept that. He eventually did. I could get that sap to do anything I wanted to do. Which I did, until I didn't want him around anymore."

It sounded cold and callous, and I really wanted to hate Rebecca Steffani for what she'd done. But I realized how hypocritical that would be of me. Because I had done pretty much the same thing with my baby daughter as she had. Got rid of her quickly so she wouldn't interfere in the life I wanted to live. Rebecca just made it sound a lot worse than I did when I've tried to rationalize my own actions over the years since then. But it was still the same. We'd both walked away from our daughters at birth.

Believe me, the irony of that comparison with this cold, unfeeling woman was not lost on me.

"When did you marry Zachary?" I asked.

"When he came back from New York."

"Why did you marry him? You said you didn't want to be tied down . . ."

"I thought Dave was a pretty good catch back then for a husband."

"You mean because of the rock star persona appeal you mentioned?"

"Nah, I'm talking about the money."

"What money?" Manning asked.

"Dave came back from New York with a lot of money. Enough for us to buy a nice house. Travel around the world. Buy me all sorts of expensive jewelry and clothes. That was okay. For a while, anyway . . ."

"Where did he get the money?"

"He said he'd gotten it in New York."

"Dave didn't have much money in New York."

"That's all I know. I didn't ask any questions. Anyway, that's why I married the guy. He was loaded."

"So why didn't the marriage work out?" I asked.

"The jerk gave all the money away."

"Huh?"

"The money. One day it was just all gone. He said he'd given it away, but he wouldn't tell me why or where the money had gone. He said we'd be happier without it. Can you believe that? Then he told me about how he was going to become a friggin' teacher or whatever. Well, there was no way I was going to stay with some loser who would wind up being a schoolteacher. I wanted a better life than that. And that's what I got."

She looked at us defiantly. As if challenging us to make something of it. This was a woman who cared only about herself. Who went after whatever she wanted. Who seemed to have no conscience or sense of morality or right or wrong.

I knew one other woman that had been described like that.

And when you put those two facts together, everything suddenly made sense.

"Did you ever find out what happened to your baby, Mrs. Steffani?"

"Like I said, she was put up for adoption."

"Do you know where the family was?"

"They told me the name once, but I forgot."

"Did they live in Pennsylvania?"

"I think so."

"Was the family that adopted your daughter named Mancuso?"

"Yeah, Mancuso. That sounds sort of right."

"Did you tell Dave when he came to see you recently that your daughter's adopted name was Mancuso?"

"I might have mentioned it. I was just trying to tell the creep whatever he wanted to hear so he'd leave. Why? Is this important or something?"

I thought about Grace Mancuso's battered body lying in that apartment.

From the very beginning, I'd always believed this was a case of passion, by a killer who was angry about something more than just money.

Like a lover.

Or a jealous spouse.

Or a heartbroken father.

CHAPTER 54

"So WHERE IS David Zachary now?" Brendan Kaiser asked.

"I think he's somewhere in New York City," I said. "Assuming he's the one who murdered Grace Mancuso and left that note—and we certainly have to assume he is at this point—he came back to New York, killed his own daughter, then tied you and the others into it with that note, for some reason, because of the picture. There's no sign of him back in Chicago. It only makes sense that he's still here on whatever twisted mission of redemption he's determined to carry out. Which means, of course, he may not be finished. He could have something else he wants to do here before he dies."

I was back in Brendan Kaiser's office again. Sitting there with the owner of the station and all those other media properties, along with Jack Faron, going over the details of the story just like I would in one of our daily news meetings. I wasn't in charge here; Kaiser was running the show. But I was clearly the star. Not Kaiser. Not Faron. Not Maggie or Brett or Dani or any of the other people in the newsroom. I was the big star again on this story. I kinda liked that.

"Before we go any further," Faron said now, "we need to talk about what we do next with the story we have. Do we put it on the air tonight—or do we wait?"

"We've got plenty of good stuff already," Kaiser said. "The identification of Zachary as the likely suspect. And you've been able to confirm with Pennsylvania authorities and the Mancuso family that he was indeed Grace Mancuso's biological father. That's a big story right there. Even if we don't have all the rest of the answers."

"On the other hand," Faron pointed out, "we have all this information exclusively at the moment. Once we put it on the air, everyone will know what we know. We could just hold off for another night or two in hopes of finding Zachary—and being able to report the whole story. Now that would be a blockbuster ratings win. Which way do we go?"

"I have an idea about that," I said.

I laid it all out for them. I would go on the air that night with what we had, all right. Zachary. The Mancuso connection. His illness and terminal prognosis, plus his apparent goal of going back over events in his life to somehow tie up loose ends—or clean the slate, as his wife said—before he died.

But there was more.

I also would make a public appeal on air for Zachary to turn himself in. Well, I wouldn't do it. I'd bring Manning, his old friend from when he lived in New York all those years ago, to make a personal appeal for him to surrender.

Maybe we could smoke out Zachary that way.

I told Kaiser and Faron I thought it was worth a try. Even if my idea didn't work, I pointed out—and I guess this was the strongest part of my argument, the one that convinced Kaiser and Faron in the end—it would get us a huge amount of media attention and ratings.

And so that night I led our Channel 10 newscast by reporting everything we knew so far to the viewers.

The segment then ended with a personal appeal from Manning, who spoke to the camera for several minutes and ended with: "Joey—I'm calling you that again, just like I used to back when we had the band and the apartment in New York City—I'm your friend. I've always been your friend. You can trust me. I know you're going through a very hard time right now, and I'm sorry about that. But this will only get worse for you unless you let me help you. Contact me immediately [a telephone number and an email address flashed onto the screen] and I'll meet you anytime, anywhere you want. Just you and me, Joey. Like the old days . . ."

*　*　*

I met up with Janet for a drink afterward at a bar near the TV station.

"Where's Scott Manning now?" she asked me.

"He went home."

"To his wife?"

"That's usually the definition of home for a married man."

"How do you feel about that?"

"I'm fine."

"How do you feel about that, Clare?" she repeated.

"It sucks. Okay, is that what you want to hear from me? But I can't do anything to change things. I just have to live with it."

We talked about the things I'd done with Manning over the past few days. About how he'd been working with me on the story. About his unhappiness at still being under investigation by the NYPD in the Nazario death.

"Are you sure this is a good idea, Clare?" Janet asked when I was finished.

"What do you mean?"

"This guy seems to be involved in a lot of messy stuff. Not just the death of the guy who went out the window. He's also clearly tied in somehow to these things happening with the Mancuso murder. He's the one who was the friend of Zachary. He's the one that the photograph of those five people on the list was supposed to be sent to. This all looks like it is revolving around him. How can you be sure he's telling you everything? How can you be sure he's not a big part of this? How can you be sure you can trust him, Clare?"

Jeez, first Maggie and now Janet. Both of them were questioning my judgment in working on the story with Manning's help. That pissed me off. What made it even worse was they were pretty much the two people whose judgment I trusted the most. That pissed me off even more.

"My instincts tell me I can trust him," I said.

"Your instincts about men have been wrong plenty of times in the past."

"That was personal, this is professional."

"Is it?"

"All right, maybe a bit of a combination of both. But I trust him. I really do. Sure, he might not be telling me everything. But I think he's a good guy, And, in the end, he's always going to do the right thing."

"I hope you're right about that, Clare."

CHAPTER 55

NOTHING HAPPENED FOR a few days after that.

Which is the way it sometimes works with the arc of a big story. There's a rush of breaking news, one new development after another—and then everything grinds to an agonizing stop.

I'd been in the news business for a long time so I understood how this worked. But that didn't make it any easier for me. I still had to come up with something new to put on the air every night about Grace Mancuso and Dave Zachary and all the rest. I'd ignited the audience's interest with my big exclusive. Now they wanted more.

We told the Dora Gayle story again, replayed the interviews with the surviving people on the list—even went back to get a jailhouse interview with Lisa Kalikow about her love for Mancuso and the temporary insanity she said drove her to murder Atwood. None of it was groundbreaking, but it still pulled in good ratings because of the interest in the case.

Feeding the beast again—that's what being a TV news executive's job like mine was really about.

But I was running out of ideas to keep this story going. I remembered back when I still worked at a newspaper, and Michael Jackson died. There was such interest in his tragic and unexpected death that our newsstand sales soared with the story. That meant we had to keep doing Page One follow-ups for days afterward. By the eleventh day of this, we had completely run out of ideas. That's when someone suggested we go with a front-page headline that said: "Michael Jackson Still Dead." I wasn't quite there yet, but "Grace Mancuso Still Dead" was certainly a possibility if something didn't happen soon.

Sitting in my office thinking about all this now, I decided to call Manning. I wanted to ask him again if anyone had contacted him after his appearance. Or maybe I just wanted to talk to him. Everyone—Janet, Maggie, the other people at the station—all seemed confused by my interest in Manning. How much was personal and how much professional, they wanted to know. That was a good question. I was confused about my feelings for him too.

"Have you gotten any response?" I asked when he came on the line.

"Oh, lots of responses. I've gotten calls and emails from a bunch of people claiming to be Dave Zachary—but who know nothing about him except what we ran on the air. There's also a few anonymous confessions to Grace Mancuso's murder; one person who said they had evidence she was killed by the CIA; another who believed it was done by an alien from Venus in a UFO; a half-dozen people who wanted to know why I wasn't in jail for the Manny Nazario death; some suggestions on changes I should make in my clothes and hairstyle before I went on TV again; and—oh, yes—there was even a marriage proposal along the way. It's been fun."

"I guess my idea isn't going to work."

"It was worth a try."

"Maybe Zachary's already dead—that's why he hasn't responded."

"I don't think so."

"Why?"

"Cop instinct. I feel like he's still out here waiting for something."

"Me too," I said.

We talked for a while about the case, going through all the possibilities for what seemed to me like the zillionth time. But I always did that when I was working on a story. Sometimes you eventually stumbled across something you've missed all the previous times. That's what happened now.

"Why would Zachary come to New York?" I asked.

"To track down and, for some reason, murder his daughter, who turned out to be Grace Mancuso. That's the obvious thing."

"But that was a while ago now. Assuming he's still here, and we are assuming that, what's here in New York for him?"

Manning couldn't think of any reason, but I did.

"He came here in the eighties for the music. He wanted to be a rock star, just like you did. He would walk around the streets of the city where you lived back then and dream about being Bob Dylan or Bruce Springsteen, that's what you told me. Now he's going back over his life, trying to revisit all the places and people from that time on whatever redemption trip he's on. So why wouldn't he come back to the place where he lived when he still had all those dreams and was a young man with his whole life ahead of him?"

"The old neighborhood we lived in?"

"It makes sense. Goes along with the other stuff he's done. And the picture with the five of you from back then whose names he put on that list. Where did you say you lived then?"

"Sullivan Street, in the Village."

"I think we should go back there and check it out."

"We?"

"I'm going with you."

"Clare, Zachary could be dangerous at this point."

"He's your friend."

"He used to be my friend. I don't really know him anymore. There's no telling what this Dave Zachary might do."

"I'm heading down to that address where you lived on Sullivan Street right now. You can come with me or not. Your choice."

"Okay, but I'm going to be ready in case there's any trouble."

"Are you bringing your gun?"

"I'll be ready for him," Manning said ominously.

* * *

Manning's old apartment building was still there, but it had been completely renovated. There was a sign in front from some real estate agency indicating that the rental for one-bedroom apartments started at $5,000 a month. Manning shook his head in dismay when he saw that, telling me how he and Zachary had paid under $600 for their two-bedroom apartment there back in 1986. Just another reminder of what New York City had once been and where it seemed to be headed now.

Had Dave Zachary stood here and looked at his old building like this too?

I was still betting he had.

We began to make our way through the neighborhood to check out stores, apartment houses, hotels—showing the picture of Dave Zachary to everyone we could find and asking if they'd seen him.

At a coffee shop a block away, we got the first positive hit. A waitress said a man who looked like Dave Zachary had been there a few days ago. He'd ordered a sandwich—a BLT, she thought—coffee, and a piece of pie. He paid in cash, walked out, and she hadn't seen him again.

There was another sighting at a bar a few blocks away. Someone fitting Zachary's description had been there one night and drank a couple of beers. The bartender remembered because he caused a kind of a stir by playing a Ramones song on the jukebox twenty-one times in a row. A young guy in the house wanted to hear something else and complained. Manning and I looked at the jukebox. There were two Ramones songs on it. "Blitzkrieg Bop" and "I Wanna Be Sedated." "He used to play both of those over and over in our apartment when we lived together," Manning said.

The manager at a small residential hotel in the area remembered him. He didn't want to talk to us until Manning flashed his NYPD shield. Like I said before, working with a cop sure did have its advantages.

"Yeah, he was here," the manager said. "Came in about ten days ago. Stayed maybe a week."

"What happened then?"

"He didn't pay his bill."

"You evicted him?"

"That's what we're in business for. People don't pay their bill, we don't let them stay here." The hotel manager looked down at the picture again. "What'd he do?"

"Why do you think he did something?"

"Cops don't go looking for people who are innocent."

When we were finished at the hotel, we walked over to Washington Square Park. It was late afternoon, and the sun was blazing down. There were people sitting on benches, sunbathing on the grass, throwing Frisbees in the park. There were mothers with their babies, students, businessmen on a break, homeless people, and a few drug dealers.

It had been a long day. I suggested we get something to eat. So we bought hot dogs and sodas from a street vendor near the entrance to the park, then took them in and sat down on a bench.

While we were eating, a man sat down on the bench next to us. He was wearing a tattered pair of jeans, a T-shirt that said "Welcome to New York," and carrying a newspaper. He looked tired and weak, like it took all of his strength just to make it to the park bench.

"Hello, Scott," Dave Zachary said. "It's been a long time."

"A long time, Joey."

"I guess you've been looking for me, huh?"

"You've been watching?"

"For a while."

"We need to talk."

"So let's talk, old buddy."

CHAPTER 56

"I DIDN'T EXPECT you'd bring someone else with you," Zachary said, looking over at me.

"She's—"

"I know who she is. I watched the TV newscast the two of you did. That's how I knew you'd come looking for me here eventually. I knew if anyone would figure it all out, it would be you, Scott. You always were smart."

"So are you. And the smart thing to do now is to let me take you in."

"Just like that?"

"We can help you. You're not well, I understand that. The illness has caused you to do things you wouldn't normally do—that's not your fault. It's not really Dave Zachary who committed murder, it's the illness that's doing it. I really believe that. I can get you to a hospital, get you whatever treatment you need right now."

"I can help too," I said. "We'll talk about your condition on the newscast, we'll get public compassion on your side. Whatever you have done, it's not your fault—just like he said. Let us both help you. This has gone far enough already. Please don't make things any worse, Mr. Zachary."

Zachary had the newspaper folded over his right arm. He lifted it slightly now so that we could both see what was underneath. He was holding something silver and metallic in his hand. A gun. He kept it pointed at us. Hidden by the newspaper, no one else could see the drama that was being played out here.

"I used to always love this neighborhood back in the old days," Zachary said, looking around at the village streets around the park. "It was so exciting in the Village back then. We all had this energy, this commitment, this feeling that everything mattered so much. That's why I wanted to come back here and see it again before ... before it was too late. Except it isn't the way I remembered. It's different. Everything has changed."

"Maybe we're different too," Manning said.

I kept my eye on the newspaper with the gun underneath it in Dave Zachary's hand. He held it like a prop, as if he'd almost forgotten it was there. I was hoping Zachary wouldn't use it, hoping he was still the kind of person Manning remembered, hoping he'd come here to listen to his old friend and let this all end peacefully.

But that was the Dave Zachary that Manning had described to me back then, a long time ago.

Not necessarily the Dave Zachary who was sitting next to us with a gun in his hand on a park bench right now.

"We were really something back then, weren't we?" Zachary said. "Playing our music, dreaming of making it big, being around all the incredible energy of New York City during the eighties. We were so young and so optimistic about the future back then, Scott. Sometimes I close my eyes and I can still see you and me and the rest of the band going onstage to play."

"Hey, ho, let's go," Manning said.

Zachary smiled sadly. "Yeah, like that night at the Domino Club, huh? Jeez, it just felt like everything came together that night—us as a band, the Mets with their miracle comeback, the people in the crowd all going wild. That was like a perfect night to be young and living in New York City with all these great hopes and expectations we had for the future.

"But it was never the same after that. Once you quit to join the police force, the band fell apart. I went back to Chicago and married Rebecca, the one great love of my life. She was the only thing I ever felt as much passion for as my music. But, as I guess you found out, that didn't work out. I never became Bob Dylan or Bruce Springsteen either. The two things I loved the most—Rebecca and my music—both broke my heart.

"And so I did the best I could with my life—and the hand I'd been dealt. I married Maureen, the woman you met. She's a good woman. But I just never felt the same passion for her as I used to for Rebecca. The same thing with my work. I became a schoolteacher. I taught kids about music. I thought at the time I was helping and making some kind of a meaningful contribution. But, once I found out I didn't have much time left, l realized that's not much of a legacy for five decades on this planet. Before I died, I wanted something more. I wanted to tell myself that I left something good behind. Something that showed I'd been here and that I'd made a difference. The way I wanted to do with my own music back here in the old days.

"They always say your life flashes before your eyes when you die. Amazing concept, isn't it? I mean there you are falling off a tall building to your death, and fifty years of stuff are fast-forwarding and replaying in your mind. I've never been sure I really believed that. I mean at best you'd only have time for a few images. Marriage, kids, job, or whatever. Come to think of it, how would anyone even know if it were true? Because even if it does happen to you, you can't tell anybody about it. You'd be dead. That, I believe, is the biggest flaw in the whole your-life-flashes-before-your-eyes-when-you-die theory. You'd have to talk to a dead man to prove it.

"Anyway, I've been thinking a lot about this—life, death, and all that stuff—since I found out I don't have a lot of time left. Let's just say it would be a lot easier to go off a tall building or die in a car accident or drop dead of a sudden heart attack. Because what happens to you then—whether you get one last look at your life or not—only takes a matter of seconds. Me, I have weeks, months to think about dying. And that's the tough part, old friend. That's tougher than dying.

"I guess that's what I was doing—trying to watch my life pass before my eyes. And it took a long time. Plenty of time to realize I didn't like who I was and what I had become. So I tried to remember who I used to be. I wanted to be that person again, just a little while, before I died.

"Then I was watching television one night and I saw the piece about the homeless woman who died destitute and alone on the streets of New York City. About how she'd once had all these big hopes and dreams, just like I had then. The woman who called herself Cinderella and believed that fairy tales really did become true. And I recognized her from the picture. The one you used from college, when she was so young and pretty," he said, looking over at me.

My God, I thought to myself.

The Cinderella story.

It had gotten picked up by cable news networks and shown in a lot of places around the country, including Chicago.

And now Dora Gayle, whose murder had seemed so insignificant to nearly everyone at the time, had somehow become the catalyst for all this.

"I remembered her from the picture taken that night at the Domino Club," Zachary said. "The one that got sent to our old apartment after you moved out. I've kept it all these years for some reason. I guess because that was such a special night and I wanted to have something to remember that good feeling. And there Dora Gayle was in the picture again, looking just as beautiful as she did in the one you ran from her college years. That really got to me."

"But you didn't know her or any of the other people in the picture, except Scott," I pointed out.

"Actually, I did." He turned to Manning. "I wound up talking to Atwood at the Domino Club that night and then—after you moved out—I hung out with him a few times afterward. He had a lot of money, he liked to party, and he was a real ladies' man, even back then. He told me he was with the Gayle woman for now, but he wasn't going to let himself be tied down to one woman. How he was headed for England on the Rhodes scholarship and was going to make it with all these British chicks while he was there.

"Then one night we were drinking at some place on the Upper West Side, across from Central Park, and he picked up this girl who said she had some mind-blowing pot. So we walked into the park to smoke it. At some point, things started getting heavy sexually between Atwood and the girl. They went off into a nearby woods together while I just sat there and smoked my joint. Dreaming about Rebecca. Hell, you remember me back then—she was the only girl I wanted to be with.

"Suddenly, Atwood came running out of the woods in a panic. He said things got out of hand, the sex got rough, and now she wasn't moving. Sure enough, when I followed him into the woods and saw the body, I realized she was dead. I don't think Atwood meant to kill her. It was an accident, something had gone wrong—maybe because of all the dope we'd been smoking.

"I wanted to call the police, but he said we couldn't do that. That his career would be ruined. He told me we needed to just leave the body there, since no one could ever connect us to her. Maybe I wasn't thinking clearly because of the pot—and I guess I was worried about being implicated in a murder too—so that's what we did.

"When I woke up the next morning, I thought it all might have just been a bad dream. Until Atwood and his father showed up at my door. They said how important it was that he not be implicated in this in any way. All about the big future he had ahead of him. They offered me money—a large amount of money, enough money to go back and marry Rebecca—for my silence. I took the money."

This was the money Rebecca had talked about with us. The reason why she decided to marry Zachary. And then the reason why she left him when the money was gone.

"Your ex-wife said you gave away the money," I said.

"I did."

"Why?"

"To save my life. Or least to try to salvage whatever was still left of it."

"Because of guilt over letting Atwood get away with murder."

He nodded.

"But you took the money. You went back to Chicago with it and started a new life there with Rebecca. Why the sudden change of heart?"

Zachary looked down at the gun in his hand. For a second, he seemed to drop it a bit, and I thought maybe he was going to put it down. But he didn't. The gun was still pointing at us. This was his story, and all Manning and I could do was let him keep talking and see how this all played out.

"One day after I was back in Chicago with Rebecca," he said, "I decided to see if I could find out what had happened with the dead girl in the park. It turned out that some kid they found in the park got arrested for the murder. I'm not sure what evidence they had against him, but it didn't really matter. He wound up getting stabbed to death in a prison fight before the trial.

"I didn't know what to do. I couldn't come forward and tell the truth without implicating myself—both of being at the murder scene and taking the money to keep quiet. But I had to do something; the guilt I felt over what happened was overwhelming. So I did the only thing I could think of. I gave the money away to charity. To some big music schools and for scholarships to music students. All anonymous. I didn't want anyone to know what I did with that money, I just wanted to know that I did the right thing in the end. Even if it was too little, too late.

"I stopped dreaming about being a big music star after that and settled for a life as a high school music teacher. And, as the years went by, I almost forgot about that long-ago night. Until I saw the story on TV about Dora Gayle and went back to look at that picture of the five of you at the Domino Club."

He talked about writing the original comments on the picture when he'd first gotten it in 1986. He said he'd been so inspired by everything that happened that he wanted to preserve the memory of that special night.

"You all seemed to have such dreams and optimism back then. Atwood talked about one day becoming a politician who would make the profession seem noble again, like the Kennedys had once done; Kaiser wanted to travel the world and experience life, not be all about money like his father; Lehrman was dedicated to using the law to help the homeless and other needy people; Gayle wanted to write poetry and great literature; and you, Scott—well, you and I were going to turn the music world upside down.

"But, after I saw that newscast about the Gayle woman, I thought about what had happened to everyone else in the picture since then. Atwood and all his scandals. The Lehrman woman defending drug dealers and mob bosses. Kaiser becoming a money-grubbing billionaire who stepped all over people to get what he wanted. And, of course, you, Scott. I felt the saddest about you. I always had such high hopes for you."

"And I let you down?" Manning asked.

"I read about you and that kid who got pushed out a window. You lied, man. Why did you lie? You used to have such high ideals and hopes and aspirations. What happened to you? What happened to us all? I couldn't stop thinking about that. About how we had all thrown everything away. My life—all of our lives—seemed to have no point whatsoever. I only had one hope left for some sort of salvation. A long time ago, I had a daughter. I'd never seen her, and I wanted to find out about her before I died. So, after I talked to Rebecca, I came to New York to try and find her."

CHAPTER 57

I WAS PRETTY sure I knew where this was going.

Grace Mancuso had been blackmailing Bill Atwood in the days leading up to her murder. Until now, we never knew what she was blackmailing him over. Just that it had to be something really bad—something even worse than the sex scandals that had dogged Atwood over the years.

Now it turned out that he had killed a woman a long time ago as a young man and that someone else died in jail for the crime.

And Dave Zachary—Grace's long-lost biological father—was there when Atwood killed the girl.

It wasn't hard to figure out what happened next.

"I had one big thing I wanted to do before I died. A long time ago, I had a daughter. I'd never seen her, and I wanted to find out about her before I died. So, after I talked to Rebecca, I came to New York to try and find her. This was my daughter, my legacy from the eighties, my one remaining hope for the future.

"When we first met, I tried to explain that to her. About my music, my love for her mother then, and about the mistakes I had made. I told her everything, including about that night in the park when I had helped to cover up a murder. About how no matter how much money Atwood and his family paid me to keep quiet, it wasn't worth it. About how that decision had haunted me ever since then.

"My daughter was the only thing left that mattered for me. I wanted her to understand, so she never made the same mistake herself. I wanted a better life for her. That was all I cared about now. If I knew she was all right, I could die happy.

"But when I came back to see her again, she laughed about it all in my face. She said I was just a silly old man. She bragged about how she'd first come up with a scheme to defraud investors at the company where she worked. Now she said I was going to help her make even more money because I had told her the secret about Atwood. How she was blackmailing him for enough money to get a big score to set herself up big in a new place.

"I was devastated. I told her I loved her. I told her how important she was to me. I told her I needed to know I did one thing right before I died. But she just kept laughing. Then she told me if I really loved her, I could do one more thing for her. She said she'd invited Atwood to come over there at ten that night. He thought it was for sex, but she was going to drop the hammer on him for the money—either pay up immediately or go to jail for the long-ago murder. And, just to make it even more convincing that she had the goods on him, she wanted me to be there. The only witness to that murder. The man he'd paid to cover it up and allowed police to put the wrong man in jail for the crime. She said she wanted to see the look on Atwood's face when he saw me there and realized who I was. Then all that money—the blackmail money from Atwood—would be hers, she gloated.

"'C'mon, Daddy, do me this one last favor,' she said in this mocking tone. 'Help your little daughter get fuckin' rich tonight!'

"When I told her I wouldn't do it, she called me a loser. She said she was a winner and all the rest of us were losers. She said she was ashamed to have someone like me as her father. Then she told me to get out. She said she didn't need me anymore. I'd given her enough damaging information about the murder Atwood committed to get the money from him.

"I was devastated. On that first day I'd come to see her, I'd brought her a present. The wooden statue of the Empire State Building. I knew it wasn't much, but it somehow symbolized New York City and my new hope for my daughter once I found her. I wanted her to have it. I wanted her to have a piece of me after I was gone.

"But at the end, when she was telling me to get out, she made fun of the statue. Said it was just like me . . . cheap and useless and an embarrassment to her. I guess something snapped in me, it was too much to take. She's taken my innermost secrets and left me with nothing. The statue was right in front of me, the statue she made fun of. I'd like to say that I didn't know I was capable of that kind of violence. But I discovered that I was."

"What happened then?" I asked.

"I'm not sure. This brain tumor . . . well, it plays tricks on my mind. Big chunks of my memory these days are sometime just gone. The next thing I remember was waking up in a hotel room. I went back to Grace's apartment. When I saw her lying there dead, that's when I realized just how much rage I was capable of."

"Were you the one who called the police afterward to lead them to the body?" Manning asked.

He nodded.

"She was just lying there. All covered in blood. Beaten so badly. I was so ashamed of what I'd done. I didn't want to just leave her there like that. I couldn't just walk away. She was my daughter."

"And then you left the note next to her body for police to find with the names of me and the other four people?"

"Yes."

"Why did you do that?" Manning asked.

"I don't know. I guess I just wanted to send you all some kind of a message. The five of you in that picture. I blamed you for all the lost hopes and lost dreams we had on that night when the picture was taken. I was mad at all of you for what you have become, and I was disappointed by you. I know that probably doesn't make a lot of sense, but I felt you had all played some role in what happened inside my daughter's apartment. That's why I did it.

"I wrote down all five of your names as being complicit in what I had done. And used the verses of two of my favorite songs from the past too, because they seemed appropriate. '. . . for sins committed yesterday' is from the Rolling Stones song on their *Between the Buttons* album. And 'a little help from my friends', of course, is from *Sergeant Pepper* and the Beatles. I used to play those songs a lot in our apartment, Scott. Just like I did with the Ramones. They were all my favorites."

Manning nodded. "I should have recognized that sooner, I guess. Except I had no idea you were involved."

"But you did find me in the end. Which is what I wanted to happen. One way or another, I wanted it to be you that found me. It just felt right that way."

I looked around the park. There was no sign that anyone else was aware of what was going on. People continued to lounge on the grass, play games, read on park benches, and do all the other things that people do on a hot summer day in New York City.

"So what happens now?" I asked.

"I can't just walk away. I need to take you both out of here with me so you don't try to stop me somehow. I'm not going to shoot you, unless I have to. I just wanted to talk to you, Scott. I've done that. I didn't know you were going to bring the TV woman. But now I need to go ahead with the rest of what I have to do here. Give me your gun."

Manning hesitated for a second or two, looked down at the gun in Zachary's hand, and then over at me. He shrugged, took out his gun, and handed it to him. Now, I was really scared. But it turned out he knew what he was doing.

"There's backup officers watching us," Manning said.

"What?"

"There's been police officers watching us the whole time."

I thought at first he was bluffing.

But then he pointed toward a clump of trees and made a signal. There were two police officers who stepped out from behind them now. They had their weapons out. Manning hadn't been bluffing at all. He really did make preparations, like he'd told me, before coming here to find Dave Zachary.

"You get up and try to walk us out of here, they'll stop you. Someone might get hurt. So just give my gun back and give me your gun. I can help you. I'll do everything I can to help you. I'll get you a lawyer . . ."

"To do what? Get me a shorter sentence? I'm afraid it's a bit too late for that."

"You need a doctor."

"A doctor can't help me. A lawyer can't help me. No one can help me anymore. This is something I'm going to have to do on my own."

"If you try to take us out of the park with that gun, they're going to give you one warning to drop it. If you don't, they'll have to shoot you. That's the police procedure for a case like this. Don't do this. You don't have a chance. If you don't give yourself up, it's just like committing suicide."

"Tell me something I don't know." He smiled sadly.

At that moment, I suddenly understood. I understood what Dave Zachary's plan was. His grand finale. Zachary wasn't trying to get out of here alive at all. He wanted to die.

Suicide by cop, they call it.

When a person is too afraid to kill themselves but puts themselves deliberately into a situation where the police have to kill them.

The officers began moving toward us.

"Don't do this," Manning said softly to Zachary.

"Police," one of the officers shouted. "Drop your weapon!"

It was like a slow-motion film, everything happening in a relentless sequence with us powerless to stop it. Zachary throwing away the newspaper now and turning toward the two approaching officers, with the gun in his hand. The cops yelling out a final warning. Zachary pointing the gun in his hand at them.

"He's not going to shoot!" I wanted to scream out, but I didn't.

"Drop the gun!" one of the cops was yelling at Zachary.

Don't shoot . . . I thought to myself.

But I knew it was hopeless.

These were cops.

And they would do what a cop was supposed to do.

Protect a fellow officer—as well as an innocent civilian—they felt was in danger.

Zachary continued to move forward toward them now waving the gun his hand, ignoring their repeated demands that he drop the weapon.

In the end, they had no choice.

There was a single gunshot, and Dave Zachary fell forward, blood spurting out of a hole in his chest.

He was dead before he hit the ground.

CHAPTER 58

I'D NEVER SEEN a person shot and killed before. Not right in front of me like this.

Oh, I'd covered a lot of bloody murders and police killings over the years. Written about them for newspapers, talked about them on the air, seen graphic video and pictures of crime scenes. I was certainly no stranger to death and tragedy and bloodshed and gore. But this was different. This was the real thing.

I also realized at that moment how traumatic it had all been for me. I'd been scared the whole time. I admitted that to myself now. From the moment Dave Zachary sat down on the park bench and showed us the gun he was carrying. Scared that he'd shoot me or Manning. Scared that one of the police officers might hit us too with one of their shots. Scared that something else terrible could happen in the volatile situation we were in. Well, something terrible did happen. But at least Manning and I were okay.

All this was running through my head as I looked at Dave Zachary lying on the ground in a pool of blood next to me, almost feeling paralyzed and in a state of shock. But I also knew what I had to do now. I was a professional. A professional journalist. I needed to do my job.

And so I did all the things a journalist should do in that situation. I called the story into the Channel 10 newsroom. I got a video crew and reporters to the scene. We broke into the daytime programming with urgent bulletins. We shot interviews with the people there, including me, for the 6 p.m. newscast and on our website.

Manning was acting like a professional too. Working with the two police officers to control the crime scene. Bringing in an ambulance and the ME's office for Zachary's body. Briefing detectives, CSI, and the other authorities who showed up on what had just happened. I realized that he'd gone through the same emotional ordeal as I had. Maybe even worse, because he'd lost a person who was once his best friend. But he was still all business. I respected that.

It turned out that the gun Zachary had been holding wasn't a real one at all. Just a toy that looked authentic. He'd probably bought it at some novelty store, just like he did with the Empire State statue he'd given to his daughter. Not that police would have had any way of knowing the gun was fake in the split second they had to make a decision. All the investigators at the scene seemed to feel that the shooting of Dave Zachary by police had been justified.

* * *

Later, back in the newsroom, I worked furiously to pull everything together for the 6 p.m. newscast.

"How come you didn't bring a video crew with you?" Faron asked me at one point.

"I didn't know I was going to be almost killed."

"You could have pulled out your iPhone and recorded it all."

"Someone—Zachary or one of the cops—might have thought I was going for a weapon and shot me too."

"Well, at least it would have been good video."

That was the kind of gallows humor I'm used to in a newsroom.

I was glad for the jokes.

They helped me stop thinking about the reality of it all.

At 6 p.m., I was ready for showtime. The introductions played for the Channel 10 newscast. Brett and Dani did their opening. And then the red light went on for me to be on the air.

> ME: A suspect in the murder of Wall Street financier Grace
> Mancuso was shot and killed by police today in Washington
> Square Park. Channel 10 was there and has this exclusive
> story...

Afterward, a whole group of people took me out to a nearby bar where there was a lot of drinking, a lot more bad jokes about me being in the middle of a fatal police shooting, and—most importantly—a lot of compliments and acclaim for me. Even Brendan Kaiser showed up. No one had ever seen him at a Channel 10 function before. But he toasted me, told everyone how I'd proved again I was a Pulitzer Prize journalist, and how I'd exceeded every expectation of his over the course of the past few weeks.

It was heady stuff, I gotta admit that.

I had a great time. It was just what I needed.

I also drank quite a bit.

Actually, too much.

Which is probably why I was in a pretty emotional state by the time I got back to my apartment.

Sitting there alone after all the euphoria and acclaim I'd been getting from everyone, I began thinking again about the fear

and the shock and all the rest of the emotions I'd been sup-
pressing all day.

The fear I'd felt in the park.

The shock of seeing a dead David Zachary in front of me.

And I started to cry.

I knew I didn't want to be alone tonight.

I could call Janet, I thought to myself.

Or even Maggie.

But in the end, when I picked up my phone, I knew the number
I was going to punch in.

"Scott, I need you to come here!" I said.

* * *

A short time later, Manning was at my door.

He let me talk about all the things that were racing through my
mind at what seemed like 100 mph now. We did that for a long
time, sitting on the couch in my living room. He put his arm
around me and hugged me when I got especially emotional. And
then, as I guess I knew we would when I made the phone call to
him, we wound up in the bedroom.

I've had sex with a number of men in my life. Okay, a lot of
men. I've found that my sexual experiences generally broke down
into two categories: The passionate, but ultimately meaningless,
sex-for-sex's sake type like I had with Alan Paulus and many other
men in the past. Or the more meaningful sex I've experienced
with men who truly mattered to me—my ex-husbands, at least in
the beginning, and a handful of others along the way. The first
type of sex is easy. No worries, no risks, no emotional investment
of any kind. The second type of sex is trickier and—at least for
me—rarer. But every once in a while, these two different types of

sex—the passionate physical and the deep emotional bonding—come together in one glorious package. Well, without going into all the X-rated details, that's what happened with Scott Manning and me that night.

The next morning, when I woke up, I looked over and saw he was still there.

"You didn't get up afterward and go home to your wife," I said.

"I'll go home later."

"Won't she ask you where you were all night?"

"I just lost a good friend," he said. "I think that gives me a special dispensation for one night of sex."

More gallows humor.

Just like a newsroom.

I liked that.

"We talked a lot about me last night, but what about you?" I said now. "How do you feel about the way things wound up with Zachary? It's got to have been quite a shock the way it all played out like that."

"I keep going over the whole thing in my head. Wondering if there was anything I could have done differently."

"There wasn't."

"Sure there was. I didn't have to ask my friends on the force to be there for backup. I knew in my heart that Zachary wasn't even going to be of any serious danger. He didn't even really have a gun. We weren't in any immediate danger at all."

"But you didn't know that at the time."

"I should have sensed it. I feel terrible."

"If you didn't bring those cops as backup and Zachary's gun had been real and he would have killed me—or both of us—"

I shook my head. "You did the right thing. You're a cop. You did your job."

I asked him some more questions, like how he'd convinced the two officers to follow him there. If he was on restricted duty, why would they even agree to help him on a case? He said they were friends of his—and, more importantly—fellow police officers. Cops always backed up other cops on the street, he told me.

Just like he'd backed up his partner, Tommy Bratton.

The question I really wanted to ask him was still out there though. I knew I shouldn't bring it up again, but I couldn't help myself. I'm an investigative journalist. I ask questions for a living. So I asked him the big one.

"What's going to happen now between you and your wife?"

"I don't know, Clare."

"How about us?"

"I don't know that either."

To be honest, that was the only answer I'd expected from him. If it had been anything else, I probably wouldn't have believed him anyway. I reached over and hugged him. Then I gave him a big kiss. He might not be here with me tomorrow night or the night after that. But he was here now. That was enough for me at the moment.

CHAPTER 59

THE BOTTOM LINE was, the Grace Mancuso story was finally over.

Dave Zachary had killed his biological daughter in a rage fueled by his brain disease when he saw what she had become. Then he left behind the list of names from that long-ago picture, including Dora Gayle—whose senseless murder had ignited Zachary's quest for answers in the first place. That bizarre confluence of events had led to all that happened afterward, including the tragic death of Bill Atwood.

There were still some unanswered questions, of course, but there always were on every story.

I spent my first day back in the office after Dave Zachary's death working at being a news editor again. I sat in a lot of meetings, worked on budget numbers, read the latest ratings and marketing demo reports, and dealt with a few personnel problems.

The biggest one was Dani Blaine wanted to know if she could file a sexual harassment complaint against Brett Wolff for sleeping with her. I asked her if she'd agreed to have sex with him. She said she had at the time, but since then changed her mind and decided it hadn't been a good decision. And besides, she said, he'd been a real jerk afterwards. I told her I didn't think that quite met the bar for sexual harassment in the workplace.

I figured it was only a matter of time until Brett wanted to file a sexual harassment complaint against Dani.

Welcome to my world. I was back in my old job.

Even when I was a reporter on newspapers, I'd always felt a letdown after the end of a big story. All the adrenalin and energy and excitement over breaking a front-page exclusive was gone—and I had to go back to covering routine news again. It was even worse now. I'd gotten a taste of being a reporter again and I'd broken one of the biggest stories of my career. I sure missed that feeling.

But I wasn't really a reporter anymore.

I was a TV executive, and I had a job to do.

It was time for me to move on from Grace Mancuso and all the rest.

Or so I thought, at least until Maggie came into my office.

"You're always preaching to us about not jumping to conclusions on a story, right, Clare?"

"Glad you've been listening, Maggie," I said distractedly as I pored over some of the ratings numbers.

"Well, I think that's what you're doing now."

"What are you talking about?"

"You—and everyone else—is taking it at face value that Zachary killed Grace Mancuso."

"He admitted it to us in the park."

"No, he didn't. He admitted he was in her apartment. He admitted he was furious at her. He admitted he saw the body. But he also said he didn't remember actually killing her. That he remembered leaving the apartment, blacking out, coming back again to see her dead and realized then 'I must have killed her.' Those were his words, according to your account. But what if he didn't really remember killing her because he didn't really do it? What if someone else did? Someone who showed up there in between those last two visits of his?"

"That's a pretty far-fetched scenario."

"Is it? Dave Zachary never committed a violent deed in his life, from everything we've been able to find out. And the one violent act he witnessed—the killing of the girl by a young Bill Atwood—traumatized him so badly that he carried the guilt with him all of his life. And even at the end, when he supposedly murdered his daughter, what was his first reaction? To call the police so her body didn't just lie there alone in the apartment. Does that sound like the act of a man who could have brutally beaten a woman to death? And I'm not sure Zachary could have had the strength to beat her like that. He was very sick and weak, people said. You said that too when you saw him in the park. Mancuso was a young, reasonably fit woman. Does it not seem hard to believe that he could overpower her like that? No, everything we know about Zachary tells us he was a good, kind, caring, compassionate man. No indication ever that he was a killer. And certainly not someone who could be capable—psychologically or physically—of such a bloody, brutal beating as the way Grace Mancuso died."

I stared at her. Like I've said, Maggie can really be annoying sometimes. Especially when she's right

"The story's over, Maggie."

"I think we should still keep digging for more answers."

"Okay, let's just say hypothetically that you're right. Who else could have killed her then? There's a lot of suspects out there, especially with the Revson scandal. Hundreds of people involved in that who could have wanted her dead for revenge. But it would be like trying to find a needle in a haystack at this point."

"Maybe the Revson stuff is just a sideshow in Grace Mancuso's murder. There's passion about money, and then there's real passion. I think this all comes back to Bill Atwood. We know she was blackmailing him about that girl's death a long time ago in the park. He tries to bed her, she threatens him with exposure until he pays her big bucks."

"Except Atwood didn't do it. He couldn't have. He was at college meetings across town when the Mancuso woman died. We've been through all of this before. It's like this story just keeps going around in circles."

"No, Atwood wasn't the killer."

"Huh?"

"He was the reason for the killing."

And, just like that, it all came together for us.

"This was a crime of passion," Maggie said. "A crime of sexual motivation. A crime of anger. And if Atwood was having an affair with the Mancuso woman, who would be angry and jealous and capable of that kind of passion?"

"His wife," I said.

CHAPTER 60

NANCY ATWOOD BROKE down and confessed very quickly.

The police brought her to the same interrogation room where her husband had been questioned and laid it all out for her. As soon as they did, she began to cry. Her body trembled, her shoulders sagged, and she sobbed uncontrollably. She looked like a broken woman, a woman who had held on to her secret too long and now needed to bare her soul.

Nancy Atwood then waived her rights and agreed to make a statement.

"I killed her," she said. "There had been so many women over the years, but this time it was too much. Bill had promised me after the last time that there'd be no more affairs. I don't know if I believed him or not, but I wanted to. I let myself believe that we could finally have a real marriage.

"I'd put up with it for a long time, but I guess this time something just snapped. I waited for him outside the college and followed him to that woman's apartment. I didn't know what to do, I was so upset. I thought about it for days. Finally, I went back to her apartment that night and knocked on her door. I figured she probably wouldn't let me in. But she did. She didn't even seem surprised when I told her what I wanted. Like she'd had visits like this from wives before. I begged her to leave my husband alone. But she refused. She said she could get him to do anything she wanted—and she would. Then she laughed at me. That's when I lost it. I killed her."

Under questioning, she gave a lot more details about what happened in Mancuso's apartment. She talked about how she had overpowered Grace Mancuso, and then beat her to death. How, in a jealous rage, she battered her face beyond recognition. How she then fled the apartment, leaving the dead Mancuso woman's body behind.

It was a helluva story.

The only problem was—none of it was true.

Nancy Atwood couldn't accurately describe the inside of Grace Mancuso's apartment. She stood barely five foot tall and weighed only about 110 pounds and was twenty years older than Mancuso. Making it unlikely—even more so than with Zachary—that she could have overpowered the victim the way she said she did. And, most importantly of all, there had been other people's fingerprints found in Mancuso's apartment. One of the sets of prints belonged to Dave Zachary. Another to Bill Atwood. A third set of prints was still unidentified. They did not match Nancy Atwood's fingerprints. It was clear she had never been there.

So why would she confess to a crime she didn't commit?

There was an obvious answer to that, of course.

She was protecting someone else.

There was only one person a mother would be willing to go to jail for.

Her daughter.

* * *

Miranda Atwood was a lot tougher than her mother to crack. She denied vehemently at first that she had anything to do with Grace Mancuso's murder. She refused to answer questions without a lawyer present. And she even argued—without success—that police had no right to take her fingerprints.

But the case against her was building in other ways now that she had been identified as a suspect.

A tenant at the Mancuso building picked her out of a lineup and said she'd seen her on an elevator there on the night of the murder.

A coed from her college remembered Miranda drinking heavily on campus after that. When a newscast came on TV about the Mancuso killing at a bar they were at, a drunk Miranda declared in a loud voice: "I guess I showed her, huh? That ought to shut her up!" No one knew what she was talking about at the time. But now it certainly seemed to be one more nail in the case against her.

It also turned out that, in addition to being a star athlete on the lacrosse and soccer teams at Yale, she had taken a number of self-defense and boxing courses—where she had excelled. She clearly had the physical strength and ability to overpower Grace Mancuso the way the killer had done.

And, when Miranda Atwood's fingerprint results came back as a match for the set found in Mancuso's apartment, she finally broke down and the whole tragic story finally spilled out of her.

Later, I watched—and, of course, eventually put on the air— the police video of her interrogation. Just like I'd watched and put on the air the interrogation video with her father before he died.

"Why did you do it, Miranda?" one of the detectives in the interrogation room asked her.

"Because she tried to take him away from me."

"Who?"

"My father."

"You mean she wanted to take your father away from your mother?"

"No, not her. Me."

"But you're his daughter."

"He loved me more than any of the rest of them."

* * *

The secrets came tumbling out then, secrets about a young woman's bizarre father fixation that were in some ways more sad and more tragic than anything else that had come before in this story.

She told how she'd called her father one night and said she wanted to meet him in the city. He said he was going to be tied up in meetings. She knew what that meant. He was seeing another woman again. She was so angry at him over this that she showed up anyway and waited outside his office until he left. There was an argument, then he walked away from her. He'd never done that before. Afterward, she followed him to the apartment on the Upper East Side. She found out he'd visited Grace Mancuso.

She became obsessed with the thought of her father being with this woman. Sure, there had been other women in her father's life before. Lots of them, she knew that. But this one seemed different. He seemed more preoccupied, more serious about her. She didn't know why Grace Mancuso was so important to him, of course. About dealing with the blackmail threat. She was just afraid she was going to lose him to Grace Mancuso.

And so she'd gone back to the apartment where she'd followed him that night. She knocked on Grace Mancuso's door, told her who she was, and tried to reason with her. But Mancuso just laughed at her. Bragged about how she had Miranda's father wrapped around her little finger. About how she was going to use that to destroy him.

That's when Miranda picked up the statue in front of her and hit her. She hit her again and again and again.

At that moment, it wasn't just Grace Mancuso she was hitting. She represented a lot of women. Every other woman Miranda's father had ever been with. She didn't stop until this woman—the woman that had once been Grace Mancuso—was an anonymous mass of flesh, something so horrible that her father would never look at her again.

*   *   *

Later, Nancy Atwood—in an exclusive on-air interview with me—tried to explain the motivation behind what her daughter did. She actually had requested the interview because she wanted to set the record straight about Miranda and Bill Atwood and everything else.

"When Miranda was growing up, it was very difficult for her. Her father was always on television and in the newspapers and everyone knew him. But Miranda never did. She hardly ever saw him. He was always out on the campaign trail or meeting with people or making speeches. For most of the time when she was a young teenager, in her formative years, he was in Washington— while we continued to live up here. I didn't realize the repercussions of that absence from her father would be so severe.

"The stuff with the women made it worse. All her friends and classmates knew about Bill and his scandals, of course. They were always throwing it up in her face. For a young girl growing up, just having her own first sexual feelings, it got very confusing. So confusing that at some point she retreated into a fantasy world.

"She became obsessive over Bill. He was the most important man in her life. She would do anything for his attention. She blamed me for driving him away to other women. I think she blamed herself sometimes too. And—this is very difficult to put into logical words—it was almost like she was competing with me for Bill's love. She wanted him all to herself. She wanted him to love her more than any other woman, even me."

I tried to phrase my next question as delicately as I could, but there was no way to avoid the obvious.

"Are you sure your husband didn't do anything sexually with her?" I asked her.

"Yes, I'm sure. There was never anything sexual. It was all in her head. I knew Bill. He was a bad husband, but he wasn't a bad father. We sent Miranda to a psychiatrist after we found out about this fixation on her father. She's been going for sessions ever since. There's been a lot more we tried—the group counseling sessions, the hospitalizations, the therapy. You always hear about the damage a cheating husband does to his wife. But you never really think about what it does to a child. I could handle what Bill was, but Miranda couldn't. So she created a fictional father she could live with. The father of her dreams."

I believed her. Miranda Atwood, in a sense, was just as much a victim as all of the rest of them. There were no really bad people here, except for maybe the murder victim herself—Grace Mancuso.

"It's not fair," Nancy Atwood said, then began crying.

That clip would be played over and over again hundreds of times on stations all across the country, on websites and on

Twitter and YouTube. It was trending and viral and everything else hot in this era of social media for days afterward.

"It's not Miranda's fault. I know she did a terrible thing, but you can't take away her whole life for that. It's my life too. She's all I have left. Someone has to understand that . . ."

CHAPTER 61

MURDER IS A numbers game for us in the media. Sure, every human life is supposed to be important, every murder victim should matter—but that's not true in the world of TV news where I work. Sex sells. Sex, money, and power. Those are the only murder stories really worth covering.

I've heard that from bosses and editors my entire career, and I've taught it to the reporters who worked for me.

I've pretty much always followed that rule myself too.

Until Dora Gayle.

We'd set everything in motion at Channel 10—Maggie and me and the rest of us—by just following our instincts this one time. Ignoring the murder-by-the-numbers stuff and covering the seemingly meaningless death of a woman we had no reason to care about.

The results had been staggering. Three more people dead—Bill Atwood, Dave Zachary, and, of course, Grace Mancuso. Other lives—Lisa Kalikow, Miranda Atwood, Nancy Atwood—ruined or dramatically altered. So many stories intertwined, so many repercussions. It was like throwing a stone in a silent pond, then watching the ripples spread relentlessly through the water. We made a lot of ripples with Dora Gayle.

All because of one homeless woman.

Someone who wasn't even supposed to matter had changed everything.

* * *

I'm back "feeding the beast" every day at Channel 10 News, chasing after more stories to put on our newscast.

I did get a big raise and a promotion and even a new job title because of my work on the Grace Mancuso story. It came from Kaiser himself, so I guess I'm sitting pretty in terms of my future at the station.

The new title part was very cool. He offered me the choice of two options: Senior News Director or Vice President of News. I liked the sound of both "senior" and "Vice President," so I asked him if I could be Senior Vice President of News. He said no. So I took Vice President of News. I always wanted to be a Vice President of something, even though I'm not exactly sure what the title means and I basically do the same job I did when I was a plain old news director.

Jack Faron got a raise and a promotion too because of the story. And I made sure Maggie got more money for her invaluable contributions. So everyone at the station was happy.

* * *

Miranda Atwood got a plea deal for manslaughter—not murder—in the death of Grace Mancuso. Which seemed kind of ludicrous given the brutality of the killing. But the DA's office took into consideration her mental state at the time and her lack of any previous criminal record and a lot of the other mitigating factors to cut her a break. She was sentenced to fifteen to twenty-five years in prison, with a chance to get out on parole in ten years. Maybe she'll still have enough time left then for a chance at a life.

Her mother, Nancy Atwood, was a sad figure at the sentencing, sobbing uncontrollably in the courtroom as her daughter was being sent to prison. A few days later, Nancy Atwood took an overdose of sleeping pills and was saved by ER personnel just in time. She was later taken to a hospital to be treated for severe depression.

Emily Lehrman was still practicing law, but she no longer represented mob bosses and drug kingpins. It wasn't like she had suddenly gone back to working for the homeless or anything; she was still making money. But it sounded as if she'd taken another look at herself in the light of everything that had happened, didn't like what she saw, and decided to make some changes in her life.

* * *

Meanwhile, Scott Manning did go back to his wife.

He was very honest with me about it. He said he had a responsibility to his wife to try to make their marriage work. He had a responsibility to his son to try and repair their broken relationship. He also changed his testimony about the Manny Nazario murder; admitted he now suspected that his partner, Tommy Bratton, had indeed pushed the suspect to his death. Manning said he cared very much about me, but these were all things he needed to do in order to make things right.

They were noble things to do on his part, and a big person—a compassionate, understanding person—would have praised him, respected him, and supported him for the decisions he had chosen.

Unfortunately, I was not that person.

I was stunned, disappointed, and angry at him, and the final meeting between us ended badly.

But I suppose I always knew that it was going to wind up for me like this in the end.

Because I—unlike Dora Gayle—never believed that a Prince Charming was going to come along and the two of us would live happily ever after.

That only happens in fairy tales.

And fairy tales don't come true.

*   *   *

I still think about Dora Gayle a lot.

I look at that college picture of her—the beautiful, brilliant, poetry- and literature-loving Dora Gayle with her whole life still ahead—and can't reconcile that with the sad, homeless woman who died in that lonely bank vestibule.

How could that have ever happened?

I recently reread Sylvia Plath's *The Bell Jar*, Dora's favorite book when she was in college. I'd read it a long time ago myself, but now I thought maybe it could help me better understand Dora Gayle. My overwhelming reaction when I finished the book was one of sadness. Not just about the words on the page, but for the author too. Sylvia Plath killed herself at the age of thirty, before much of the acclaim for *The Bell Jar* and her other works turned Plath into a literary icon. Dora Gayle hadn't been recognized by anyone until after she died too, just like Sylvia Plath. I wondered how Dora would feel about that.

All I know for sure is that I feel worse about Dora Gayle than any of the rest of it.

And angry at her, too.

Yes, she'd had some bad breaks in her life. Her alcoholic parents. Her breakup with Bill Atwood, the man of her dreams. The loss of her unborn baby. And all the other things that had happened to her which started Dora on her downward spiral to a life on the streets. No question about it, she was a victim of a lot of events she couldn't control, just like the other four people on that Grace Mancuso list.

But they had persevered—and built meaningful, even if flawed, lives for themselves.

I believed there must have been moments when Dora Gayle could have made different decisions—as difficult as they might have seemed to her at the time—and turned her own life around.

Moments when she had the opportunity to find happiness but didn't take advantage of them.

And I suppose that was the worst tragedy of all.

CHAPTER 62

I WAS THINKING about all this as I sat in a rental car outside a house in Winchester, Virginia.

Linda Nesbitt's house.

The woman I believed used to be Lucy Devlin.

My daughter.

It was a little after eight a.m. Other houses on the block were springing to life, with people emerging to start their day. Finally, the door of the house I was watching opened, and a woman came out with a little girl. She walked the girl to a waiting school bus, kissed her goodbye, and began heading back toward the house. Just before she got there, she turned around to wave goodbye to her daughter one more time.

I could see her face clearly now.

And I knew.

God help me, I knew it was her.

This was Lucy.

I've always had this dream about meeting my daughter again.

Well, two dreams.

The first dream is the happy one. When Lucy and I meet for the first time, she tells me she's watched me doing the news on television and always admired me from afar. Even before she knew

I was her mother. She tells me all about her own child, an adorable little girl too—and how I'm a grandmother now. Then I take her in my arms and I hold her. I tell her that I'm sorry I left her for so long. I tell her that I'll never leave her again. I tell her she's the one good thing I've ever done in my life.

The second dream is different. In this one, I'm sitting in a car outside a house that I've never seen before. I know Lucy lives there, but for some reason I can't go up and knock on the door. Instead, I just sit in the car and do nothing. Eventually, Lucy comes out of the house. Again, I want to run to her, but I can't—my legs won't move. I simply watch as she walks away down the street outside of her house, just like she did that long-ago day in New York City, and disappears on me all over again.

I thought again now about Dora Gayle.

The beautiful, brilliant young woman who called herself Cinderella, believed in fairy tales, and waited in vain for her Prince Charming to come save her.

Yes, Dora's life ended tragically.

But maybe—just maybe—she was right about believing in fairy tales though.

Except sometimes you just have to make your own fairy tale come true.

I opened the door, got out of the car, and went to meet my daughter . . .

AUTHOR'S NOTE

BELOW THE FOLD takes place in a TV newsroom in New York City. I know a lot about newsrooms. I've worked in plenty of them over the years. NBC News. NBC local stations. *New York Daily News. Star* magazine. *New York Post.* And, so, what I've tried to do in this book is give you a real-life look at what it's like behind the scenes in the high-stakes world of news media.

It's not always the same as you see on TV or at the movies. Not everyone is as likable as Murphy Brown or Lou Grant or Jane Craig in *Broadcast News.* Not every story turns into Watergate. And not every journalist comes to work every morning hoping to right the wrongs of society and make the world a better place, as we're frequently led to believe.

Do you know what the biggest motivation in a real newsroom is? Fear. Fear you're going to screw up. Fear you won't get the story. Fear someone else is going to beat you to it. Funny, but the stories you remember aren't just the ones you got. They're the ones you missed, too.

I talk in the book about "feeding the beast," and that's what a news journalist has to do every day. Come up with a big story that's better than the story your competition is doing. And, as

Clare Carlson points out, the beast is never satisfied. No matter how many stories you feed it, the beast always wants more.

There's a classic anecdote about a reporter who won a Pulitzer Prize for his newspaper. His editor held a big party in the newsroom after the announcement to celebrate this great honor. They congratulated him, praised him, and did toasts in his honor. At the end of the party, the editor called the reporter over to the side and asked him: "So what have you got for tomorrow?"

Then there's the title of this book itself. "Below the fold" is a newspaper term—which Clare uses in the TV newsroom, since she's a veteran of print journalism—to indicate a story that's not important enough to be displayed prominently at the top of the front page. Except it's not always that easy. Sometimes a "below the fold" item—like the seemingly meaningless death of a homeless woman like Dora Gayle—can explode into a huge Page One phenomenon of its own. I've seen this happen many times, which is why I wanted to write a book about this kind of story.

All of this pressure to produce day after day takes a real toll on a journalist. Frequently, the result is someone like . . . well, Clare Carlson. Three failed marriages, uncertain about her role as a mother, a personal life that is in constant turmoil—but she's still one helluva journalist!

Readers ask me if the Clare Carlson character is based on a specific person. My answer, of course, is no. Clare Carlson doesn't actually exist. But she is an amalgamation of many real journalists—both women and men—that I've worked with in newsrooms over the years. People who literally live their lives from deadline to deadline.

Let's just say I've known a lot of Clare Carlsons in my life.

And that's what *Below the Fold*—and Clare—is all about.

Not necessarily journalism the way we think it should be.

Or the way we imagine it from TV and movies.

Just the way things really do work in a big-city media newsroom.

—R.G. Belsky

CPSIA information can be obtained
at www.ICGtest
Printed in the U
BVHW030846C
539186BV00004B/4/P

31901064820246

9 781608 093243